MW01451122

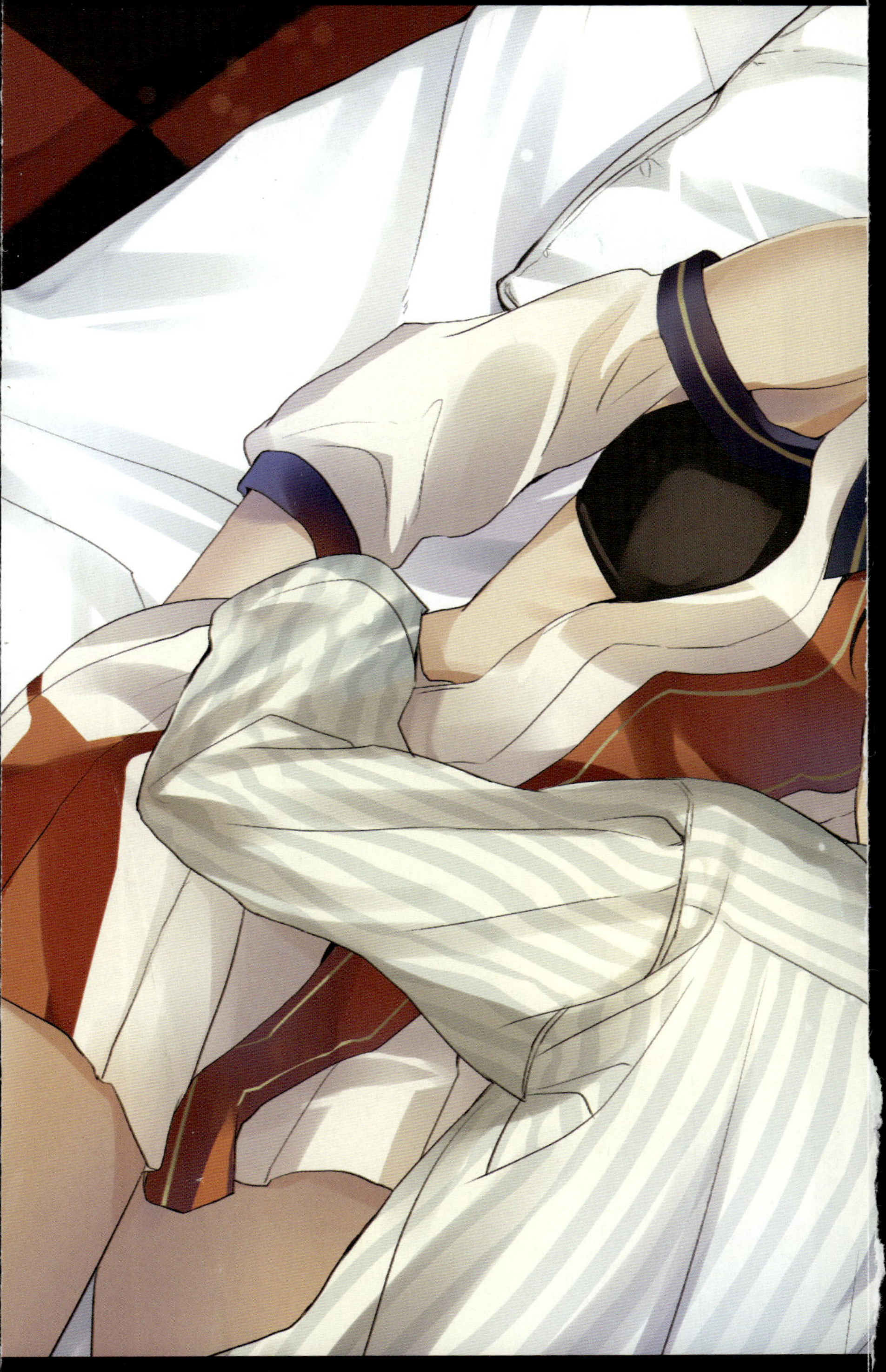

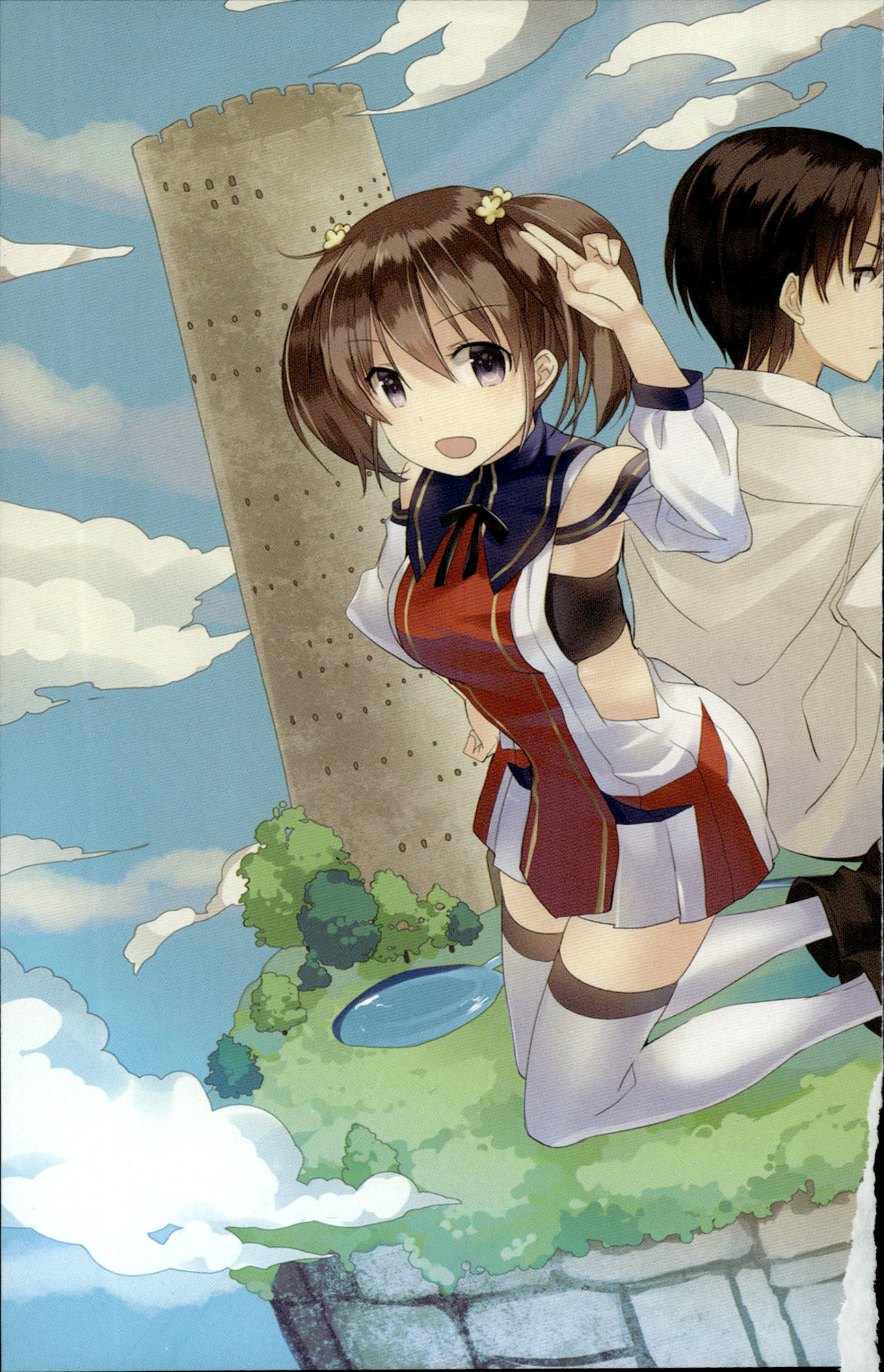

Illustration: Chisato Naruse

My Instant Death Ability Is So Overpowered, No One in This Other World Stands a Chance Against Me!

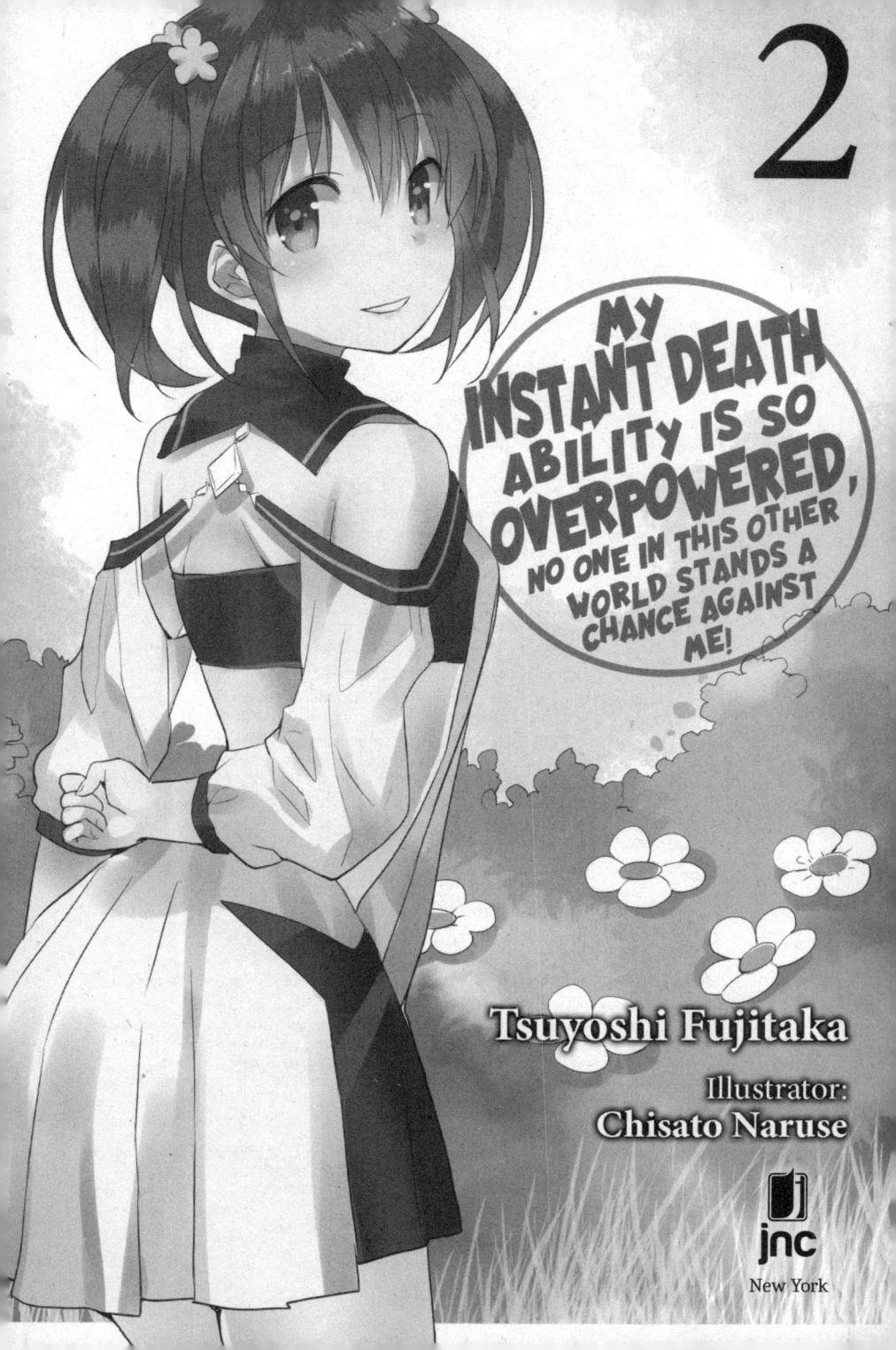

"My INSTANT DEATH ABILITY IS SO OVERPOWERED, NO ONE IN THIS OTHER WORLD STANDS A CHANCE AGAINST ME!"

2

Tsuyoshi Fujitaka

Illustrator:
Chisato Naruse

jnc
New York

MY INSTANT DEATH ABILITY IS SO OVERPOWERED, NO ONE IN THIS OTHER WORLD STANDS A CHANCE AGAINST ME! 2

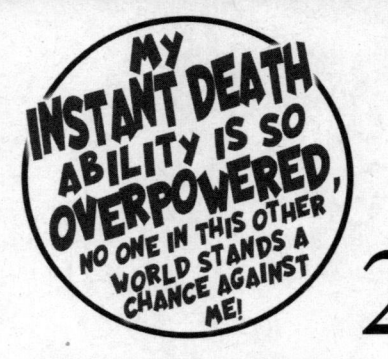

Author: **Tsuyoshi Fujitaka**
Illustrator: **Chisato Naruse**

Translated by Nathan Macklem
Edited by Tess Nanavati

This book is a work of fiction. Names, characters, places, and incidents are the product of the author's imagination or are used fictitiously. Any resemblance to actual events, locales, or persons, living or dead, is coincidental.

SOKUSHI CHEAT GA SAIKYO SUGITE, ISEKAI NO YATSURA
GA MARUDE AITE NI NARANAIN DESUGA.
© Tsuyoshi Fujitaka / Chisato Naruse 2017
EARTH STAR Entertainment All Rights Reserved
First published in Japan in 2017 by EARTH STAR Entertainment, Tokyo.
English translation rights arranged with Earth Star Entertainment
through Tuttle-Mori Agency, Inc, Tokyo.

English translation © 2020 by J-Novel Club LLC

Yen Press, LLC supports the right to free expression and the value of copyright. The purpose of copyright is to encourage writers and artists to produce the creative works that enrich our culture.

The scanning, uploading, and distribution of this book without permission is a theft of the author's intellectual property. If you would like permission to use material from the book (other than for review purposes), please contact the publisher. Thank you for your support of the author's rights.

Yen Press
150 West 30th Street, 19th Floor
New York, NY 10001

Visit us at yenpress.com · facebook.com/yenpress · twitter.com/yenpress
yenpress.tumblr.com · instagram.com/yenpress

First JNC Paperback Edition: September 2023

JNC is an imprint of Yen Press, LLC.
The JNC name and logo are trademarks of J-Novel Club LLC.

The publisher is not responsible for websites (or their content) that are not owned by the publisher.

Library of Congress Cataloging-in-Publication Data
Names: Fujitaka, Tsuyoshi, author. | Naruse, Chisato, 1978– illustrator. | Macklem, Nathan, translator.
Title: My instant death ability is so overpowered, no one in this other world stands a chance against me! / Tsuyoshi Fujitaka ; illustrator, Chisato Naruse ; translated by Nathan Macklem.
Other titles: Sokushi cheat ga saikyou sugite, isekai no yatsura ga marude aite ni naranai n desu ga. English
Description: First JNC paperback edition. | New York : JNC, 2023.
Identifiers: LCCN 2023015011 | ISBN 9781975368302 (v. 1 ; trade paperback) | ISBN 9781975368319 (v. 2 ; trade paperback)
Subjects: CYAC: Graphic novels. | Fantasy. | Ability—Fiction. | LCGFT: Fantasy fiction. | Light novels.
Classification: LCC PZ7.1.F87 My 2023 | DDC [Fic]—dc23
LC record available at https://lccn.loc.gov/2023015011

ISBN: 978-1-9753-6831-9 (paperback)

10 9 8 7 6 5 4 3 2 1

LSC-C

Printed in the United States of America

Contents

ACT 1

Chapter 1	Why Are You Guys Always So Naive?	003
Chapter 2	It's Like a Scene You'd See in a Pesticide Commercial	013
Chapter 3	You See These Kinds of Things in Other Worlds All the Time	019
Chapter 4	He Seems Like a Decent Person… But I Won't Trust Him So Easily!	027
Chapter 5	You Say That Like You're a Famous Person in Disguise	033
Chapter 6	Why Is Someone Like That Trying to Be a Knight of the Divine King, Anyway?!	041
Chapter 7	I Would Have Died Without These Apology Stones	049
Chapter 8	I Feel Like the Definition of "Swordsman" Is Being Stretched Too Much!	057
Chapter 9	What Kind of Crappy Game Is This World?!	065
Chapter 10	Think of It as One of Those Ghost Stories You Normally Hear About at Old Inns	073
Chapter 11	Interlude: I Don't Know What I'm Doing Here Either	085

ACT 2

Chapter 12 I'm Not So Rude as to Complain to the Person Who Saved Me ······ 097

Chapter 13 Horizontally Challenged ······ 107

Chapter 14 I Figured if It Had Already Happened Anyway, I Might As Well Enjoy It ······ 117

Chapter 15 What Makes You Think That Talking Will Work This Time?! ······ 127

Chapter 16 You Picked a Fight With the Wrong Guy ······ 137

Chapter 17 This Feels an Awful Lot Like a Last Boss ······ 147

Chapter 18 I Don't Know What Will Happen if I Kill Space Itself ······ 155

Chapter 19 Your Luck Really Is the Worst of the Worst ······ 167

Chapter 20 Aren't You, Like, a Perfect Example of an Enemy of the World? ······ 177

Chapter 21 Was There Actually a Reason for Us to Get This Close to You?! ······ 185

Chapter 22 I Might End Up Falling for You Anyway ······ 195

Chapter 23 Interlude: Why Are You Using Such an Annoying Method? ······ 205

Side Story: The Agency ······ 217

Afterword ······ 243

MY INSTANT DEATH ABILITY IS SO OVERPOWERED, NO ONE IN THIS OTHER WORLD STANDS A CHANCE AGAINST ME!

CHARACTERS

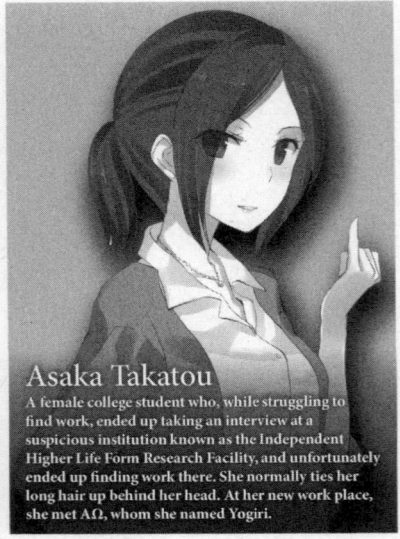

Yogiri Takatou
High School Year 2. Although he seemed unmotivated and was always sleeping in school, when he gets serious, he is surprisingly attractive. He didn't receive the Gift, the special power of this world, but he already had the power of Instant Death from his original world. Also known as AΩ.

Tomochika Dannoura
High School Year 2. Although she looks quite attractive and has quite the ample chest, her role is unfortunately that of the Straight Man. Like Yogiri, she did not receive the power of the Gift, but she is trained in a martial art derived from the ancient Dannoura style of archery.

Mokomoko Dannoura
Tomochika's ancestor and guardian spirit. As a ghost from the Heian era, she was the one responsible for reviving the Dannoura School of Archery... or so she says. She looks exactly like Tomochika's older sister (in that she's fat), and wears a kimono in the fashion of the Heian-era nobility. Apparently, she is well acquainted with digital technology.

Asaka Takatou
A female college student who, while struggling to find work, ended up taking an interview at a suspicious institution known as the Independent Higher Life Form Research Facility, and unfortunately ended up finding work there. She normally ties her long hair up behind her head. At her new work place, she met AΩ, whom she named Yogiri.

Sage Sion
The Sage who summoned Yogiri's class and their bus into this world. The white dress she's wearing looks like a magical girl cosplay. She herself was formerly summoned into this world and became a Sage at the end of her own adventure, but due to her immense magical power, her common sense has lapsed somewhat since.

Sage Lain
One of the Sages that protects the world, and also the highest class of vampire. Unhappy with her inability to die, and the numerous obligations she held in life, she challenged Yogiri seeking her own death, and her wish was granted. A clone of herself in a newly designed body was left behind, and has now been entrusted with her final wish.

Euphemia
A half-demon girl turned into a slave by the power of one of Yogiri's classmates, Yuuki Tachibana. After Yuuki was killed while attempting to fight Yogiri, she encountered Lain on a mission to fight off an Aggressor, who sucked her blood and turned her into a vampire. She has long silver hair, dark skin, and wears a white dress.

Daimon Hanakawa
One of Yogiri's classmates. Having been summoned to this world for a second time, he had already reached the highest level as a Healer of 99. As that level is only the limit for humans, he is not actually all that strong. He's a little plump, a big nerd, and speaks in an old-fashioned dialect. Besides that, he has a tendency to be pretty gross.

ACT1

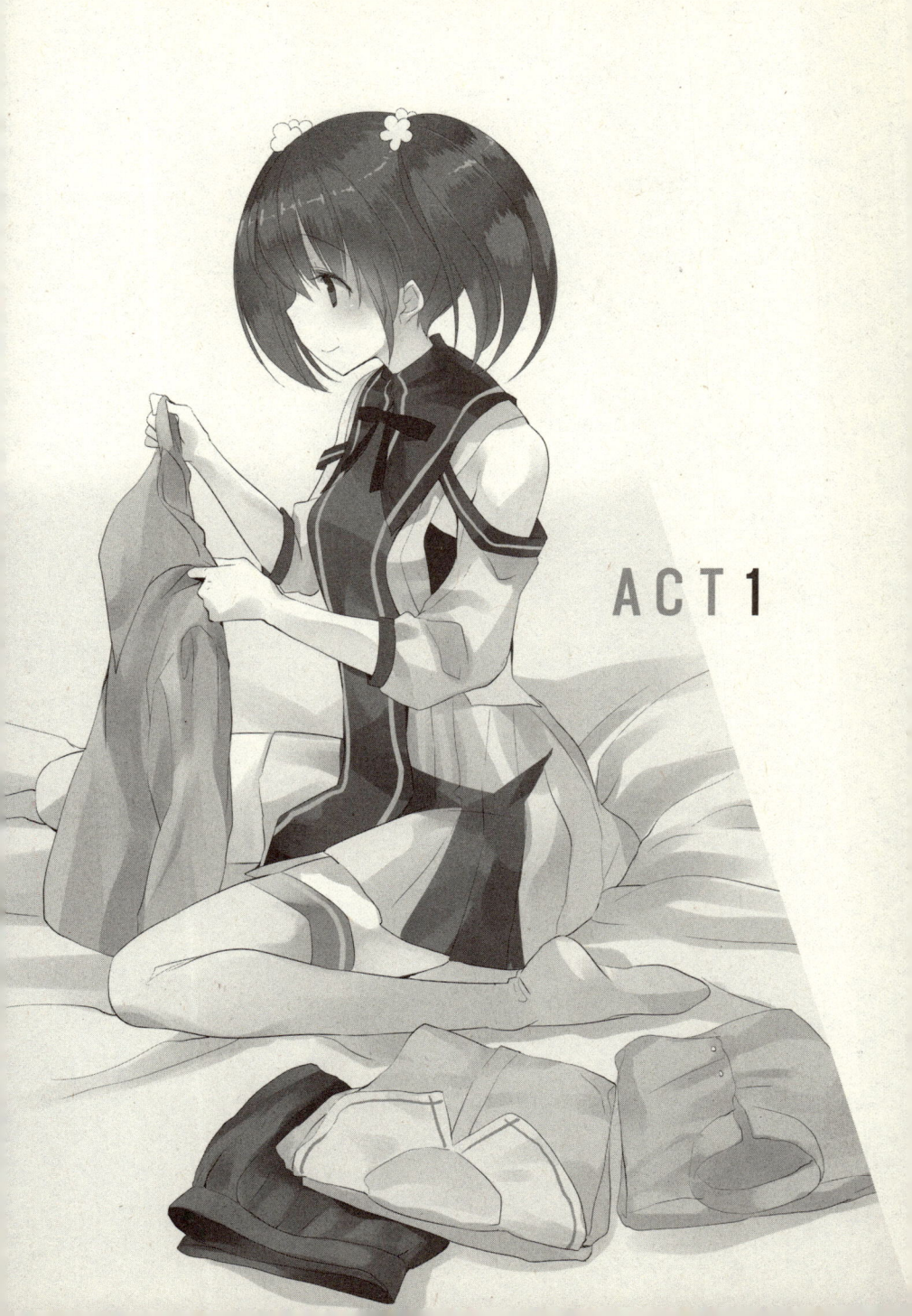

Chapter 1 — Why Are You Guys Always So Naive?

A lone girl walked through the forest of monsters, the territory of the Beast Kings. She wore her hair in a short, tomboyish cut, but there was no way she could have been trying to disguise herself as a man; her figure was indisguisably feminine.

The girl walked through the dappled sunlight filtering through the trees as if she didn't have a care in the world. Aside from the knife at her waist, she was completely unarmed and she carried no luggage. For those who knew the forest, she must have looked insane.

The forest itself wasn't particularly harsh terrain. The trees were spaced out enough to let ample light through, and the ground was flat and even. But this particular region was populated by monsters; to walk within its borders was to step into the realm of the inhuman. Ordinary civilians would be devoured in an instant. Yet she wound through the trees as if strolling through nothing more than a park.

"Why is he hiding in a place like this anyway?" she complained, as if it were all too much trouble for her to be there.

"Well, it makes more sense than people who don't want to get involved with others yet still live in cities," a voice answered the girl's complaints, despite the fact that she was entirely alone. Rather than a person, the voice had come from the knife at her hip.

"You're talking about the last guy, right? For all his complaints about not wanting to be involved with other people, he had no problem getting a mansion in the city and setting himself up as an aristocrat. I don't really understand it, but it does sound like a much easier life to me."

"This is the best place to hide, though, don't you think? People so rarely come into the forest."

"How do they survive here?"

"It's simple. Monsters won't attack those who are clearly stronger than them."

That made sense. The forest around her was overflowing with the presence of monsters, but none of them dared approach the girl.

After walking for a while, she arrived at a clearing. The first thing she noticed was the rice paddy. Golden heads of rice swayed in the breeze as far as she could see.

"The maps didn't say anything about a huge clearing like this, did they?"

"The residents must have cleared it themselves. But for the monsters of the forest to leave this place untouched, its owner must be rather powerful."

"You know that has nothing to do with it. But still, this is pretty nice. Otherworlders always need rice, right?"

Besides the rice paddy, the clearing also housed a field for cultivating crops and pens for livestock. Whoever made it must have been dead set on self-sufficiency. Of course, there was no way a place this large could be managed by one solitary person, so it was hardly surprising to see numerous workers out in the fields.

"I wonder why they're all girls. And *so* many elves, too…they're everywhere!" The workers were exclusively attractive young women. More than half of them were elves, but there were also a few with animal ears and even some who had bat-like wings as well.

"Must be his personal preference."

"Everyone always wants an elf bride for some reason. No clue what they see in those fake humans."

"I think you are much more beautiful, personally."

"Thanks. But moving on…" She headed for one of the nearby elven workers. "Hey, you. Is the guy in charge of this place around?"

Chapter 1 — Why Are You Guys Always So Naive?

"Huh? Umm, how did you get here?" the elf girl asked, clearly surprised by the stranger's presence. She must have thought it was impossible for outsiders to reach them so deep in the forest. There were, of course, no roads there, and there was no way to drive a vehicle through the brush.

"I walked. Why so surprised, though? Didn't you have some other visitors recently?"

"I wouldn't know. Do you have some business with the master?"

"Yeah. Business. You can call him if you want, but just telling me where he is would be fine."

"Okay, I will take you to him." Putting her work on hold, the elf guided them farther onto the plantation.

Their destination was an enormous mansion in the distance, large enough that the girl felt a guide wasn't particularly necessary.

"Hey, I know it's kind of weird for me to ask, but are you sure you're allowed to take random strangers to meet your master?"

"There's no problem," the elf replied with an easy smile. "There's no one who can harm him, after all." She must have had absolute faith in the guy.

After walking for a while, they reached the mansion. Before they could so much as knock on the door, it swung open to reveal a young man. It seemed he was already aware that someone had come to visit.

"No matter how many times you ask, I'm not going to do it. That Sage thing or whatever? I'm not interested in that kind of annoying work."

The man was Japanese. Of medium height and build, his appearance was inoffensive but unimpressive. His clothes weren't particularly fancy, but he did have a longsword at his hip.

He was a Rogue Sage. That was the name Aoi and her group had given to those who had the power to be a Sage, but refused to join them.

"Don't worry, I'm the last one who'll come and ask you. Would you mind at least hearing me out?"

"Fine. But I can tell you right now, you won't change my mind. So say your piece and leave us alone," the man said with clear exasperation.

"First, just to make sure, you are Rikuto Saitou, correct?"

"Yup. And you're Aoi Hayanose? I'm surprised they finally bothered to send an actual Sage."

Rikuto must have been trying to surprise her by showing that he knew her identity, but for Aoi, it simply meant she didn't have to waste time introducing herself. She was well aware of what he was capable of.

"I'm here to invite you to join us, but you've heard that speech plenty of times, so I'll leave out the boring parts. This is the third time, so I'll just tell you what's different now. If you refuse this time, I'll have to kill you."

After a short pause, Rikuto burst out laughing, the laughter quickly devolving into a coughing fit. "You're gonna kill me, huh?" He finally recovered enough to respond and turned to the elf at Aoi's side. "That's a good one, don't you think, Layla? It's been a while since I've heard a good joke."

"No, it's not funny at all! You!" she snapped at Aoi. "What are you saying?! Apologize to him immediately! If you make Mr. Rikuto angry, things will get bad fast!"

"Okay, just to confirm, you plan on refusing the invitation again, correct?" Aoi asked, completely ignoring the elf. "Just remember, the moment you officially decline, we'll be enemies." She already knew what he would say, but she needed a formal answer.

"I refuse."

"I see," Aoi said with a smile. From the start, she had wanted to kill him, so it would have been unfortunate if he had suddenly changed his mind and joined them.

"Come on, now. There's no way you can kill me. You know how much stronger I am, right? God gave me the best possible power in this world."

"If we're talking pure specs, then sure, I'm definitely weaker," she confessed. She was strong enough that the monsters of the forest were afraid of her, but compared to the other Sages, she wasn't especially powerful.

"Given how this usually goes, you'll attack me regardless and I'll wipe the floor with you, but I'd appreciate it if you just gave up and left instead. A fight with no chance of losing is such a waste of time. Or...did you want to join my harem? More than half the girls here originally came to kill me, you know."

"I agree that this is all a waste of time, but it's my job."

"If you're planning on using her as a hostage, you can forget that too," Rikuto continued, glancing at Layla. "All that will do is upset me more."

"Oh, don't worry about that. I'm strictly targeting you. There's no reason to get powerless bystanders involved. Which reminds me, could you step back a bit, Layla?"

The elf immediately looked at her master, and after seeing his silent nod, she complied, stepping away from the pair.

Aoi looked around her. A number of the workers had stopped what they were doing to watch, but none of them seemed especially worried. This must have been an everyday occurrence for them.

"I can't imagine this being much of a fight, but are you so confident because of your magic eyes? Fair warning: petrification and charms don't work on me."

"Ah, maybe you can't get a good grasp of my eyes' abilities because they are linked to Fate? These are Hero Killer eyes. It's a fancy name, but for the most part, all they can do is see."

"Hero Killers, huh? Are they going to be that useful against me, then?"

"Well, you're not a Hero, so no, not really."

Rikuto seemed bothered by that. Although he was trying to maintain an air of detachment, he wasn't holding onto it that well. "You realize what those girls out in the field actually are, right? They're the Beast Kings of this region, dragons incarnate, Demon Lords, and things like that." He acted as if this made him a Hero, but Aoi wasn't impressed that he'd shut himself away in the depths of the forest. She certainly wasn't prepared to consider him heroic.

"Well, arguing won't get us anywhere, so should we just get started?"

"All right, then. Don't worry, I won't punish you too badly."

Flesh-colored strands suddenly erupted from the ground around Aoi. The numerous leathery appendages were slick with some sort of liquid.

"Starting off with tentacles? That's kind of gross, don't you think?" His intention must have been to restrain her. "*Just World!*" Aoi activated her own power — "A Cruel World That Rewards Only Effort." The official name of the skill was a bit long, so she normally shortened it as she had just done.

"What?!" Rikuto's eyes went wide in surprise. Ignoring his spell, Aoi was walking straight towards him. The tentacles themselves had stopped moving — another set had sprung up from the ground, wrapping around and restraining the first batch.

Rikuto had gone stiff. He must have never encountered someone who was able to oppose his power before. He seemed to be hesitating over what to do next.

"I would prefer to finish this quickly, but I was told to set an example, too," said Aoi dismissively.

"Don't look down on me!" Rikuto threw his hand outward, palm facing towards her. A thick beam of light shot forth, hot enough to reduce anyone who touched it to ash. At this rate, the farm workers behind Aoi would be incinerated along with her.

Aoi mimicked Rikuto's action, opening her own palm towards him. An equal beam of light shot out of her hand, intercepting and neutralizing Rikuto's attack.

"Seems to me like you're the one who's taken hostages here," she said exasperatedly to an awestruck Rikuto. "Why are you guys always so naive? Your power was *given* to you. What makes you think it wasn't given to someone else as well?"

Aoi had grown tired of these exchanges. All of them were the same in the end. These people all started out timidly testing their limits, then immediately grew full of themselves, becoming arrogant enough to believe that the power was all their own. And after receiving said power without any work whatsoever on their end, they scorned those who had actually worked hard for their gifts.

"Did you also get your power from him?! Dammit! Aren't I meant to be the strongest in the world?!"

"I have no idea who you got your power from. But if a pathetic person like you can do it, I figured it would be easy enough for me, too."

"Shut up! Take this! Funeral Pyre!" He tried to activate another skill, but nothing happened. "What? Why isn't it working?! Black Centipede!

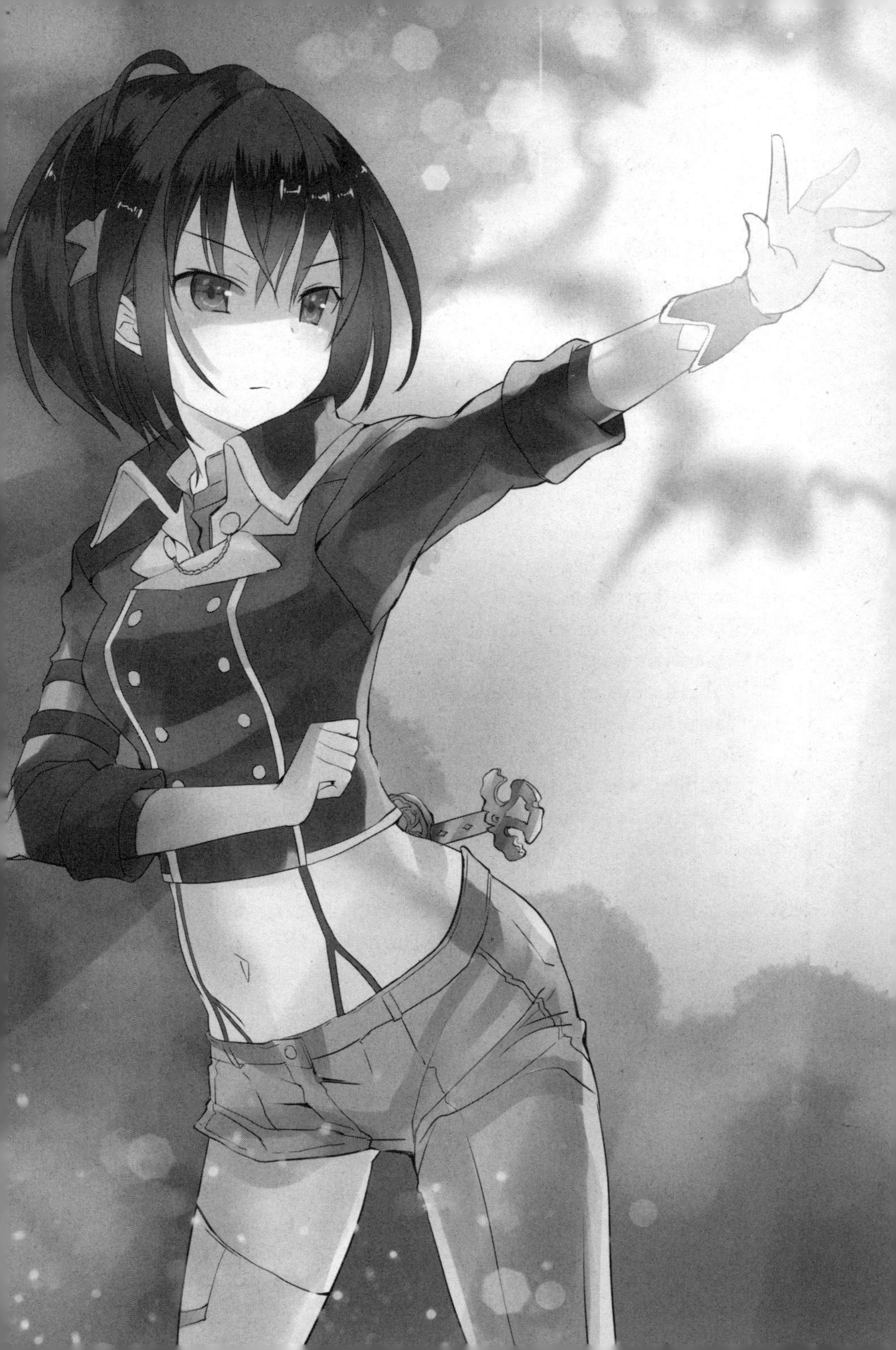

Type 100! Dark Scripture! Why isn't anything happening?!" Rikuto's voice began to tremble.

"Like I said, it's just a power that someone gave you. Is it that surprising it was taken away?"

"I don't understand! I'm supposed to be stronger!" he shouted, trying to cover the fear in his voice.

"Hmm, how do I phrase this? Your Fate level is really low, so countering it with something similar or taking it away entirely is easy."

"Taking it...away?" Rikuto's face blanched. He had finally realized that the invincible power he had freely wielded up until then was gone.

"It's not hopeless, though. My power isn't completely one-sided. If your skills were something that you had built up yourself, I would lose easily." As she approached Rikuto, she drew her knife.

The young man began to laugh madly. "That's right, I still have this!" Seeing her pull the knife, he drew the sword at his hip. To some degree, the action helped him to calm down. The sword had an unnatural air about it, clearly a weapon of some power.

"Yeah, that sword's Fate level is rather high, so I can't nullify it." An instant later, Rikuto's throat was torn open. Aoi, now behind him, slid her knife out from the back of his neck. "But it doesn't really matter if the one using it is weak."

"Was it really necessary to use me?" the knife in her hand complained as Rikuto collapsed to the ground.

"Hm. Looks like his underlings didn't have much love for him," Aoi remarked. At some point, the people who had been watching the conflict had disappeared. "Well, as long as they spread the word of how gruesome his death was..."

No one could be allowed to defy the Sages. Making that clear was one of Aoi's jobs.

"Sorry to bring it up so soon after finishing this job, but we've been assigned a new one already. The targets this time are two otherworlders, Yogiri Takatou and Tomochika Dannoura. Oh, this is rare. It looks like they're Sage candidates."

The knife that Aoi held could also send and receive messages. Communicating over long distances required an enormous amount of magical energy, so it was rarely used, and its usage was sign enough of it being an emergency.

"Really? I wonder what that's about. Are Sage candidates important enough to get me involved?"

"Who knows. First, let's head to Hanabusa. The details for our mission are there."

"Jeez. They won't even give us time to catch our breath, will they?"

As Aoi complained to herself, she heard footsteps from within the mansion. "Are there still workers inside?"

She waited to see who would come out, and soon a plump young man leaped through the doorway. To Aoi's amazement, he immediately threw himself to the ground, prostrating himself as he crawled toward her.

"My name is Daimon Hanakawa! I was caught up in the machinations of this Rikuto's disgusting cheat harem and forced to live out my days here, but now that he has been slain by your hand, I am without recourse! Would you perchance assist me in some way?! Otherwise, all that remains for me is death!"

"Um…what the hell is this?"

"A rather odd creature, indeed."

Unsurprisingly, Aoi was at a total loss.

Chapter 2 — It's Like a Scene You'd See in a Pesticide Commercial

Garula Canyon was an area dominated by its namesake river, carving a meandering path of cliffs and valleys through the landscape. The reddish brown rock of the canyon had been cut through, revealing countless layers of geological strata. Perhaps due to this harsh environment, it was rarely visited by people. Until the development of the road between Hanabusa and the capital, it had been an often ignored territory. Even now, besides the train that ran through it, it was virtually unexplored.

There had once, however, been a tribe of people living in the region who had called the canyon home, and thanks to their efforts, a network of what could technically be called roads had been left behind. At a dead end on one of those roads, a single armored vehicle was parked. The large, many-wheeled truck was a rare sight.

"Not another dead end..." The girl sitting in the driver's seat, Tomochika Dannoura, breathed yet another sigh. She was wearing a new outfit that she had picked up in Hanabusa — a dress with open sides. Having bought a large number of clothes during their journey, she enjoyed a different fashion each day, as her mood dictated.

"Hey, why are we going to the capital anyway?"

The grumbling reply came from a boy sitting in the passenger seat, Yogiri Takatou. As always, he was wearing his school uniform, as if choosing new clothes every day was just too much work. The supplies in their truck included a number of sets of clothing for him as well, but he only ever changed his underwear and the shirt under his uniform jacket.

"You say that now?! Could you come up with these complaints before we leave, please?" Tomochika snapped back at him.

"I just think it might be best to reevaluate our situation. Getting through here isn't our only objective."

The cliffside road they had been following had come to an abrupt end. There seemed to be the remains of what was once a bridge, indicating they were on the right path, but that was little consolation.

"True, but Ryouta didn't seem to think it would be a problem, did he?"

Ryouta, the lord of Hanabusa, had told them that, thanks to roads that were built during the railway's construction, it should have been possible to drive to the capital.

"Now that the railway's been built, they don't actually use these roads anymore, though, so they probably don't know what condition they're really in."

The railroad that passed through the area had been constructed a long time before. It was hardly surprising that a previously functional road was no longer in good shape.

"Our objective is to get back to Japan, which means making contact with a Sage," Yogiri continued. "I thought it would be faster to work with the rest of the class, but don't you think a Sage will come to us eventually anyway?"

"Are you saying we should have just stayed and relaxed in the city?"

"I thought we might have been able to, but who knows. If they just attack us out of the blue, it'll be pretty hard to hold a conversation." And if Yogiri fought back, their opponents would always die. Waiting around to be attacked wasn't going to yield much in the way of results. "Besides, they don't care about the lives of the people in the cities at all. I don't particularly care either, but that bothers you, doesn't it?"

"Right..." Tomochika replied with an unpleasant expression, remembering the scene from Hanabusa.

"Anyway, I thought maybe we could talk to this Sage named Sion. She *is* the one who summoned us here, after all."

Chapter 2 — It's Like a Scene You'd See in a Pesticide Commercial

The two of them had been called to this strange world by a woman named Sion, who had forced their class into a trial to become powerful Sages. Becoming a Sage required clearing the missions that Sion had laid out for them, and the surviving candidates would eventually meet her again. If Yogiri and Tomochika could connect with their classmates and find the Sage, they could ask her how to return to their home world.

That was the extent of their plan for the moment, anyway. Of course, they hadn't bet everything on Sion — they just assumed it would be easier to talk to her than going to one of the other Sages. If Sion wouldn't speak with them, they would have to find another way.

I had a look ahead as you asked, and even if we cross this ravine, there will be another dead end shortly afterwards, Tomochika's guardian spirit Mokomoko said as she floated into view.

As a spirit, she could freely navigate the landscape regardless of obstacles. They had sent her ahead to scout out the land in front of them, but clearly the news wasn't good.

"It doesn't look like we'll make it to the capital at this rate — wait! I've got it! We know of one sure way to reach the capital, right?" Looking up at the nearby train tracks, Tomochika spoke as if she had struck a gold mine of an idea.

"Are you going to suggest that we drive along the rails? You know if a train comes, we'll be toast."

"But it doesn't look like the trains are running right now. And with Hanabusa in its current state, they probably won't resume service for a while."

"That's a good point. And if a train does happen to come, I can always kill it. I have no idea what would happen if I did, but the results probably wouldn't be great."

"Fine! We'll just go back and try to find another road, then!" Tomochika slowly turned the armored truck around. But as she began to accelerate, the vehicle ground to a stop with a loud thump. They had hit something.

"Hey, what?! I'm pretty sure there was nothing there a second ago..."

She couldn't see anything in the side mirrors. More importantly, given how narrow the road was, if there had been any obstacles earlier, they wouldn't have been able to reach the location they were currently in, so it must have just appeared.

Tomochika opened the door to peek outside. A split second later, she jumped back into the truck, hurriedly closing the door. "Th-There's something out there! Something wiggly! Like a tail!"

"That's weird," Yogiri said, opening his own door and looking around. An enormous face, somewhere between that of a bird and a reptile, stared back at him. "Oh, it's another dragon. This is the same type as the one that attacked the bus. They really do like cars, don't they?"

"I don't need to hear about any more weird fetishes! Can you just get rid of it?"

"I don't know. If this is its nest, it's kind of our fault for driving through it. Just waltzing in and killing it for no reason feels kind of mean."

The truck began to shake. The dragon had started ramming its body into it. Luckily, the vehicle was sturdy enough to take the blows, but they were near a steep cliff. If the assault continued for much longer, they would be thrown off into the ravine.

"This isn't the time for your bleeding heart act!"

"Fine, then." As requested, Yogiri killed the dragon. Of course, ending its life didn't actually get rid of the body, so in the end they were still stuck.

As Yogiri was considering what to do about that, a roar filled the canyon. In response to that roar, more dragons took to the sky one after another, flying straight towards the vehicle. They appeared to be the same species, their reddish brown skin matching the color of the rocks around them.

"Where the hell did all of these come from?!" cried Tomochika.

As they watched, the number of dragons continued to increase, gathering in the sky around the cliff. They began to open their mouths wide, each giant maw filling with flames. No doubt they would soon be breathing fire down onto the truck. The angry creatures were more than ready to fight.

"Seems like we're at a real disadvantage here. Oh well, it's not like we can reason with them." Yogiri unleashed his power again, and the

Chapter 2 — It's Like a Scene You'd See in a Pesticide Commercial

dragons simply dropped out of the sky one by one, fire still burning in their mouths.

"Wow, it's like a scene from a pesticide commercial..."

Despite being more than twenty meters long from head to tail, the enormous reptiles had immediately lost all strength and plummeted to the earth. It was a rather impressive sight. The canyon soon returned to silence, as if nothing had happened at all.

"I really don't want to think about what's going to happen to the canyon now, with all of those bodies lying around," Tomochika sighed.

"More importantly, we're still stuck."

"I guess we'll have to do something about that one dragon behind us."

No problem at all, offered Mokomoko. *Just use your weapon on it. Either cut it to pieces, or use it as a lever and push the carcass into the canyon.*

The weapon that Tomochika had received from the Aggressor was currently masquerading as part of her outfit. It could freely change shape, so it could become a sharp blade or a strong metal beam as needed.

The pair disembarked from the truck. Glancing at the fallen dragon, it seemed like they could stick the weapon between the body and the cliff, have it expand, and send the creature toppling over the edge.

"Wait a second," said Tomochika. "Couldn't we make a bridge out of this?"

Beyond this point, the road has crumbled away. It wouldn't be possible to make it all the way to the capital regardless.

"Well, maybe there will be more places later on where we can use this — hold on, something else is coming!"

Although his sight wasn't nearly as good as hers, even Yogiri could see a wyvern flying through the sky towards them. But something about it was different from the others.

"Great, now we've got a Golden Thunder Dragon on our hands?" asked Tomochika.

The newly arrived monster was a sparkling gold in color. Clad in lightning, it had a powerful, divine air about it.

17

Chapter 3 — You See These Kinds of Things in Other Worlds All the Time

Yogiri and Tomochika watched the new arrival hovering beside their cliffside road. The golden dragon maintained its place in the air, beating its wings slowly. Wyverns were different from other dragons in that they only had two legs rather than four. But its enormous body, wreathed in lightning, was far larger than the other dragons they had come across so far. The talons on its feet were easily large enough to pick up their entire vehicle. Its enormous eyes were locked on the two of them, weighing them down with an oppressive air.

"It's definitely glaring at us," Tomochika said, voice shaking. The dragon should have been able to attack them at any time, but for now it was merely hovering.

"It's only watching us right now. If it's not going to do anything, we can probably just leave."

"No, no, no, we can't just go! It looks like it's going to hit us with lightning or something!"

In spite of Tomochika's words, it was actually impossible to read any sort of expression on the dragon's inhuman face. In addition, Yogiri couldn't sense the slightest bit of killing intent coming from it. If it was planning on attacking them, he would certainly feel something, so they appeared to be safe for the moment.

With that in mind, Yogiri decided to wait and see what happened.

He was curious about what this dragon had come there to do, but it wasn't doing anything just yet. It was simply bobbing in the air, watching them.

Although she had been unsettled at first, the oddness of the situation gradually caught up with Tomochika, and she cocked her head at the creature in confusion. She was just about to tell Yogiri that maybe they should leave after all when the wyvern finally spoke.

"You pass."

Its voice was deep and heavy. With a powerful flap of its wings, it lifted itself away.

"Uhh, pass? I have no idea what just happened, but it looks like it's leaving, so that's a good thing, isn't it?" Tomochika was relieved. She wasn't too concerned about understanding the exact details of the exchange.

But Yogiri called out to the dragon before it could depart. "Wait."

"What are you doing? Just let it go!"

"We could leave it alone and go, sure, but if it actually understands us, we should ask it a few questions."

"Haven't you ever heard of letting sleeping dragons lie?!"

Despite her warning, Yogiri continued to speak to their flying visitor. "If you saw what happened before then you know that if you try to run, I can easily kill you."

In reality, it was an empty threat. Even if it did flee, Yogiri had no intention of harming it. But the dragon's wings immediately froze, and it began to simply float in the air.

"What are those wings for if you don't need them to fly?!" Tomochika asked as the dragon remained suspended in the sky — an odd sight considering its wings were no longer moving.

◇◇◇

"Gah! I should have just left without saying anything! I thought it would be best to speak, but I was wrong!"

"Yeah, I probably would have ignored you and walked away if you hadn't spoken."

"Umm, Takatou? Why are you acting as if this is a perfectly normal

Chapter 3 — You See These Kinds of Things in Other Worlds All the Time

conversation?" A small girl was now lying on the ground between the two of them. "How did that dragon suddenly turn into a human?!"

"How should I know?"

What Tomochika had called a Golden Thunder Dragon had suddenly taken on the form of a young girl.

It is a normal enough occurrence in a world like this. Things like dragons and wolves always end up turning into little girls that talk like old men, Mokomoko observed, nodding to herself as if it were the most obvious thing. But it was the first Yogiri had heard of such a trope.

After writhing around on the ground for a while, the dragon-turned-child collected itself, rising up to sit on its knees. "Actually, I was told that when speaking to human males, a form like this is ideal."

"Where the hell did you hear that?" asked Tomochika. "What is wrong with the people in this world?"

Yogiri remembered the robot that had stopped their train earlier saying something similar. "Okay, putting all that aside for now, why did you attack us? Those other dragons were here because of you, weren't they?"

"It was a test to see if you were worthy of meeting the Swordmaster."

"Swordmaster?" Yogiri felt the spark of a memory stirring inside him. "Ah, the cat girl mentioned that to us before. Something about a Swordmaster's Gift, wasn't it?"

It was during an encounter they'd had in the first city they had visited. A beastkin had briefly brought up Swordmasters after volunteering to show them around (and then betraying them).

"What?! You aren't here to meet the Swordmaster?!" The girl opened her eyes wide in shock.

"Talk about unnecessary collateral damage," Tomochika muttered to herself.

"We're just trying to get to the capital."

"That's impossible! No one passes through here simply to reach the capital!"

"The lord of Hanabusa told us we could do it."

"Those people only use steam engines! They don't drive through!"

"Huh, that's true; I guess Ryouta would never have made the trip like this himself…" mused Tomochika.

"There are roads for people to go out and do maintenance on the tracks, so you should be able to make it." Those had been Ryouta's words, though he had likely been offering a reasonable guess rather than speaking from personal experience.

"No matter. This canyon houses a Swordmaster, who has the power to bestow the Gift upon others. Of course, we cannot permit just anyone to stand before him, so we sift out those who are unworthy ahead of time."

Tomochika frowned. "Can anyone in this world make it past that many fire-breathing dragons?"

"If one cannot withstand such an attack, then they have no right to meet the Swordmaster," the girl answered, sounding quite proud for some reason.

"Well, I guess it has nothing to do with us, then," Yogiri said with a shrug. "Let's go."

"Okay."

The two of them turned back to their truck. As they did, the dragongirl stood up to block their way.

"I told you, you passed! Will you not go to meet the Swordmaster?!"

"Why would we? I was just wondering if you were targeting us specifically, but that doesn't seem to be the case." Yogiri had only been interested in finding out who was orchestrating the attack on them, but if there was no grand plan behind it, he didn't particularly care to know more.

"Err, that's…not good — for me! I was told to bring those who are worthy!"

"Didn't you just try to run away?"

"Isn't it normal to flee the scene when all of one's comrades are annihilated?"

"So why did you appear to us at all?"

"After someone is attacked by my underlings, seeing my majestic form in the sky strikes an inescapable despair into their heart! I flew over here to wrap things up, but by the time I realized the others were dead, it was too late to run away without looking like a fool. So I figured I should tell you that you had passed and then fly away to maintain some semblance of dignity."

"Okay, so you're just an idiot, basically. But why should we go meet the Swordmaster? Do you really think we look that promising?"

Neither of them possessed the Gift. Although they had used the camouflage rings to present themselves as normal residents of this world, they still looked totally powerless to an outside observer.

"I do not judge based on the power of the Gift. The fact of the matter is, you killed all of my underlings. To accomplish that, you must have considerable strength."

"Okay, but really, I don't care about this Swordmaster person," Yogiri replied bluntly.

"This is a Swordmaster we're talking about! An equal to the Sages! Do you not wish to see that power for yourselves?!"

After hearing the comparison to the Sages, Yogiri stopped and thought. If a Swordmaster was really on the same footing as a Sage, it was possible that person might also know how to return them home.

"What do you think?" Yogiri asked, turning to Tomochika. "Maybe it's worth our time to meet this guy after all."

"I don't know. We're already lost. I'm not sure we're in a position to be getting sidetracked like this."

"Aha! Very well, then! Allow me to guide you! There is no way you can reach the capital on your own. It's a good deal, don't you think? After you've met the Swordmaster, I can take you straight to your destination!"

Hmm. That doesn't sound like such a bad idea. We're probably just going to get more and more lost on our own.

"Oh, all right, why not," Tomochika conceded.

"Okay," Yogiri told the dragon-girl. "We'll go with you to meet the Swordmaster, then."

After all, heading to the capital to meet up with their classmates wasn't their primary objective. Yogiri felt that expanding their knowledge of the world around them was also important. No matter what they planned on doing next, they would still need information.

"Very well. My name is Atila. What are your names?"
"Yogiri Takatou."
"Tomochika Dannoura. Nice to meet you."
And with that, they were off to meet the Swordmaster.

◇◇◇

Returning to the truck, the four of them set out at once. As usual, Tomochika was driving while Yogiri sat in the passenger seat, now with Atila on his lap.

The canyon was like a maze. Getting out of it without a guide would have been extraordinarily difficult. Apparently, few people attempted to cross it except by train. Before the construction of the railway, locals had taken a wide arc to avoid the area entirely.

After traveling for a while, the green of distant trees came into view. Yogiri more than welcomed the change from the desolate brown tones of the canyon. It relieved him to know that there was an oasis even here in this wasteland.

Passing through the trees, they eventually came upon a large clearing. Aside from the low-growing flowers, the space didn't seem to house anything particularly special. Even so, Tomochika looked at the clearing in open-mouthed shock. It was overflowing with people.

Upon hearing that a Swordmaster lived there, they had assumed there would be a considerable number of followers with him, but even at a glance it was easy to see that there were more than a hundred gathered in the clearing alone. It was far beyond Yogiri's expectations. The mixed gathering seemed to have no uniformity, meaning they had most likely all traveled there independently to meet the Swordmaster.

"Is this guy especially popular?" Yogiri asked Atila.

"If you don't know of him, I suppose you really were just passing by! Today is the day of selection for the Knights of the Divine King. Those who are selected will be allowed to become the Swordmaster's own disciples. In short, everyone gathered here is aiming to be a Swordmaster in the future."

"You're getting us involved in something annoying, aren't you?

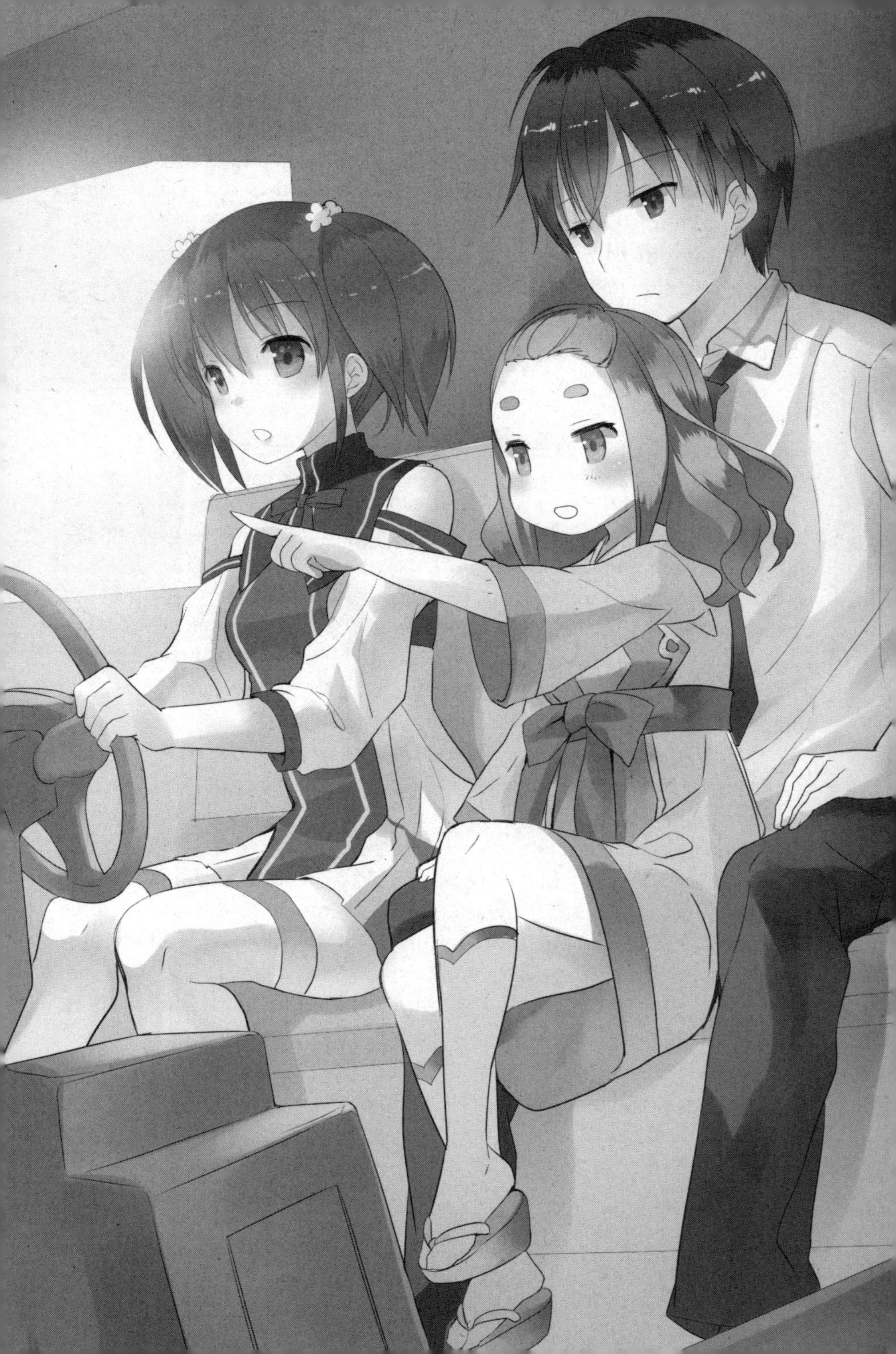

You'd better keep your promise to us, at least." Yogiri had initially thought that meeting this Swordmaster would be a good idea, but things were looking a bit more complicated now.

Stopping in front of the crowd, the travelers climbed out of the armored truck. A hooded man immediately accosted them.

"Hey! Since when are vehicles allowed to come here?! I thought that getting here on your own strength was part of the trial!"

"It's not like we ever intended to do any trials in the first place," Yogiri answered.

"Ha! Sorry for your trouble, but I guess you all fail then! Sucks to be you!"

In the face of the man's obvious scorn for them, Yogiri didn't have anything to say. He saw little point in feeling bothered by something he didn't even care about in the first place.

But a voice did answer. An old man behind Yogiri spoke up as he pushed his way to the center of the crowd. "You can't fail before the trial has even started. Although I suppose getting here at all is a trial in and of itself." The deep wrinkles on his face spoke to his advanced years, yet there was no sign of that age in the way he walked.

Hm...so this is a Swordmaster, Mokomoko mused, already sounding impressed, as if she could sense his mastery of the craft just from the way he carried himself.

Though he wore eastern-styled clothing, he wasn't carrying a sword. As he reached the center of the crowd, the old man looked around. "There are a lot of people here, eh?" he muttered to himself. He seemed to consider that for a short while, then continued. "Start killing each other until I say to stop. Whoever survives will begin the trial."

"Ugh. Just a minute ago I was thinking, 'Hey, maybe this guy is better than the other people we've met so far!' God, I feel stupid for believing that for even a second," Tomochika said in disgust.

Within moments, the entire clearing around them was overflowing with killing intent.

Chapter 4 — He Seems Like a Decent Person… But I Won't Trust Him So Easily!

The crowd that filled the clearing around the Swordmaster included all sorts of people from far and wide. Yogiri and Tomochika stood at the outer edge of the gathering, and although the area was now filled with killing intent, no one had made a move just yet. Some of them were probably waiting to see what would happen next, while others were waiting to hear if the Swordmaster had anything more to say.

"Can I ask a question?" Despite the nervous atmosphere, a confident voice rang out. "If I kill everyone else, does that mean I automatically pass?"

The speaker was the man who had been harassing them. He wore a black shirt, black pants, and a black cloak. The scabbard on his back was black as well, and so was the handle of the weapon sticking out of it.

"No comment. But if this were a test of character too, then you would have already failed."

"What?!" The man went stiff at the unexpected reply.

"Come now, you can't just ask whatever comes to mind. Think before you speak. It's possible that asking any questions at all might disqualify you off the bat, don't you think?" the Swordmaster said, making no attempt to hide his disdain. At his words, the crowd around him grew steadily more cautious.

"Hmm, is he actually nicer than he seems after all?" Tomochika wondered, although Yogiri had the opposite impression.

"If he was nice, he wouldn't be telling people to kill each other. Excuse me, can I ask a question too?" Yogiri called out to the Swordmaster, raising his hand. The gaze of the crowd immediately shifted to him.

"What is it this time? Were you even listening?" The Swordmaster was sounding increasingly exasperated.

"I don't really care if I fail. We're only passing through, and I don't feel like killing a bunch of people, so can we just walk away?"

They had only gone there to gather information, but Yogiri certainly wasn't interested in going through a battle royale to get to it.

"Wh-What?!" Atila stammered, before the Swordmaster could even answer.

"Well, we've met this amazing Swordmaster now, haven't we? So it's your turn. You're supposed to lead us to the capital," he replied before turning back to the older man. "So, can we go?"

"Oh? You made it all the way here by sheer coincidence? It doesn't seem like you're a coward, but if I simply let you go, things could get messy. So let's do this: if anyone escapes this clearing, everyone fails. Think that over."

"Ah, that's annoying," Yogiri grumbled. They were now fully committed to being a part of the trial, one way or another.

"Hurry up and get started. A Knight has to be more bloodthirsty. I didn't come here to watch you all stand around and have a chat. Do I have to set a time limit too? You have ten minutes. If more than half of you are left by then, you all fail."

With those words as the trigger, the tense atmosphere broke. The man clad in black drew a sword from his back. Perhaps he was just that fast, but despite everyone around him being on guard, the man next to him barely had time to react as the blade slashed through him. With a single stroke, he had been cloven cleanly in two, the upper half of his body sent flying. His torso careened towards Tomochika, who nimbly stepped back to avoid it.

It seems you've grown rather accustomed to this, Mokomoko observed.

Chapter 4 — He Seems Like a Decent Person... But I Won't Trust Him So Easily!

"After all we've been through, this isn't that weird," Tomochika replied as an angry roar filled the clearing.

The fighting had begun in earnest.

"Whoa!" Yogiri suddenly raised his voice in surprise.

"What's wrong?!"

"Even the blade of that guy's sword is black."

"Oh, you're right. Who cares?!"

"What do we do now? Running away would be easy, I guess..."

But if they did run, some of the people around them would certainly try to stop them. Before Yogiri could even put that thought into words, it became a reality. A small crowd had started moving towards them. Either they looked like easy pickings, or they'd been pegged as the most likely to run away. It seemed like Yogiri was going to have to use his power.

Just then, a swordsman appeared in front of them. Despite being in silver full plate armor, he moved as if it weighed nothing at all. Each individual piece seemed to be as slim and lightweight as possible. His lack of a helmet served to strengthen that impression.

"Please rest assured, I shall keep you safe!" Flashing them a bright smile, he turned back to face the coming crowd. "You fools! Do you not understand the Swordmaster's intentions at all?! He will never recognize those who kill indiscriminately! This is a trial to determine who will take actions befitting a Knight of the Divine King!"

"He seems like a decent enough guy...but I'm not going to be fooled again." Considering her experiences thus far, Tomochika was naturally suspicious.

Impressive. For someone to make it here they must have some measure of strength, but it seems this man is leaps and bounds above the rest of them.

The silver swordsman met the crowd that approached him head-on, dispatching them handily with his blade and shield. He was clearly skilled enough to not only thrash those around him in spite of being outnumbered, but to do so without using lethal blows. No matter how strong he was, however, he was still just one swordsman. There was no way he could defend the pair against magic or ranged weapons.

The moment Yogiri felt a clear killing intent aimed at him, he discharged his power. As he did, ten members of the melee immediately collapsed.

"What on earth...?" Seeing their sudden deaths, the silver swordsman paused for a moment.

"Well, actually—"

"I see! This is the power of the Swordmaster! It is no wonder he doesn't carry a sword! I didn't see him move at all, but a feat like this would be no challenge for him! This must be his judgment against those using dastardly means to triumph!"

Tomochika had been trying to think of a way to cover up Yogiri's power, but it was totally unnecessary. Seeing the strength of the swordsman and the bizarre deaths of those around him, their attackers moved on in search of easier prey.

"Hmm. It seems we are safe for the time being," the swordsman said, watching the mob retreat. "You said you ended up here by happenstance. While this must seem like quite a cruel sport to you, this trial is a matter of great importance. Could I ask you to stay at my side for a while longer?"

They had been warned that if a single person escaped, all of them would fail. Yogiri didn't know what all of this Swordmaster business was really about, but he was hesitant to ruin it for everyone else.

"All right, we'll stick around for a bit."

"Thank you for understanding. I will make every effort to shield you from harm, so please rest easy."

With the people targeting Yogiri and Tomochika having moved on, the area around them quieted down.

"Please...help..."

Breaking through the calm, a weak voice called out, drawing Yogiri's attention. It was the man who had been cut in half at the very beginning. All that remained was his head and right arm, with just enough of the torso left to connect them. It was incredible that he was alive at all.

"This is...most unfortunate." The silver swordsman shook his head, clearly deciding that there was nothing to be done for the poor man. Yogiri felt the same way.

"No, please, don't give up on me!" Mustering what little strength he

Chapter 4 — He Seems Like a Decent Person... But I Won't Trust Him So Easily!

had left, the man called out to Tomochika. "You, the girl over there, please come here! Help me!"

He has an impressive voice for someone with barely any lungs left, Mokomoko mused.

"Umm, what should I do?"

"He's not giving off any killing intent, so it doesn't seem like he's planning anything."

"Really? Well, I guess I can go help him a little." Tomochika approached the fallen man. "Are you okay? If you want me to hold your hand or something, I can do that much."

"Pick up those rainbow-colored rocks over there, please." He pointed at a number of shining, colorful rocks that were scattered about him. They must have been sent flying when he'd been cut down.

Tomochika gathered them up. "What are these?"

"These are...Apology Stones..."

"So what should I do with them?"

"Please put them in my right hand."

Tomochika did as she was asked. As she pressed the stones into the man's hand, they began to glow. Within moments, the mutilated fellow had completely regenerated. Although less than a quarter of him had previously remained, he was now restored to perfect condition, with a fully functional, tall, and slender body.

"What the...?"

"Thank you so much! I thought I was done for!"

He now looked just as he had before the black-clad man had cut him in half. Even his clothes were intact, with not a scratch to be seen on them. Yogiri looked around, but the other half of the man's body was no longer on the ground. It had probably disappeared as part of the regeneration process.

"These are Apology Stones. They are star crystals given away as an apology. They can heal you from serious injuries, or they can be used to roll the *gacha*, so they are extremely useful items!"

"What is this, a mobile game?! Who was apologizing to you anyway, and for what?"

"Stop!"

The Swordmaster's shout filled the air. Everyone in the clearing froze at once.

"We've cut the numbers down significantly. Let's move on to the next phase. Come with me."

With those words, the old man made his way out of the clearing, which was now covered with a gruesome pile of bodies. Only about half of the crowd had survived.

"You said he was testing for how a Knight should act, but I'm pretty sure he just wanted to reduce the number of people applying."

"No, I'm confident that there is some deeper meaning to all of this. We ordinary people cannot fathom the thoughts of a Swordmaster."

Despite Tomochika's commentary, the silver swordsman was unshaken.

"Takatou, this is getting kind of dangerous, don't you think? We met the Swordmaster, now let's get going to the capital."

"No. I will have to ask you to continue with the trials…" Atila piped up, somewhat hesitantly.

"Why? You asked us to meet him and we did."

"Well, see, if the person I recommend becomes a Knight, then I myself will become the Knight's attendant. But don't worry, I won't ask you to become the Swordmaster's disciple or anything!"

Yogiri sighed. "I guess it would be a waste of an opportunity if we left before getting any information."

It was definitely a frustrating situation, but getting out of the canyon without a guide would have been difficult anyway. And although this Swordmaster's power was supposedly equal to that of the Sages, they had yet to see it in action. Yogiri was curious to know more.

He decided to participate in the trial for the time being.

Chapter 5 — You Say That Like You're a Famous Person in Disguise

The Swordmaster left the clearing, heading into the forest with the survivors hurrying to follow him. Yogiri stayed at the back of the crowd, walking at a leisurely pace. Beside him was Tomochika, with the tall man who had used the Apology Stones next to her, and the heroic swordsman in silver plate armor beside him. Atila walked a little ways ahead of the group, as if to guide them forward in response to Yogiri's total lack of motivation.

The guy with the Apology Stones was chattering away with Tomochika. "My luck has always been terrible. It's honestly a miracle I survived long enough to become a high school student. I can't even count the number of times I've been hit by cars. It got to the point where people were calling me Lucky Shin. Of course, I was compensated with lots of money, but that didn't really help. My parents would throw it into their wallets and that was the end of it." Perhaps because she had helped him out, he was being oddly friendly with her. Apparently, he was originally from Japan, like they were, but unlike them, he had been killed and then reincarnated in this world. "I was abducted by a cult and used as a human sacrifice in one of their rituals," he explained.

"Sounds like you had a rough time."

"Indeed. That is how I got these Apology Stones."

"Wait, we're talking about how you got the stones?! I thought you were just telling me a very sad life story."

Believing himself to be dead, he came face to face with a woman who claimed to be a goddess. She had brought him over to this world for a fresh start, but after being reborn, his terrible luck had continued, so he was given the star crystals as an apology.

"You mean a goddess is powerful enough to decide where you go when you die?" Tomochika mused.

It depends on the person, I suppose, Mokomoko answered, although only Yogiri and Tomochika could see and hear the Dannoura guardian spirit. *Just as there are some who are protected by guardian spirits like myself, there are those whose fates are dictated by the gods.*

"And you said you can use the Apology Stones on the *gacha*? So, umm…" Though she felt it was a little rude to ask, Tomochika couldn't help her curiosity.

"Yeah, you can get amazing items or new companions from it, so why am I in this situation? That's what you wanted to ask, isn't it? I told you, my luck is terrible!"

"Uhh, yeah, now I get it." Basically, no matter how many times he played, he would probably never get anything good from it.

"I'm saving them up. If I do ten rolls at once, then at least I get a rarity guarantee!"

"I see. Good luck." She had no idea what to think of this mysterious *gacha* system he was talking about.

Seeing that they had reached a natural pause in the conversation, the silver swordsman took the opportunity to jump in. "Now then. Since we have become so well acquainted, is it not strange that we still do not know each other's names? Perhaps we should introduce ourselves."

They had developed a sense of camaraderie while walking together, so none of them objected.

"I suppose I will go first. Perhaps you have guessed my identity by now, but please, just call me Rick," the swordsman said with a wink.

"You make it sound like you're some famous person trying to keep your identity a secret, but we have absolutely no idea who you are, sorry," Tomochika replied.

Despite clearly having expected them to know his identity, the silver-clad man remained unperturbed.

"My name is Lynel," offered their second companion. "I don't have much interest in becoming a Knight, to be honest, but my friend kind of forced me to come." He scratched his head, as if wondering how he got there.

"And where is that friend now?"

"She probably assumed I was dead and went on ahead."

He really did seem like a man who had nothing but bad luck.

"I'm Yogiri Takatou."

"And my name is Tomochika Dannoura. We were heading for the capital and somehow ended up here. Don't ask."

Walking ahead, firmly keeping herself separate from the rest of them, Atila seemed to have no intention of sharing her name with the group.

Yogiri used the momentary silence to finally ask a question that had been bothering him from the start. "So what exactly is this Knight thing all about?" Everyone spoke about the process as if it were common knowledge, so he hadn't been able to glean any helpful details.

"Ah, yes. It appears you two are foreigners here, so of course you wouldn't know," Rick said. "Let me give you a simple explanation. First, as you must have seen, this world is beset by a number of threats. These threats can generally be divided into two categories. The first are the Aggressors, also known as 'invaders.' They are said to come from a place beyond this world, but most of them are dealt with by the Sages. You do know of the Sages, I'm sure?"

Yogiri nodded. Having encountered both categories already, he was well aware of the relationship between the Sages and the Aggressors.

"The other primary threats are the sealed deities, also known as Dark Gods. As far as we know, they too came from beyond the bounds of this world, but that was over a thousand years ago. Now they are considered a threat from within our world. The Divine King's role is to dispatch those creatures."

"Do the Sages not deal with them at all?"

"For the most part, the Sages and Swordmasters work separately.

35

Since they each have their own specialties, it has become an unwritten rule that they do not interfere with each other's opponents. That said, the Sages are a rather arrogant bunch, so the two groups often come into conflict regardless. At any rate, the Dark Gods were locked away by the Divine King over a millennium ago."

"And they're still a threat, even though they've been sealed off?" Tomochika asked.

"Correct. The Dark Gods have produced their own powerful spawn and adherents who survive to this day. These groups act in the shadows to revive their masters. The Divine King's Knights work to thwart their efforts, and the leaders of those Knights are the Swordmasters."

"Wait, the Divine King isn't the leader?" Considering the flow of the conversation, that's not at all what Yogiri was expecting to hear.

"The Divine King is currently sealed away herself, holding back one of her enemies."

"For over a thousand years?!" Tomochika was surprised. If the title wasn't passed down from one generation to the next, then that would mean a single person had been doing the job for all that time.

"That is what we've been told."

Of course, with the story being over a thousand years old, it was likely little more than a myth. It was hard to tell how much of it was actually true at this point.

Having been wrapped up in their conversation, the group suddenly looked around and realized that they were alone.

Yogiri immediately shrugged it off, looking ready to turn right back around and leave. "Huh, looks like they left us behind."

"Wait! Here! You just need to keep going in this direction!" Atila pointed ahead, but she was pointing into the forest, where there was no sign of anyone else.

"There's nothing there, though."

"This is merely a barrier. You cannot see the inside from out here."

"Hmm."

He supposed it *was* rather strange that such a large group of people had suddenly disappeared without a trace. But when they went to continue forward, Atila remained where she was.

Chapter 5 — You Say That Like You're a Famous Person in Disguise

"This is as far as I can accompany you. Only those who are invited can enter."

Yogiri didn't remember being personally invited anywhere, but they must have been at some point without realizing it.

"So how are you going to take us to the capital, then?"

"Simply call my name once you have finished the trial. I shall appear before you."

It was starting to feel like she had no intention of guiding them anywhere at all, but they couldn't exactly force her to do it.

"This is getting to be a real pain, you know that?" Yogiri sighed, leading the other four onwards and through the barrier.

As they passed into the interior, a tower suddenly appeared, looming before them. Tomochika looked up at it with a surprised gasp. The others made no effort to hide their shock either.

Aside from the tower, the scenery within the barrier was the same as what they had seen from the outside, but the atmosphere was completely different. Yogiri could feel a sharp cold in the air. The crowd they had been following was once again within view, walking towards the tower as if it were the most natural course of action. Clearly, that was their destination.

Hey! Leave here at once! Forget this Swordmaster! Mokomoko's shocked voice had a layer of urgency to it that took them by surprise.

"What's wrong? It's weird that it's hidden, but it's just a creepy tower..."

That's not it at all! Can't you tell? The dark aura surrounding this place is so thick! Something truly evil lies ahead!

Tomochika looked around her, but she didn't feel anything like Mokomoko was describing. Yogiri, however, could sense a general killing intent hovering over the entire area, all but clinging to them.

"Lynel, are you okay?!" Tomochika cried out as their new friend suddenly doubled over and vomited. Looking around, she saw a number of other people in the crowd collapsing and falling violently ill as well.

The miasma of evil surrounding us must have gotten to him.

"But I don't feel anything..."

I am protecting you, and I'm sure the boy can handle himself.

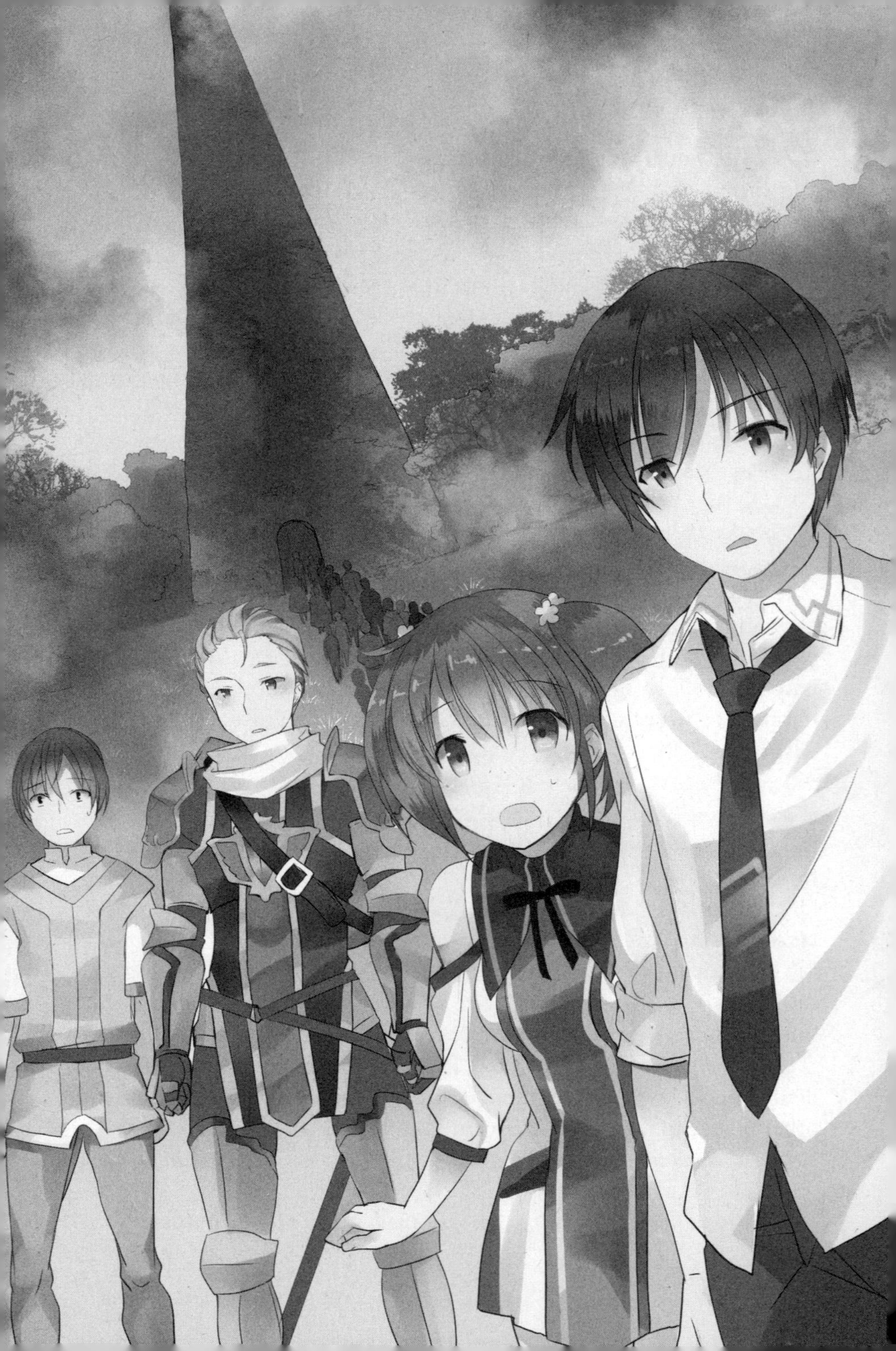

Chapter 5 — You Say That Like You're a Famous Person in Disguise

"An evil aura of this strength will have no effect on me, but it seems Lynel isn't so lucky," Rick noted. He appeared to be perfectly fine, but it didn't look like there was anything they could do for their other companion.

As they were trying to take in what was happening around them, Lynel's body began to glow. Before long:

"Thank goodness. Saved by the Apology Stones again!" he gasped, climbing back to his feet.

"Are you sure you should be wasting those stones on something as basic as throwing up?"

"Well, given how sick I felt, I wasn't going to be able to move at all without them."

Tomochika didn't know the extent of the Apology Stones' abilities, but they seemed to have given him some sort of resistance to the tower's dark aura.

"Well, what do we do now? This place seems pretty unhealthy, and Mokomoko did tell us to leave," she said, turning to Yogiri.

"Yeah, ever since we came through the barrier, there's been a faint feeling of death around us. It's almost like this whole area is in the shade." Still, it wasn't an urgent threat, and it didn't feel pressing enough to force them to leave right away. "It seems fine to me for the moment. There's no immediate danger, at least."

Well, this is you *we're talking about, after all. You* may *be able to protect yourself, but please keep your guard up just in case.*

"Is something wrong?" Rick asked. Their odd conversation had piqued the silver swordsman's interest.

"Oh, no, we were just surprised. We should head that way, right?" Yogiri brushed off his question and began walking towards the tower.

The structure was built as a circle, probably about a hundred meters in diameter. Looking upwards, the top of it disappeared into the haze, so it must have been fairly tall. At ground level there was an enormous door, through which the crowd of people was slowly moving.

Yogiri's group followed them inside. There was a large circular chamber within, in the middle of which was yet another tower. This inner tower was a cylinder about ten meters wide, reaching right up to the room's ceiling. The building appeared to consist of an inner and outer layer.

Within the interior tower was another door, inside of which was the Swordmaster himself, surrounded by the surviving Knight hopefuls.

"You lot are so slow. Hurry up or we'll leave you behind."

"I wouldn't particularly mind if you did," Yogiri muttered, brushing off the Swordmaster's complaints as he and his group stepped into the inner tower. The door abruptly slammed shut behind them and the room began to shake with a loud rattling noise.

It appeared they were inside an elevator, which had now begun to climb.

Chapter 6 — Why Is Someone Like That Trying to Be a Knight of the Divine King, Anyway?!

The top of the tower offered an unbroken view of the surrounding canyon. It was a desolate wasteland of stone and earth stretching as far as the eye could see. The greenery around the tower seemed to be the only exception.

Standing at the edge of the roof, the Swordmaster pointed downwards, directing the crowd's gazes to a truly bizarre sight. A large, spherical hole had been gouged into the canyon. The sphere itself ran ten kilometers across, as if a bomb had gone off there, vaporizing everything in its path.

Within that space was a huge crowd of horrible creatures. Countless monsters glared up at them, but they seemed to be frozen in place. Tomochika's superior eyesight could make out two particular figures standing right at the center: a woman in white and a man dressed in black. They looked like they were hugging each other, but there was no doubt that they were locked in combat, as the woman's sword had punched through the man's back and into her own stomach, clearly in an attempt to keep him trapped there with her.

Tomochika instinctively understood that this was where one of the Dark Gods was imprisoned — where the Divine King had sacrificed herself to hold him prisoner.

"This is where the world ends. It is always on the edge of collapse, ready to fall at any moment. Swordmasters aren't anything special. All we do is watch over those below."

"Of course we know that!" A woman in fancy clothing stepped out from the crowd. "I came here to put an end to that thousand-year-long struggle. This conflict between the Knights and the Dark God's spawn is a wasted effort! Let us end the conflict once and for all!"

"You seem to be absolutely brimming with motivation," the Swordmaster observed with amusement.

"Yes. Your job ends here. Feel free to retire in peace!"

The woman raised the staff that she was carrying. The heat that it gave off sent a murmur through the crowd. A ball of intensely hot light had appeared just above it, and even without any knowledge of magic, Tomochika could tell that it contained an enormous amount of energy. That brilliant, blinding fireball was like a tiny sun.

The woman swung the staff downwards and the ball of light seemed to vanish, catapulted towards the barrier at an incredible speed. Her confidence was understandable — certainly, anything it touched would be utterly destroyed.

But something changed the moment the sphere struck the barrier. The light visibly began to slow, and in no time at all it had come to a complete stop. The woman looked at the now-frozen fireball in confusion, not comprehending what she was seeing.

"Time within the barrier moves much more slowly," the Swordmaster explained. "The farther in you go, the slower time will move. Once you reach the center, time has essentially stopped. It will probably take a few hundred years for that attack to reach its destination, so I suppose my retirement will have to wait a while longer!

"Now, let's start with the trial of selection. Generally speaking, anyone who makes it to the bottom of the tower will pass, but there are some rules. I'll leave the explanation to you." As he spoke, the crowd realized that a woman in a black dress had appeared beside him. "I will see you all later. Oh, and due to the proximity of the barrier, time here moves a bit more slowly as well. If you waste too much time, the rest of the world will move on without you."

With those parting words, the old man stepped into the elevator.

Chapter 6 — Why Is Someone Like That Trying to Be a Knight of the Divine King, Anyway?!

The door closed with a sharp sound, transporting him back to the bottom of the tower. Naturally, those remaining would not be able to use the elevator themselves.

"All right, then, everyone. Please pay attention. I am Magic Puppet A, and I have been appointed to oversee this trial."

Tomochika looked at the woman. As the newcomer had announced, she was clearly a doll. Her skin was far too smooth for a normal human being.

"Within this tower are numerous other dolls like myself. They all look identical, so please don't be alarmed. Now I shall explain the rules of this tower. As the Swordmaster said, we will have you descend from the one hundredth floor, where we currently are, back down to ground level."

"Hey, what happens if we just jump off the side?"

The speaker was a girl whose maid outfit looked totally out of place on her. She had a rather high-class air about her — a sharp contrast to her choice of wardrobe. Tomochika could hardly imagine her ever serving someone else.

"Such an action will not be sufficient to pass."

"I figured that would be too easy." The girl spoke as if she could indeed fall a hundred stories and be just fine. At that point, Tomochika noticed that something else was off.

"Hey, Takatou, was she with us earlier? Do you remember anyone like her?" Tomochika couldn't recall seeing the girl beforehand, but she could hardly imagine failing to notice someone that flashy and eye-catching.

"She wasn't in the clearing. It looks like a bunch of other people have joined us since then."

Tomochika looked around. Their numbers had been significantly reduced by the original massacre in the clearing, but the size of the crowd seemed to have somehow increased again.

"In order to pass, you must reach the first floor after accumulating one hundred points, all within twenty-four hours. The time is currently fifteen hundred hours, so you must complete this task by the same time tomorrow. You will discover how to obtain points on your own. There

43

are numerous hints scattered throughout the tower. To keep the explanation to a minimum, the tower is divided into two areas. Please look at the floor. You can see that here it is white. That makes this a safe zone. Engaging in any form of combat inside a safe zone will immediately disqualify you. The other areas are battle zones, which are gray in color."

Tomochika was starting to get a very bad feeling.

"You may ask any Magic Puppet to determine your current total points along the way. This ends the explanation and the trial has now begun. There are numerous ways to leave this rooftop, so please take whichever one you prefer."

A number of structures were scattered around the platform, each one presumably an entrance to the tower interior. A large portion of the crowd had jumped into action the moment the signal was given, heading straight for those entrances. They must have thought that starting as soon as possible would be an advantage, considering the time limit.

Rick, however, raised his hand. "May I ask a question?"

"You may, although I will not answer anything regarding the rules, so you're likely better off just getting started instead."

"If memory serves, that woman in the maid uniform is Lady Teresa of the Thunderous Blade. Why is someone who is already a Knight involved in the selection process?"

Tomochika realized that the girl in question must be quite well known.

"She is participating under special circumstances. There are various reasons for an established Knight to be here, but in her case, her qualifications have been revoked and she must retake the trial."

The unexpected increase in participants must have been those with other special circumstances. Rick seemed to accept her explanation, but his face still turned grim.

"May I have a word, everyone?" he said, gathering their group together.

"What's up?"

"If the explanation we've been given is correct, I suspect we will not be able to avoid combat within the tower. If that is the trial, then unfortunately there is nothing we can do about it. But between us, there are some participants we should absolutely avoid fighting."

"Like that thunder girl?" Tomochika asked, glancing at the former Knight. Clearly not in a rush, she was still standing around, perfectly relaxed.

"Yes. Her name is Teresa. She is a swordsman of the Thunderous Blade and was once royalty."

"I don't know what Thunderous Blade means, but I guess she's pretty strong?" Tomochika had no idea how powerful the girl might be. She obviously stood out, but she didn't have the same aura of mastery that Tomochika was used to seeing in their stronger opponents.

"The 'Thunderous Blade' denotes her rank as a swordsman, with that particular rank being third. In comparison, my rank is Royal Blade, which is seventh. In short, she is not someone we could hope to challenge in combat."

"Seeing as she used to be royalty, did her family fall from grace or something, for her to be dressed up like that?" Tomochika wondered if she was simply disguising herself as a maid for some reason.

"Is that what you're worried about?" Rick asked in a tired voice. As he did, Teresa herself answered. They had been speaking quietly, but she'd had no problem overhearing them.

"This is just my personal taste in clothing. I'm rather surprised to see you here, Richard," she said, approaching them with a smile.

"I'm also quite surprised. Why *are* you here?" As if dreading the conversation to come, Rick's voice was flat.

"It seems I was killing people too recklessly, so my qualifications were revoked. But without the title of Knight, I'll have significantly less clout within my household, and I'll lose my personal standing as well. I spoke to the Swordmaster about it, and he agreed to give me a second chance."

"I see," Rick responded, still visibly tense.

"I can tell that I'm not welcome here, so I will take my leave. I look forward to meeting you inside." With that, Teresa left them behind, casually walking towards one of the many entrances.

The unasked question hung in the air between them, the heavy atmosphere making it difficult to speak.

There are several others that you should be wary of as well, Mokomoko whispered, prompting Tomochika to look around. *First is the one with the skull mask.* The guardian spirit pointed at someone who was wearing an outfit made entirely of black cloth. It was likely a man, but there was no way to know for sure. His white skull mask was a stark contrast to the rest of his clothing, and gave the impression that it was floating in the darkness.

"Why is someone like that even trying to become a Holy Knight?!" It was hard to think there was anything holy about such a person.

Also, that one. I am not familiar with the magic of this world, but his presence is quite different from the others.

"Yeah, I get what you mean."

Mokomoko was pointing out a man dressed entirely in gold. He wore a golden robe, with a gold circlet that decorated a face with rather delicate features. A necklace studded with numerous precious gems hung around his neck, and his fingers were thick with gaudy jewelry. In his hand was an expensive-looking golden staff, decorated with finely detailed ornamentation. One look made Tomochika think that he must be a mage of some kind. At first glance his appearance seemed ridiculous, but all of the items that he wore looked to be of very high quality.

"Really, come on. Isn't this supposed to be a selection for *swordsmen*?!"

Meeting Tomochika's gaze, the man gave her a gentle smile and a wave in response.

Next is that one. He looks like an otherworlder. He was either reincarnated or summoned here, so he likely has some sort of power. Wearing a white jacket lined with fur, the man certainly did look Japanese. He had three girls with him who appeared to be his companions.

"Seeing those girls with him makes me think of Tachibana and his bodyguards," Tomochika murmured. One was a bunny-eared girl dressed in white, another wore something like a military uniform, and the third — much smaller than the other two — wore a dress. All three seemed to look up to him with an air of respect.

Chapter 6 — Why Is Someone Like That Trying to Be a Knight of the Divine King, Anyway?!

Last is this one over here. Something about her bothers me, although I don't quite know what it is. I feel like she's hiding something. Wearing a slightly dirty overcoat, the woman the spirit was referring to seemed ordinary in every way, although her stance suggested that she had experience in combat. She possessed a definite aura of strength.

As Tomochika looked around, she noticed that most of the others had already entered the tower.

"Lynel and I each have one point, and Rick has ten," Yogiri noted. "You should go find out how many you have."

While Tomochika and Mokomoko had been reviewing the competition, the others had been finding out their current scores.

"Wait, they'll actually tell us?"

"I mean, she specifically said that she'd tell us if we asked, yet everyone just went straight inside for some reason."

Tomochika checked in with the Magic Puppet and found that she had one point.

"How does Rick have ten points already? Is it because he just *looks* like such a swordsman?"

The one-pointers among them weren't carrying any visible weapons.

"By the way," Lynel said timidly, "that girl who launched an attack at the barrier earlier was the friend I told you about. Her name is Frederica, but...what should we do? I feel like we can't just leave her like that."

Frederica was still standing as still as a statue, staring blankly at the barrier. Tomochika supposed that she hadn't yet overcome her shock at her failure.

"You're right," Rick replied. "Although, considering her behavior earlier, trying to console her will likely have the opposite effect."

At Rick's comment, Lynel continued, his voice still shaking, "Exactly...but anyway, I came here without knowing anything about Dark Gods or the Divine King. So what should I do now? She said she was going to defeat the Dark God, right?"

Frederica's magic had been completely blocked by the barrier. Naturally, if the barrier was made to seal the monster inside, outside

47

intervention would hardly be a simple task. But Tomochika, of course, knew of an attack that could bypass all of that.

"Hey Takatou, couldn't you —"

Couldn't you kill it? Tomochika cut herself off before she finished the sentence. She could almost hear him saying, "But there's no reason to kill it, right?" At this point, they had no idea what the Dark God actually was. Killing it because it "sounded evil, I guess" was definitely jumping the gun. Reflecting on her own hasty reaction, she looked at Yogiri, seeing an unpleasant expression on his face.

"What's wrong?" she asked, confused. It was a look she had never seen on him before.

"That Dark God or whatever? I thought it was the source of the evil aura here, so I went ahead and killed it already..." he said, pointing towards the center of the barrier. "But...it seems I may have made a mistake. I feel kind of bad now."

Rick had been explaining the local history to Lynel, telling him all about the millennium-long battle between the Dark God and the Divine King. It was just about the most awkward possible moment for Yogiri to cut in and say, "Oops, I killed it."

Chapter 7 — I Would Have Died Without These Apology Stones

He was one who bestowed blessings. Hearing the wishes of ordinary people, he granted exactly what they asked for — it required no special action from him, and mattered not whether the wish was good or evil. He was like a machine, producing blessings in accordance with the number of sacrifices offered.

He wandered the world of humans, granting all sorts of wishes. And naturally, the humans had fought to control him. Although he wasn't someone who could be confined to a single place, the mortals inevitably clashed over control of the land that he walked. Even if they had no wishes of their own to be granted, no one was willing to let others have unrestricted access to him.

As the humans waged endless wars over him, he continued to grant their wishes. It didn't take long for humanity to be reduced to half of its original population. The survivors finally realized that they were bringing about their own destruction. Seeing the fate that awaited them, they came to terms with their own foolishness and realized that he was something beyond their grasp — something that shouldn't even be reached for.

His destruction had been the only answer. Or, at the very least, sealing him somewhere that no human hand could touch. But it would prove to be a remarkably difficult task. He paid no mind to the attacks that they leveled against him, and he offered no counterattack. Nothing could bring him down.

Then one wise person offered the following piece of advice: "It's simple. Just wish for it. Wish for him to be destroyed."

With no other recourse, those who heard those words treated them like a gift from heaven and immediately made their wish.

But he — later to be called a Dark God — displayed his own will for the first time in response to that wish.

"Very well. As compensation, I will take all of the lives of this world."

The Dark God bared its fangs. Spreading its miasma of fear and darkness, unleashing its spawn, it began to overrun the world. Uniting in desperation, humanity took up arms to fight against their seemingly inevitable destruction — but ordinary humans couldn't hope to stand up to the creature's spawn. They were once again on the verge of annihilation.

That was when the Great Sage first appeared.

◇◇◇

Rick was explaining these details of the thousand-year-old battle to Lynel while Yogiri and Tomochika were speaking softly a short distance away, but they could still overhear his story.

"When did you even kill it?" Tomochika whispered.

"Right after we entered the barrier, I guess? Around the time we first learned about the evil aura covering this place."

"Can't you make sure that you're killing the right people?!"

"It was a reflex."

"Well, either way, according to their story, killing it doesn't seem like a big deal." It felt odd to be angry with him about it, so Tomochika tried to console him instead.

"I don't know. It sounds like humanity was just getting what it deserved. Was the Dark God actually that bad?"

"I mean, if you put it like that..."

Yogiri figured it was humanity's own fault for thoughtlessly abusing the creature's power. "I was just trying to deal with the source of the

Chapter 7 — I Would Have Died Without These Apology Stones

dark aura here. It ended up killing the monster, but listening to Rick's story, I'm not sure that killing it off that way was the right choice."

"I'm sorry. It's not surprising that you'd feel bad about it."

"I don't know how to explain it. It feels like I killed an animal from a species on the verge of extinction, or destroyed an ugly statue and then found out it was culturally significant." Yogiri seemed to be feeling the weight of the Dark God's history, which was, after all, over a thousand years old, and there were entire organizations dedicated to watching over this legendary being. It hardly felt appropriate for someone who merely happened to be there by chance to step in and put an end to it all.

Finally, Yogiri shrugged. "Well, there's no point in overthinking it. If we don't say anything, they'll never know anyway."

"Wow, talk about a quick recovery!"

"In the end, it technically did try to hurt me."

The barrier had probably been put up by the Divine King, so it would continue to exist even after the Dark God's death. No one would know about its passing for quite some time. Obviously, it was pointless to seal the beast away now that it was dead, but revealing that fact would throw off the balance between the many groups that were based around its existence.

Yogiri sorted through his feelings and moved on. "All right, let's get to the bottom of this tower. If we can talk to the Swordmaster properly, we can get on with our trip to the capital."

At some point, the roof had almost entirely emptied of people. The only ones left were their own small group and Lynel's friend, Frederica. Even the doll that had given them their instructions had disappeared at some point.

Finally seeming to snap out of her stupor, Frederica walked over to join them.

"You have more of those stones, right?" she said sharply to Lynel, holding out one of her hands. "Give me one!"

"Uhh, why?" Lynel asked, recoiling a little. Tomochika didn't think they looked much like friends at all.

"I want to regenerate my magical energy. And you can use those to give yourself a boost, right? I'm going to try firing off another blast, even faster this time."

"Uh, I think I explained this before, but these are bound to me specifically. Other people can't use them..."

"What?! Then why did you even come here?!"

"I didn't really want to in the first place —"

"God, you're useless! Fine, whatever!" With an angry huff, she left them behind and stalked into the tower. Yogiri's company was now alone on the roof.

"Should, uhh, should we get going too?" Lynel suggested, still rattled by his encounter with Frederica.

Given the numerous entrances to the tower that were scattered about the rooftop, picking one seemed like part of the trial in and of itself.

"All right, let's take this one." Yogiri picked a door at random, actively avoiding the one that Frederica had chosen. There were no objections.

◇◇◇

Lynel screamed as a spear shot out from the wall, punching straight through his stomach. He had triggered a trap, proving once again just how awful his luck was.

Yogiri could sense the danger from the traps and thus avoid them easily enough himself. And most had already been triggered by those who had gone ahead of them, but Lynel had managed to step on one of the few that hadn't been activated beforehand. Their group was just inside the entrance to the tower and hadn't even had a chance to get their bearings before it was triggered.

"Lynel, are you okay?!" Tomochika rushed over to him in a panic as Rick calmly drew his blade, cutting off the part of the spear that was jutting out from the wall.

With the spear handle broken and no longer holding him up, Lynel collapsed to the floor, struggling through the pain to reach for his pocket. A moment later, his body began to glow, and he once again stood back up as if nothing had happened. The spear through his stomach had been

Chapter 7 — I Would Have Died Without These Apology Stones

pushed out and was now lying on the ground. Just like before, even his clothes had been repaired.

"Man, without these Apology Stones, I'd be dead right now," Lynel noted, wiping the sweat from his forehead. He seemed remarkably relaxed considering what had just transpired.

"If you act so casual about it, I'm going to stop worrying about you when you get hurt!" Tomochika said, a bit flustered. If Lynel could simply use the Apology Stones to save himself in every situation, there seemed to be little cause for concern regardless of what happened.

"That was still dangerous, though. I can't use the Apology Stones if I can't touch them with my hands."

"Then why aren't you always holding on to one, just in case?"

"Oh, that's a good idea! I can't believe I never thought of that!" As Lynel spoke, he reached into his pocket and took out one of the stones. "Hmm, this still seems a bit dangerous. Oh, I know, can I get one of you to wrap something around my hand? It's me, after all, so I'd probably just drop it the moment it actually mattered."

"That's so true..." Tomochika quickly tied a piece of cord around Lynel's hand, tight enough that it wouldn't be possible for him to drop the stone.

"You called them star crystals, right? I don't know much about them. What are they actually capable of? They appear to be something of a lifeline for you, so it might be useful for us to understand what they do," Rick suggested.

"Ah, that's a good idea too! Just calling them star crystals doesn't really tell you anything about them, does it?" At Rick's encouragement, he began to explain. "There are three ways to use the star crystals. One is a total restoration. Regardless of the injury, it will fully heal you and restore your magical energy. The second method is Boosting. All of your abilities are temporarily boosted by a significant amount. That's what I used to help me resist the effects of this place."

"You said it was temporary, right?" Tomochika cut in, suddenly curious. "How long does it last?"

"About thirty minutes, I think...uh-oh."

Yogiri realized at the same time that Lynel did — it had been about thirty minutes since he'd last used the stones for a boost. Although Yogiri had killed the source of the evil aura, the toxic smog that covered the region was probably left over from the battle over a thousand years ago. It had yet to dissipate.

"Err, finally, you can just use them to roll on the *gacha*. You can get items from it, or summon allies...anyway, I'll give it a spin!"

"Why right now?"

Reaching into his pocket with his unbound hand, Lynel took out three star crystals. After shining for a moment, they disappeared and something dropped to the floor at his feet.

"Um...is that some sort of really special brush?"

"No, it's just a normal one. A brush that lasts for one year." It seemed that his luck had failed him again. "B-But I still need something to get me out of this situation!"

"This guy's luck is really something else. I get the feeling the star crystals aren't going to be that useful," Tomochika quipped as Lynel began pulling more of them from his pockets. By the time he had acquired an item worth keeping, he was down to only three crystals left.

"Thank goodness I eventually got something helpful! It looks like this ring will protect me from status effects."

Now that Lynel was calmer, Yogiri took a look around the inside of the tower. The walls and floor were built with gray stone. It must have been one of the battle zones that the Magic Puppet had mentioned. The corridor before them ran in a straight line, then turned where it met the edge of the tower.

"Well, obviously we need to get to the bottom, but how do we get points?" Yogiri asked thoughtfully.

"If it is as straightforward as I imagine, we may just need to fight others along the way and take their points as a reward. But I really can't say for sure."

"Hmm. I guess there's nothing we can do now but go on. Lynel, please be careful," Tomochika warned, putting particular emphasis on those last words.

As they had little choice in the matter, they proceeded into the

Chapter 7 — I Would Have Died Without These Apology Stones

depths of the tower. The path soon turned white, indicating that they had reached a safe zone. A wooden chest sat in the middle of the room.

"I wonder what this is?"

"Lynel, make sure you stay away from it!"

"I'll check it out," Yogiri offered, approaching the chest himself. It appeared to be empty save for a single piece of paper stuck to it, with the words "one point" written on it.

"I guess there was one point inside but it looks like someone already took it."

"Is this how you're supposed to get them?"

"That means we're at a huge disadvantage, having entered the tower last..."

"It would be pretty hard to get a hundred points like this — hold on a second."

Seeing that the chest wasn't sitting quite level, Yogiri pushed it to the side, revealing a square metal plate about ten centimeters across. The number one was written on it in the local language, and it gave off a dull glow. When he picked up the metal plate, the glow faded.

"So...does this mean I just got a point?"

Feeling like he had been transported into some sort of video game, Yogiri was starting to warm up to this whole trial business.

Chapter 8 — I Feel Like the Definition of "Swordsman" Is Being Stretched Too Much!

The passage again continued onwards in a straight line for some time. Before long, the stones ahead changed back to gray, signifying that they were returning to a battle zone. Again, most of the traps had been triggered already, the bodies of their numerous victims scattered across the floor. There didn't seem to be much danger at this point, but with Lynel's luck, there was always the chance that something would go wrong.

With that in mind, Yogiri made a point to secretly sense and destroy the traps ahead of time. Anything that posed a danger to him was visible to his power, which in turn made it "killable."

"Are you sure you're okay with only three of those things left?" Tomochika pressed Lynel, still concerned for his well-being. If he were to experience three more fatal injuries, he would have no way left to restore himself.

"Yeah, at midnight I'll be getting another apology message. Depending on how unlucky the day was, I'll get more star crystals. So as long as I can last until midnight, I'll be fine."

"That doesn't sound fine at all! With the way things have been going, there's no way you'll make it to midnight!"

At the end of the hall, there was a door blocking their way. On it was written "Only one may leave." Tomochika still couldn't read the local language, so Yogiri read it aloud for her. He had more or less mastered the language by now thanks to having read through the dictionary they had received from the concierge in Quenza.

"I can feel magical energy coming from this door. This must be part of the trial. I suppose we're meant to abide by these words," Rick guessed.

"That's easy, then. If only one person can leave, we send one person through at a time," Lynel replied.

"Do you think it'll really be that easy?" the swordsman wondered.

"I'll go first. I have the Apology Stones, so even if something tries to kill me, I'll be all right!"

"I don't know about that. You only have three left," warned Tomochika.

"It's fine. You even strapped one to my hand, remember?" he replied, lifting his left hand with the stone still wrapped up in it.

"To be honest, your confidence is making me more and more certain that something *will* go wrong..." Tomochika couldn't suppress a very bad feeling that was welling up in her chest. Even if he was able to heal himself with the star crystals, Lynel seemed far too cavalier given their current situation, to the point where it almost felt like he had a death wish.

"Really, just leave it to me! At worst, it'll be less trouble for all of you if I die."

He opened the door, revealing a corridor that turned sharply to the right. With a deep breath, he confidently stepped through and the door automatically closed behind him.

"Sending in one person at a time is fine, but if there are multiple entrances to this place, how do we know when he's out? And what if once Lynel completes the trial, none of us can proceed? Is it just me or are there several holes in this plan?"

Before Yogiri could finish voicing his concerns, it became clear that his questions were all for nothing. Lynel had barely gone before they heard him screaming. Naturally, things had not gone as well as he'd hoped. Once again, they were faced with proof of Lynel's inescapable ill fortune.

"Let's go."

"Sending in one person at a time was totally pointless, wasn't it?"

"It feels like we sent him straight into danger all on his own."

Throwing the door open, the group entered the corridor together.

Chapter 8 — I Feel Like the Definition of "Swordsman" Is Being Stretched Too Much!

Turning right, they found that the passageway soon made another turn, this time to the left, before opening up into a larger room.

The smell of blood filled the air. Pieces of mutilated corpses were scattered about — and not just one or two people, either. *Dozens* of bodies lay on the floor, sliced apart in a way that made any hope of saving them impossible.

"Lynel?!" Tomochika called out, looking around the room frantically.

The first thing they saw upon entering was their friend's left arm lying on the ground. With Tomochika's cord still wrapped around the hand, there was no doubt about its owner's identity.

It didn't take long to find the rest of Lynel writhing on the ground a bit farther inside. He had lost only his left arm, which could be considered lucky by some. Of course, since that particular arm had held the star crystal, his luck swung right back around to being absolutely god-awful.

Rick drew his sword, advancing into the room. A woman stood in the center — the one Rick had called Teresa of the Thunderous Blade. The scene of carnage before them made it quite clear why her qualifications as a Knight had been revoked.

"Did you do this?" Rick asked, an uncharacteristic nervousness to his words.

"Of course. But can you really blame me? You know what the mechanism of this room is, right? Once two people are inside, the doors lock. When only one person is left, the doors open. In short, one has to die so that the other can escape."

"That may be the case, but you were obviously in this room alone earlier. You would have been able to leave at any time."

"Sure. The trial for this room is over now. I can leave whenever I want, and it looks like the mechanism only activates once, so even if I left, the rest of you could walk through with no problem at all."

"In other words, trial or not, you have no intention of letting us pass?"

The woman was standing in front of the exit, making her intentions quite plain.

"That guy in black said as much earlier, and I don't think he was far off. In the end, Knights are characterized by their strength. The Swordmaster shut him down earlier, but don't you think the old man would actually agree?"

The man that she was referring to must have been the asshole who had asked if he would automatically pass by killing everyone else. Teresa's intentions were clearly along the same lines — she planned to cut down as many rivals as possible early on.

"If strength was the only requirement, your qualifications wouldn't have been revoked! Do you not understand that?!"

The woman stood her ground casually as Rick faced her, his guard up. There was an incredible difference in their postures. Rick's stance displayed his fear, his choice to hold his sword in front of him an obvious attempt to place an obstacle between them. At least that's how it looked to Tomochika.

"Miss Dannoura, this is bad," he murmured. "Quite likely the worst possible situation."

"You said she's really strong, right?" Tomochika remembered that Rick had pointed her out as someone they should never try to fight.

"That is correct," Teresa answered with a smile. "I don't know how much it means coming from me, but without a Swordmaster or a swordsman of the Absolute Blade rank, I don't believe it is possible to defeat me."

Despite the fact they had been whispering, she once again had no trouble overhearing their conversation. Given that, they couldn't even discuss the option of running away.

"I've already taken measures to block the entrance," she continued, "so there's no escape for you either."

It was almost like she was reading Tomochika's thoughts. Turning around, Tomochika saw that the entrance they had used to get into the room was, in fact, now blocked. She scanned the chamber carefully. "Rick, please be careful! There are thin wires set up everywhere!"

Her superior eyesight was coming in handy even here. Wires were snaking across the entire room, so thin that they were practically invisible.

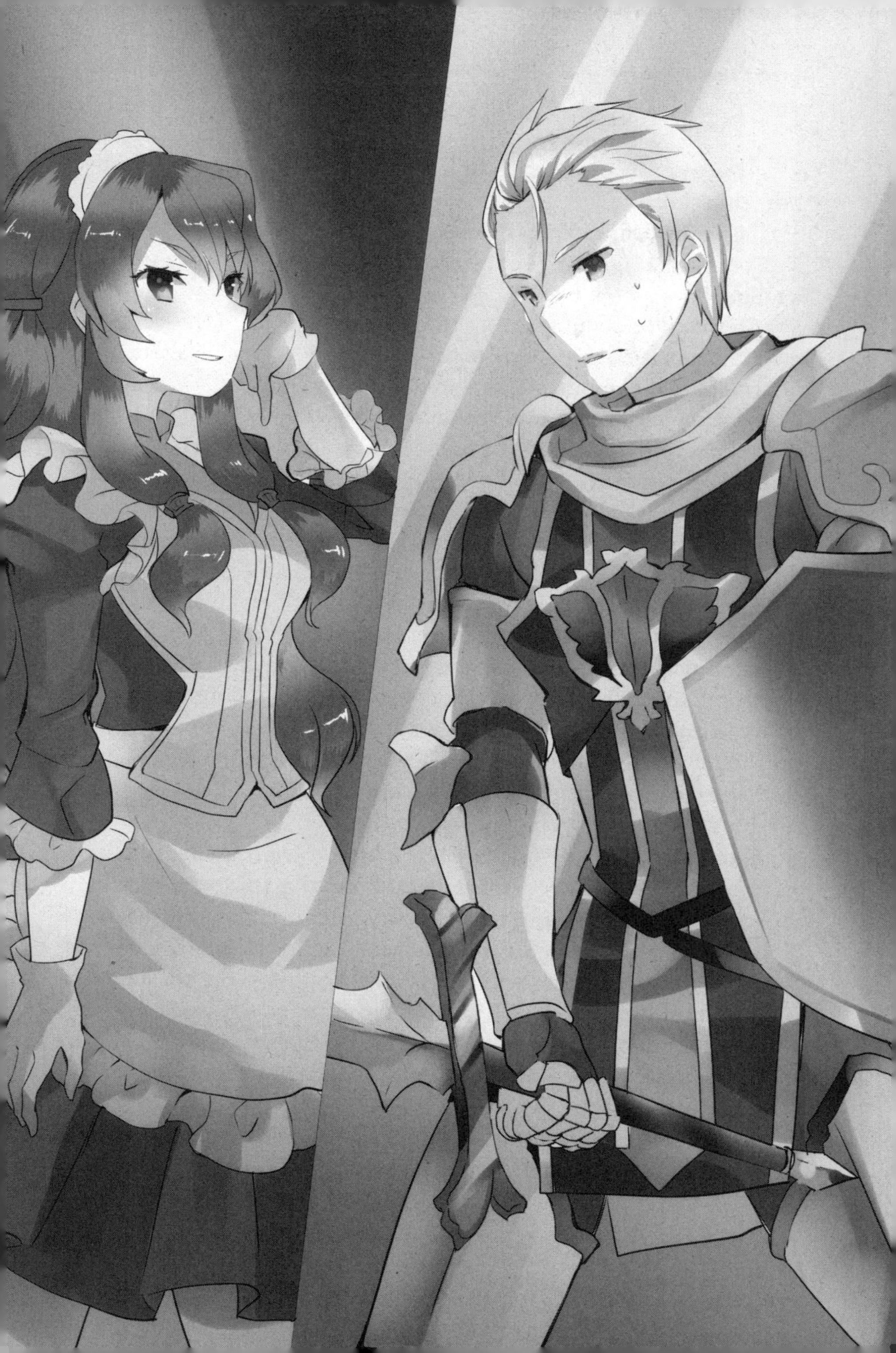

"Yes, I am aware of her techniques. She uses a sword in the form of those thin threads."

"Isn't the definition of 'swordsman' being stretched a bit too much here?" *A title like "thread user" would be far more appropriate*, Tomochika thought.

"It would be a nuisance for the Swordmaster if all of the weaklings made it through. So if you want to get past this room, you'll have to prove that you have the resourcefulness to survive my attacks."

The air itself seemed to shake as Rick suddenly swung his blade upwards, a shrill metallic sound filling the chamber. An ordinary person would have no idea what had just happened, but Tomochika could see Rick deflecting the incoming wire the moment it struck.

Rick's blade whirled around him. Sounds of clanging metal rang out one after another, with barely a pause between them. He continued to deflect the wires that were coming at him from every direction, but either due to their construction or Teresa's sheer level of skill, his blade failed to cut through them. The best he could do was deflect them, sending them harmlessly off course before they came back at him from a different direction.

"I'll do what I can to hold her here! When you get an opening, head for the exit!" As he continued to protect himself from the high-speed wire attacks, the strain in Rick's voice was clear.

But Tomochika could tell that Teresa was merely toying with him. As if the evil woman were embracing the role of examiner rather than applicant, she was throwing out attacks that Rick could only just handle. He must have realized he was on very thin ice. Teresa fully understood the limits of his ability and was forcing him to use every last ounce of skill that he possessed. If he let up for a moment, or made a single mistake, it would be over before they could blink.

But with a single word, Yogiri brought the fight to a close.

"Die."

Rick's next attack cut cleanly through one of the wires as Teresa collapsed to the floor without a sound.

"Getting caught up in an exciting fight is all well and good, but come

Chapter 8 — I Feel Like the Definition of "Swordsman" Is Being Stretched Too Much!

on, let's not forget about Lynel," Yogiri reminded them, his tone somewhat irritated.

"Oh, that's right! Lynel, are you okay?!" Tomochika ran over to their fallen friend's side.

Meanwhile, Rick could only stare at Teresa's unmoving body.

"What on earth...?"

The silver swordsman stood frozen in shock.

Chapter 9 — What Kind of Crappy Game Is This World?!

Yogiri thought for a bit about how to explain his ability to Rick. He didn't care if his enemies knew about it, since they were going to die anyway. Their impressions of him didn't matter. He also didn't mind if Tomochika knew about it, obviously. Even if she wasn't fond of it, she understood that it was necessary to protect them so that they could get back to their own world. And not only was it pretty much impossible to hide it from someone who was traveling with him long term, trying to keep it hidden would be a pointless hassle.

When it came to someone they had only known for a short while, however, things were different. He had already displayed his power, so he couldn't pretend that it hadn't happened, but it was hard to know how much he should explain to their new companions. Yogiri knew all too well how people tended to react when they found out exactly what his power was.

"I have incredibly good luck," he offered. "In a way, I guess it's kind of the opposite of Lynel."

Claiming that he had good enough luck to cause death seemed pretty absurd, but it was a lot better than confessing he could kill people with his thoughts.

"Wait, are you saying your *luck* protected me?" Rick was slowly recovering from his shock.

"Probably. Why else would she suddenly collapse like that? She was in my way so she probably had a heart attack or something."

"A heart attack? That's absurd. For a Thunderous Blade to meet such an end..." He paused. "Then again, she *was* imprisoned for a time. I did wonder how they had managed to arrest her, but if she had some sort of congenital condition..."

Yogiri hadn't actually expected Rick to believe him. After all, who would buy a story like that? But the swordsman's face showed that he had fallen deep into thought.

There was Lynel, who was living proof that some people had extremely bad luck.

There was Teresa, now dead.

And then there was the memory of the Teresa he had known before coming here.

It seemed he was trying to connect those facts in his head somehow.

"I saved Lynel, by the way," Tomochika announced happily, as if she had never been worried about him in the first place.

"Man, even with an Apology Stone stuck to my hand, it doesn't help if they just cut the hand off, does it?"

"I guess you'd really be in trouble if you lost both arms then, huh?"

Lynel seemed to be having trouble getting the remaining Stones out of his pocket, but he finally managed it with Tomochika's help.

"Anyway, let's get out of here," Yogiri suggested.

No one objected, of course — with the dozens of bodies scattered about the room in hundreds of pieces, the smell of blood was suffocating. None of them wanted to stay there any longer than they had to.

Past the door that Teresa had been guarding, they found a descending staircase. After confirming there were no traps, Yogiri led the group down, where they eventually came to a door with more words written on it.

Once one leaves this floor, they cannot return.

"I guess this is to force us closer together and make us fight," Yogiri said thoughtfully. If everyone was to walk around randomly in a tower of this size, they would rarely come across the others.

"Perhaps it is also a warning. As in, 'make sure you have finished searching above this floor.'"

Rick's idea also had merit, but Yogiri wasn't keen on the idea of turning around. "Might as well keep going forward at this point," he said, opening the door.

A white corridor extended in a straight line ahead of them. The safe zone continued for as far as they could see.

"Are you sure this is safe?" Tomochika asked, scanning the passage before them restlessly. Yogiri looked down the corridor and saw what looked like a reception desk with a magic doll in a black dress sitting behind it. The puppet looked identical to the one they had seen on the roof. Yogiri remembered the first doll saying that all of them were the same type.

"Hello. Congratulations on reaching the ninety-eighth floor. The entirety of this floor is a safe zone. As Magic Puppet A explained, any combat in a safe zone will immediately disqualify you."

"Does that mean that only the attacker will be disqualified?" Yogiri didn't particularly care about passing the test, but he was concerned that being disqualified might come back to bite him later on. As long as they followed the rules, it likely wouldn't be a problem.

"Correct. Please rest assured you will not be punished for the actions of others. However, the only punishment is the disqualification itself, so I suggest you remain vigilant." In other words, they might run into those who would willingly disqualify themselves in order to attack them. "Furthermore, there is nothing related to the trial on this floor. If you continue forward, you will find a door to another staircase. However, there are facilities prepared for you here. If you wish, you may rest here before continuing."

Looking down the hallway, they could see numerous doors along both walls, which must have led to the rest facilities she had mentioned.

"Now that we're in a safe place, I feel like there's something we should talk about," Yogiri said. "Wouldn't it be better if we went on separately?"

Up until that moment, he had been fine with working together, but if the trial was going to be this malicious, it was time to reevaluate. After all, the room they had just come from would have forced all of them to fight to the death. If there were more rooms like that later on, there would be no way for them to work together.

"Good point. This trial is much harsher than I expected. But are you sure you can manage?" asked Rick.

"We're fine," Yogiri shrugged.

"I can just hide in one of these rooms until midnight when my Apology Stones are replenished."

"I feel like that's not going to be enough to get you through, Lynel…" Tomochika seemed concerned, but Yogiri couldn't care less about Lynel. Of course he wouldn't feel right letting the guy die in front of his eyes, but if Lynel went off and died on his own, that was nobody else's responsibility.

Of course, Yogiri could simply kill all the obstacles in their path. If he did, they might safely reach the bottom without a problem, but he felt no obligation to take care of these strangers. His top priority was Tomochika's safety. He was more than confident in his ability to protect himself, so with Tomochika as his only responsibility, he figured he could manage. But each person that was added to the group increased the risk exponentially. If Yogiri was trying to keep them all safe, it would hinder his ability to protect his classmate.

"Understood. I will depart first," Rick volunteered.

For someone who was truly aiming to be a Knight, taking a rest so early in the game was out of the question. Points and other items along the way seemed to be first come, first served, so there was an advantage to going ahead as well.

"Hopefully we won't come across each other during the trial," Yogiri offered.

"I shall pray for that to be true. Good luck."

Rick proceeded down the hallway, leaving the three of them behind.

◇◇◇

The Sage Aoi was making her way out of the Forest of Beasts. A plump young man who called himself Daimon Hanakawa was following close behind her.

"And so that dastardly Rikuto fellow referred to me as a pig. Perhaps you believe I have no right to complain, seeing as he rescued me. But for even those beautiful elf girls to call me a pig was a fair bit too demeaning."

Although she had never said she would help him, nor offered to let him come with her, Hanakawa continued to follow close on her heels, rambling the whole way. At first, she hadn't really cared. Once she left the forest, she would be boarding an airship anyway, so she didn't mind acting a bit like monster repellant for the boy until then. But once he'd brought up the fact that he knew Yogiri Takatou and Tomochika Dannoura, she couldn't ignore him anymore.

"They ordered you to stay in the forest, didn't they? Are you sure you can just walk out?"

Hanakawa responded with an unpleasant laugh, annoying enough that Aoi briefly considered killing him on the spot. "Indeed, I thought such a thing might happen! But this particular slave collar was made to lose its effectiveness after three days! One must repeatedly refresh the order of subordination to keep its effects active! I needed only to bear their cruel edict for three days! My intention was to take their heads in their sleep after they had begun to fully trust me. I never imagined they would abandon me to the forest first!"

"Just to let you know," Aoi said with a snort, "an item like that won't work on me."

"Of...of course, such a thought never once crossed my mind! I hardly have need of such a device now, anyway!" Hanakawa answered nervously, hurriedly removing and throwing the collar away. His panicked response made it quite clear what he had been planning all along.

"Well, whatever. I'm going to have to ask you to come with me once we get out of the forest."

"Um, excuse me? Actually, err, I'm not all that into tomboyish types. I figured help getting out of this forest would be enough!"

"I don't have any reliable information on those two. Since you've seen their power for yourself, you might be useful, and if they know who you are then that makes things a lot easier as well."

"If that is the case, I will tell you all I know! I have been grumbling about Takatou's power, thinking that, if forced, I could turn that information into a profit with you. At least, that was my line of thinking, but never with the intention of accompanying you to face them! Besides, I am sure that the moment they see me, they will kill me!"

"If it's profit you want, I can pay you well enough. I'm a Sage, so I can get almost anything you ask for."

"Then what need is there for me to go with you at all?!"

"From here, I'm heading to a place called Hanabusa. I want you to tell me about them while we travel."

As they were speaking, they finally emerged from the forest. A wide plain stretched out before them. Called the Dragon Plains, it was the very place where the Sage Sion had transported the class of high school students during their school trip. In the middle of the field was their school bus, the back half of which was entirely missing.

"That's the vehicle you came here in, right? Looks pretty beat up."

There were traces of something passing through it and into the forest beyond, likely the result of some sort of projectile magic.

"That appears to be the case. Hm…strange, I believe on my way to the forest a few days ago, I saw the corpse of a dragon…"

"A dragon? You mean that? There's only a tail there now."

Beside the bus was what looked like the end of a tail lying on the ground. It was a pretty strange sight, since there were no creatures living in the area that would be interested in eating a dragon carcass.

"Well, anyway." Whatever had happened there, it had nothing to do with her.

As they approached the circular aircraft that Aoi had anchored nearby, the hatch opened automatically and steps descended from within.

"Let's go."

"Nooooo! I will definitely, definitely be killed! I don't want to see those two ever again!"

Aoi pulled out her knife, threatening the reluctant Hanakawa.

"Bahahaha! You think such a trinket could harm me?! I am a Healer! Such trifling wounds as that knife might cause would be as nothing, healed in an instant!"

Chapter 9 — What Kind of Crappy Game Is This World?!

"Did you not see me fight earlier? I can nullify other people's powers. Want a demonstration?"

"Why does everyone I come across have such ridiculous powers?! What kind of crappy game is this world?! It's like they didn't even try to balance it!"

"Well, from my perspective, there's a certain kind of balance."

"But if you can nullify powers, why do you have need of me?!"

"It's not like I'm omnipotent. I need to learn about my opponents so that I can decide how to best use my power against them. So hurry up and get in."

Forcing the unhappy Hanakawa forward, they boarded the ship. Their destination was the Garula Canyon, the very location where Yogiri and Tomochika had recently found themselves.

Chapter 10 — Think of It as One of Those Ghost Stories You Normally Hear About at Old Inns

Tomochika went stiff the moment they opened the door to their room. Of course, she never would have chosen to take a room by herself in a place this dangerous, but the small, cozy room had only one bed.

"Takatou, just to remind you, we're not alone in here. Mokomoko is also — wait, where is she?!" Only when Tomochika thought to warn Yogiri against any misbehavior did she realize that Mokomoko was no longer with them.

"Looks like she's not here," Yogiri observed disinterestedly.

"Why is she gone now when she's normally so irritatingly close?!"

Tomochika looked around the room in a panic. She finally located the family spirit, who had sunken halfway through one of the walls.

"What the hell are you doing?!"

I figured if I was around, there would be some things you two wouldn't be able to do. I thought it best to remove myself from the equation, but then out of sheer curiosity, I couldn't help but peek back inside.

"Make up your mind, would you?!"

Pay me no attention. Think of it as one of those ghost stories you normally hear about at old inns.

"There's no way I can ignore you when you're just sitting there, half inside the wall! And wait, why are you taking your clothes off, Takatou?! Aren't you moving a bit fast?!"

While Tomochika was speaking to Mokomoko, Yogiri had entered the room and begun to strip off his uniform.

"I'm just changing into my pajamas. Is that a problem?"

The two of them had come to the tower more or less empty-handed. Perhaps the other participants were the same, as sets of pajamas and underwear had been provided in the rooms.

Oho, you seem strangely receptive.

"What are you talking about?"

It sounds like you weren't rejecting him at all. If he's just "moving too fast," wouldn't you be happy about it if he was moving a little slower?

"That's enough out of you!"

Well, it doesn't matter all that much when he clearly has no interest, Mokomoko said flatly, pointing towards the bed. Yogiri had finished changing into his pajamas, slipped into bed, and immediately fallen asleep.

"What is with this guy? Is he interested in me or not?" Tomochika felt like an idiot, having gotten all worked up over nothing.

There was no point standing around in the doorway, so she finally entered the room, collapsing hard onto the bed. The mattress shook but Yogiri's sleep remained undisturbed.

Well, all that aside, there is something suspicious about this tower.

"You don't say."

Of course there is the issue of the tower's various mechanisms, but I don't mean something as physical as that. The truth is, ever since we arrived here, the tower has been trying to capture me.

"Why would it do that?" In spite of Mokomoko's obvious concern, Tomochika was more curious than anything else.

If you don't sound worried for me at all, it makes it a bit hard to continue.

"Well, to be honest, I don't care all that much, though I guess having you around is kind of an advantage for us."

R-Right. Anyway, back to the matter at hand. This tower is attempting to collect the souls of the dead into a single place.

"Really? That doesn't sound great."

Even putting aside the issue that this posed for Mokomoko

Chapter 10 — Think of It as One of Those Ghost Stories You Normally Hear About at Old Inns

personally, the fact that it was happening intentionally made it hard to believe the motives behind it were pure.

For someone of my level, such a trap is of no consequence. However, it deeply concerns me for numerous reasons. Please remain cautious.

"Not much I can do about it, though, can I?" Tomochika replied. Being only human, she could hardly fight against such a vague and abstract threat herself. She glanced over at Yogiri. Seeing his defenseless, innocent, sleeping face, she couldn't help but feel that he looked a little cute. "Well, putting all that aside for now...there are more important things to worry about."

Even with Yogiri fast asleep, she couldn't help but fret over whether it was safe to change in the same room.

◇◇◇

After receiving the key from the receptionist and being led to his room, Lynel entered and stopped. Any action he took was an opportunity for his bad luck to strike. He had learned from his life that in order to keep the damage to a minimum, he needed to do as little as possible.

When offered a free room service meal, he had turned it down. He had suffered from food poisoning enough over the years, and there was always the possibility of actual poison being mixed in by mistake as well.

It was a small room with just a single bed. Sitting down on it, he waited, taking care not to do anything else. Glancing at the clock that was always at the edge of his vision, he saw it was now 23:50. The date would be changing soon, but he couldn't let his guard down. If only being alone in a room was enough to stay safe, he could have avoided several deaths in the past.

He had already died fifteen times since deciding to take on this trial. Every time that he died, he was returned to the capital, but this time he had made it much farther than before. One might wonder why he bothered to come all the way out here if he knew he was just going to be killed. The answer was simple: he'd die if he stayed in the capital anyway.

It was like an incarnation of death that followed him around. It had the shape of a person but wasn't human. It was clad in a sinister black metal, covered in blades from head to toe, like a personification of pure murderous intent. No matter where he went, Lynel was always killed by the creature. But it couldn't follow him here. Apparently, the barrier around this place was keeping it out.

"It would be nice if I could change my save point already..." But the place where he regularly respawned had long since been decided on by the goddess who had brought him over, so there was nothing he could do about it now.

Lynel continued to wait, sitting on the bed.

0:00.

He had successfully made it to a new day, and a mail icon popped up in his vision to indicate that. As he was more than accustomed to seeing these notifications, he reached in to check his pocket without bothering to read the message. It was a magic pocket, specially made for holding the star crystals. Nothing but star crystals could be put into it, and it was far larger on the inside than it looked on the outside.

A huge number of crystals now sat inside the pocket, and he looked at them in confusion. It was a lot more than he normally received, certainly more than the previous day's bad luck should have warranted. He decided to read the accompanying message after all.

【Apology】 For game-breaking status effects
【Announcement】 20 Year Anniversary Present!
【Announcement】 20 Year Anniversary *Gacha*, Ultra Rare Guarantee Begins!

It had been twenty years since he had come to this world. According to the announcement, he had received a gift of eighty star crystals. Combined with the twenty Apology Stones that he had also received, that put him at a healthy one hundred in all.

Lynel decided to immediately go for the guaranteed *gacha*. The order of rarities was Common, Rare, Super Rare, Special Super Rare, and Ultra Rare.

Pulling five crystals from his pocket, he held them tight in one hand, triggering the *gacha*. The space in front of him immediately began to glow so brightly that Lynel was forced to close his eyes. It was the first time he

Chapter 10 — Think of It as One of Those Ghost Stories You Normally Hear About at Old Inns

had ever seen this happen, so he supposed it was a special animation for the Ultra Rare guarantee.

As the light died down, he opened his eyes to see a woman standing in front of him. The extravagant clothing wrapped around her voluptuous form was remarkably revealing. Her whole body glittered with gold, with lights shimmering and dancing around her. She truly looked like she belonged in the Ultra Rare rank.

Even so, Lynel felt no appreciation at having her appear.

"Ahh, what a pleasant smell...it feels like I am within his embrace..." The woman was ignoring him completely, as if in a trance. And then she opened her eyes. It was the goddess who had reincarnated Lynel into this world.

"Umm..." He timidly tried to catch her attention, worried that if he didn't, she might go on ignoring him forever.

"Oh, my apologies. I became a little too engrossed after picking up this lovely scent." Taking another deep breath, she turned to face him.

"What's going on here? Why did you appear?"

He hadn't met the goddess since he had died in his previous life. She had occasionally left hints to help him survive, but that was the most contact they'd had in twenty years.

"Ah! That is simple. I merely came here to look around. I'll be going back immediately."

"Uhh, what about my Ultra Rare companion?" Lynel asked, his expectations faint at best.

"Sorry, I didn't mean to get your hopes up like that. This body is only a copy, so it's more or less powerless. Most of its resources have been taken up by the visual effects."

"You mean that glowy stuff around you, and those clothes? No, never mind. Why didn't you just explain that from the beginning?" He wouldn't have gotten his hopes up in the first place that way — at least, that's how he felt, but he wasn't brave enough to say it out loud.

"The system has some formalities that must be followed. If I just forced my way here, they would notice me immediately and it would all be for nothing. Being summoned by you follows the rules, though, so I was able to sneak in unnoticed."

He didn't quite understand what she was talking about but there wasn't much he could do other than accept it. "Well, I did manage to get away from that thing that was chasing me. What should I do now?"

"Whatever you like. You've been given this power, so why don't you use it to enjoy your life in this world?"

"You mean Random Walk? The situation is totally different each time, so any knowledge I gain is basically useless. Like this time, the people I'm with are completely different from before."

The star crystals were nothing more than basic compensation for Lynel's bad luck. The real power that he had been given upon being reborn was the ability to skip back in time and do things over whenever he died.

"There are some powers that let you repeat the exact same events over and over again. But this way, if you come across a situation you can't deal with, you can simply choose not to encounter it again. I feel like that's a much better power. No matter how many times you choose to repeat events, you can always start fresh. It gives you a far better chance of survival."

"Aren't you the one who told me to come here?"

Indeed, she had been the one to recommend that he go along with Frederica in the first place.

"Not really. I just give you hints. You are free to do as you like."

Lynel wasn't sure that was true. He had been thinking that the goddess's hints were simply her way of trying to guide him. In this case, however, she had clearly wanted to come to the tower herself. He had no idea why, though, so he couldn't tell if she was using him for her own purposes or not.

"Well, you've already come this far, so if you're not sure what to do next, why not try to become a Knight?"

"Don't be ridiculous. I'll have to start over again. This tower is nothing but danger."

While it was true that, within the tower, he was safe from the creature that had been tracking him, the danger inside wasn't all that different. And the fact that he was stuck in this place meant the situation had actually grown a bit worse.

Chapter 10 — Think of It as One of Those Ghost Stories You Normally Hear About at Old Inns

"I'm afraid that's impossible. Since I've visited and seen you here, your save point has been moved to this room."

"No..." Lynel was filled with dread. This was tantamount to him being imprisoned in the tower.

"Well, see you later. I'm going to leave this body behind. It will take a few hours for it to disappear, so feel free to do as you like with it."

"What do you mean?"

"Sending objects to this world is relatively easy, but taking them out of it again is rather difficult. I've simply been manipulating this body from a distance. Anyway, goodbye."

With nothing more left to say, she fell to the ground like a puppet whose strings had been cut. She wasn't "dead," but her consciousness was clearly gone. All that was left now was a soulless body.

◇◇◇

The magic doll stared at the glowing wall, tilting her head in confusion. It wasn't a significant problem for the trial, so there was no urgent need to deal with it, but there were a number of events that were currently concerning her. Individually, no one issue was an especially big deal, but the collection of them all together was starting to become a problem.

She was in the basement of the tower. The room was a square, ten meters on each side carved into the stone, with a single large opening in one wall. The Garula Canyon, as well as the Dark God and its spawn that were sealed within, could be seen from the room thanks to its position on the side of the cliff.

It was dark, even with moonlight filtering into the chamber. The only sources of light were the glowing images on the wall, which lit up the area around them. The details of the tower and its barrier were displayed along that same wall. This was the control room and the core of the barrier that kept the evil sealed within.

"What's wrong?" the old Swordmaster asked as he entered.

"The selection process is proceeding smoothly. However, several points of concern have arisen. First is the situation outside the barrier. A number of individuals have appeared there. Further details are unknown."

The first barrier that surrounded the tower and its grounds hid the presence of the tower itself as well as the creatures that were sealed inside. It was impossible to see beyond the barrier from within it, so, from time to time, they sent out scouts to take stock of the situation. They had recently sent out several magic dolls to do just that, but had failed to learn anything of consequence about whoever or whatever was lurking nearby.

"There's nothing we can do but wait and see what happens. They could just be passing by."

Of course, it was unlikely that someone had come to this desolate, far-off canyon without a purpose. They would need to remain vigilant.

"Next, there is the situation inside the tower. The number of dead for the first day is greater than usual. This seems to be due to the actions of Teresa of the Thunderous Blade."

"I figured something like this would happen if we let her participate. But most of them were going to die anyway; it was only a matter of time."

"Why go through the trouble of this selection process, then?" The doll had been wondering about that for a while. Maintaining the barrier required a collection of souls, so it was necessary for many of those who entered the tower to die. It would have been much more efficient to kill the whole group the moment they entered the tower instead.

"I suppose considering the number of applicants who die, it's not strange that you'd think I bring them here just for that purpose. But that's not the point of the trial. The problem is that most of them are pathetically weak, and if they are going to die anyway, we might as well collect their mana for the barrier. So I don't think a larger number than usual dying off will be much of a problem."

"Lady Teresa was also among the dead."

"Why does it matter *who* died?"

"I understand your sentiment, but the numbers don't add up. Among the collected spirits, there are none that could be connected to her."

The Swordmaster paused for a moment. "I see. If she did truly die,

Chapter 10 — Think of It as One of Those Ghost Stories You Normally Hear About at Old Inns

it's possible that she turned into a ghost before the tower could absorb her."

If mana was the driving force that provided energy to the body, then spirit was the control mechanism that guided the mind. Both were diffused entirely upon dying, but sometimes the spirit remained intact, and that was particularly often the case for powerful mages and swordsmen.

"After inspecting Lady Teresa's body, we could not determine her cause of death." While they could actively monitor anything that was happening within the tower, they didn't have a record of things that had already taken place. "For now, a sufficient number of spirits have been collected for the tower's maintenance. However, if this were to continue in the future, it could present an issue."

A good quality spirit held many times the power of that person's mana. They were invaluable for the barrier's maintenance.

"We have enough stored up for a number of years already. It shouldn't be an issue."

"I am merely providing a note of caution. Furthermore, the number of half-demons for the underground barrier is getting low. I believe that replenishment will soon be required."

"Hmm. There was one woman who seemed fairly skilled with magic. Could we use her as a replacement for the half-demons?"

He was talking about Frederica, the one who had launched a magical attack at the barrier while they were all on the roof. The lone daughter of a proud noble family, she had an enormous amount of magical energy. Rumors of her having defeated some of the Dark God's escaped spawn — who had made it as far as the capital — had reached even this remote place.

The magic doll confirmed Frederica's current location. She was resting on the eightieth floor. While she still had a long way to go, she was making steady progress.

"What do you think?"

"For now, let her continue through the selection process. If she seems close to death, retrieve her. We can use her if she's still alive. Is there anything else you're concerned about?"

"Yes. There is an intruder in the tower. They seem to have been summoned here."

"That sounds like a rather significant problem, yet it's merely a 'point of concern' to you?"

"The one summoned appears to be a woman with no particular powers, and she is currently engaging in sexual acts with her summoner."

"That's pretty gutsy. Who would summon an outsider for something so petty in a situation like this?" The Swordmaster seemed impressed. Summoning wasn't a simple affair and it required a huge amount of magical energy. It was hard to believe that anyone would do it purely for the sake of satisfying a sexual urge.

"There is one other concern within the tower. My master appears to be among the participants."

"Aren't I your master?"

"No. I mean the one who created me, High Wizard Eglacia."

"He was one of the mages who fought the Dark God a thousand years ago, wasn't he? I'm surprised he's still alive."

"I do not know the details, but there is no mistaking it. He is the one wearing a golden robe."

"Ah! I thought that guy looked like an idiot, but I suppose he's in disguise. I know you shouldn't look a gift horse in the mouth, but does he understand what this selection process is actually for?" the Swordmaster asked with a sigh.

From the magic doll's perspective, only about half of the participants could really be called swordsmen. As long as they were strong, it didn't really matter who they were, but calling someone a Knight when they couldn't use a sword at all was highly questionable.

"Finally, regarding the Dark God's spawn: a unique type is attempting to break through the second barrier. It is expected to escape in three days, at noon."

The sealing power of the second barrier, used to keep the Dark God in place, was strongest at its center. That meant it was inevitably weaker near the outside, allowing some of the spawn that were trapped near the edge to eventually escape. It was why the Knights existed. Their mission

Chapter 10 — Think of It as One of Those Ghost Stories You Normally Hear About at Old Inns

was to slay any of the creature's spawn that escaped the barrier. The Swordmasters were those who led the Knights.

"Get ready to call them." In emergencies, the Knights could be instantly summoned to the area inside the barrier, made possible by the massive amount of magical energy held within the tower. "There are plenty of people who came here to become a Knight strictly so they could fight those things, no? It looks like this is going to be their first job."

"Should we take this into consideration for the trial?"

The magic doll thought it might be advantageous to have as many people pass the trial as possible in order to fight the spawn, but he immediately rejected her suggestion. "Anyone weak enough to die in the trial would be useless anyway."

The Swordmaster stepped over to the opening in the wall with the magic doll beside him. He looked out at the spherical space carved into the canyon. The Dark God and the Divine King remained at its center. Surrounding them were the evil spawn that had fought alongside the Dark God. Their movements were too slow to be visible to the normal eye, but they were definitely making their way towards the edges of the barrier.

"A humanoid, is it? Looks like this will be a pain," he muttered under his breath.

The creature closest to the edge of the barrier, one with a distinctly humanoid form, was laughing.

Chapter 11 — Interlude: I Don't Know What I'm Doing Here Either

Euphemia wandered through the forest. She had been struck by an overwhelming apathy towards life. With Lain's death and the dispersion of her mana, Euphemia had absorbed it and become even stronger.

But what good was that? No matter how strong she became, there would always be someone stronger than her. As long as someone like Yogiri Takatou existed, there was no point. After learning of his existence, any sort of strength she might obtain seemed empty and meaningless.

She had no idea how many days it had been since she began wandering. She wasn't hungry at all. Perhaps due to her new immortality as a vampire, she simply didn't feel the need for food. She vaguely remembered coming across someone earlier but had felt no impulse to drink their blood, either. The people that she encountered were afraid of her at first, but once they realized she was mindlessly walking through, they carefully retreated.

In the end, her wandering brought her to a destroyed village. It was a place of half-demons, Euphemia's home, which had been destroyed by Yuuki Tachibana's attack. Her subconscious had brought her there without her realizing it, but there was nothing left. More than half of the residents had been slain, and of those who remained, Yuuki had enslaved all who possessed either power or beauty.

So, what could she do now? Seeing the tragic state of her old home, Euphemia returned to her senses a bit. Once freed from Yuuki's domination, she had immediately thought of reviving her old village, believing that if she returned, others would too.

She didn't know how long it had been, but there was no sign of anyone else in the area nor were there any signs that someone had come before her. Everything was exactly as they'd left it when they were first taken away.

"What are you doing now, Teo?" she murmured.

Her sister hadn't been in the village when it was attacked, so she had never ended up becoming one of Yuuki's slaves. But after returning and seeing what had happened there, she may have gone in search of vengeance. If that were the case, Euphemia could only pray that she hadn't been killed. Her sister was just as much a beauty as Euphemia herself, so if she had fallen victim to Yuuki as well, she was likely still alive.

As her numb mind worked through these thoughts, Euphemia slowly began to move with more purpose. The first thing she had to do was clean up the village. Even if others came back, they would see only the tragedy from before and would probably leave again, discouraged.

One of the abilities that Euphemia had received after becoming a vampire was telekinesis. She used it to easily clear away the rubble and destroyed buildings, then gave proper burials to those whose bodies had been left behind. Once that was done, she began collecting materials to repair the buildings that weren't too badly damaged. The village didn't look much better after she had finished, but she felt it was a marked improvement on having collapsed rubble and bloodstains everywhere.

"Next, I suppose I should put up a barrier to prevent anyone but our tribe from entering..."

She intended to go and search for the surviving members of her village. But when she did, this place would be empty once again. Their valuables had already been stolen but vandals and other passersby could always cause further damage.

As Euphemia inspected the area, she realized that she could feel someone's presence nearby. It seemed they were heading straight for her. A small spark of hope that it might be one of her people flashed through

Chapter 11 — Interlude: I Don't Know What I'm Doing Here Either

her mind. There were few who would come to a settlement like this, deep in the forest as it was. But she couldn't feel too optimistic about it. She knew that half-demons were being targeted by something. With that in mind, she decided to await them at the center of the village.

The person who had come was a woman. Pale white skin, long black hair, red eyes, and a dress of black and red. Euphemia could tell at a glance that the woman was a vampire, and one from Lain's bloodline as well.

"What are you doing out here?"

"You don't know?" the stranger answered, surprised.

"If you came all the way here to meet me, I'm sure it has something to do with being a vampire. But unless you explain, that's as much as I know. After all, Lady Lain died immediately after I became a vampire myself."

"Ah, I see. To put it simply, I'm here to figure out who will take on the title of Origin Blood. The only ones who can do so are those who Lady Lain transformed directly."

Lain was an Origin Blood, the pinnacle of the vampire species. Euphemia didn't know much about them, but it seemed there were a number of other members of Lain's bloodline as well.

"Is that so? I'm not at all interested, so why don't you go ahead and take it?"

"Unfortunately, it's not that easy. I can only become an Origin Blood when there is only one of us left."

"Okay. So?"

"Could you die for me?"

"No, thank you."

"As expected. Of course, I can't just let you go even though you don't want the position. You're the last one, after all. After defeating the others and thinking that I was finally there, can you imagine how it felt to have one more hurdle suddenly pop up out of nowhere?"

"How unfortunate for you."

"I'm afraid I'll have to kill you." Without warning, the woman was suddenly in front of Euphemia, having closed the distance between them in the blink of an eye.

Euphemia had claimed that she didn't want to die, but in reality, she didn't care all that much. Her desire to restore the village and find the others was little more than a vague impulse, and not something that she was especially passionate about. If she died then and there, it would be fine with her.

The woman stabbed her hand towards Euphemia's chest. Vampires were more or less immortal, but their weak points were their hearts. Even if the heart was destroyed, they wouldn't die immediately, but since their power was drawn from blood, it would inevitably weaken them.

Euphemia made no attempt to avoid the attack. It was just too much effort to bother. Moving her body at all was an unwelcome hassle at this point.

The woman's hand punched through her clothes and between her breasts. Her attacker let out a surprised grunt but it took Euphemia a moment to realize why. The attack hadn't hurt her at all — it hadn't even punctured the skin. The woman jumped back, immediately on the defensive.

"What are you?!"

"Who knows? But if you want to kill me, would you get on with it? I'm not going to resist."

Irritated, the woman bit into her own wrist. Blood poured out from the wound, accumulating in the air in the form of a long, thin pole. She had made a spear from her own blood.

The woman readied her new weapon and disappeared from Euphemia's line of sight. At the same time, there was a hard impact from behind. Euphemia turned around slowly and saw that the woman had tried to drive the spear into her back.

"What the hell is going on?!"

The woman vanished again and her spear lashed out at Euphemia from all directions. But it never cut deeper than her clothes. After a while, Euphemia's eyes grew accustomed to the stranger's movements, allowing her to follow them. The woman was running circles around her, attacking her again and again. It didn't particularly hurt, but it was annoying to be hit repeatedly without a sense of the fight progressing.

Euphemia instinctively held up her arm, swinging her open hand as if to swat a fly out of the air. With a heavy slap, the woman was sent flying. Her lower body tumbled to the ground as the rest of her became a bloody mist, drenching their surroundings.

"Looks like I'll have to clean up again," she murmured as a torrent of information poured into her head. With the woman dead, the remaining property and rights that Lain had held were automatically passed on to Euphemia. She realized that she was now an Origin Blood herself.

She was the last one.

It wasn't like she had wanted to become one, but it was something she could potentially put to use while searching for her people. As she sifted through her new memories for anything useful, she remembered the house outside the forest. Rather than a torn down place like this, which had nothing at all to offer, she thought it might serve as a good base of operations.

She decided to head there at once.

◇◇◇

The house looked small and cozy, sitting on top of a quiet hill. It was, of course, much more luxurious than her old home in the forest, but it wasn't especially gaudy either. With a moat and an outer wall, it looked like it could double as a fortress, but it didn't seem like much work had been put into its defenses. It was more like a mansion or a secret hideout that might be housing a princess deep inside.

As Euphemia approached, the drawbridge descended and the gate opened, both of their own accord. The house seemed to recognize her as its owner. She walked through the gate and into the building, and immediately heard the sound of a girl shouting.

"Wait! Wait!"

Turning to look at the source of the voice, she saw a horse galloping as it was pursued by a young girl in a pink dress. She was doing her best, but it didn't look like she was going to be able to catch it. At her speed, it was hard to even call her movements "running." The horse was probably just confused by all of the excitement. As it ran around the inner garden, it eventually made its way to Euphemia.

"Stop."

At her order, the horse immediately came to a halt, waiting patiently in front of her. This was unsurprising, since vampires had the ability to charm people and control animals.

The girl gasped for air, her evident exhaustion not dampening her anger in the least as she made her way over to the newcomer.

"Thank you very much! I had no idea what I was going to do."

She seemed to have understood that Euphemia had stopped the animal somehow. As the girl thanked her, Euphemia instinctively knelt before her. The child appeared to be taken aback by her behavior.

"Huh? Umm, sorry. Who are you?"

"My name is Euphemia. I don't know what I'm doing here either." The girl was totally confused now. "By the way, are you not a vampire? Can you not control a horse this way?"

"Wait, I really am a vampire? I woke up in a coffin but I wasn't sure…"

Euphemia wondered if this was one of Lain's children. Although her face was totally different, she had a distinct vibe that was very similar to the former Origin Blood.

"Wait, wouldn't that mean it's dangerous to walk around in the daylight this way?!"

"It's okay. After all, you feel just fine right now, don't you? By the way, what were you trying to do with the horse?"

"Oh, I was thinking of riding it out somewhere. Come on! Move!" The girl pulled at the reins, but the horse remained still, awaiting Euphemia's instructions.

"Follow her orders," Euphemia told the animal, which became immediately obedient.

"Thank you so much!"

"Is there no one here to take care of this horse?"

"Umm, if I told you, you probably wouldn't believe me."

"Don't worry; I'll believe you."

"I just woke up after being asleep for a really long time. When I got up, there was no one else in the house. It seems like someone was here while I was sleeping, so I think they must have been taking care of the horse then."

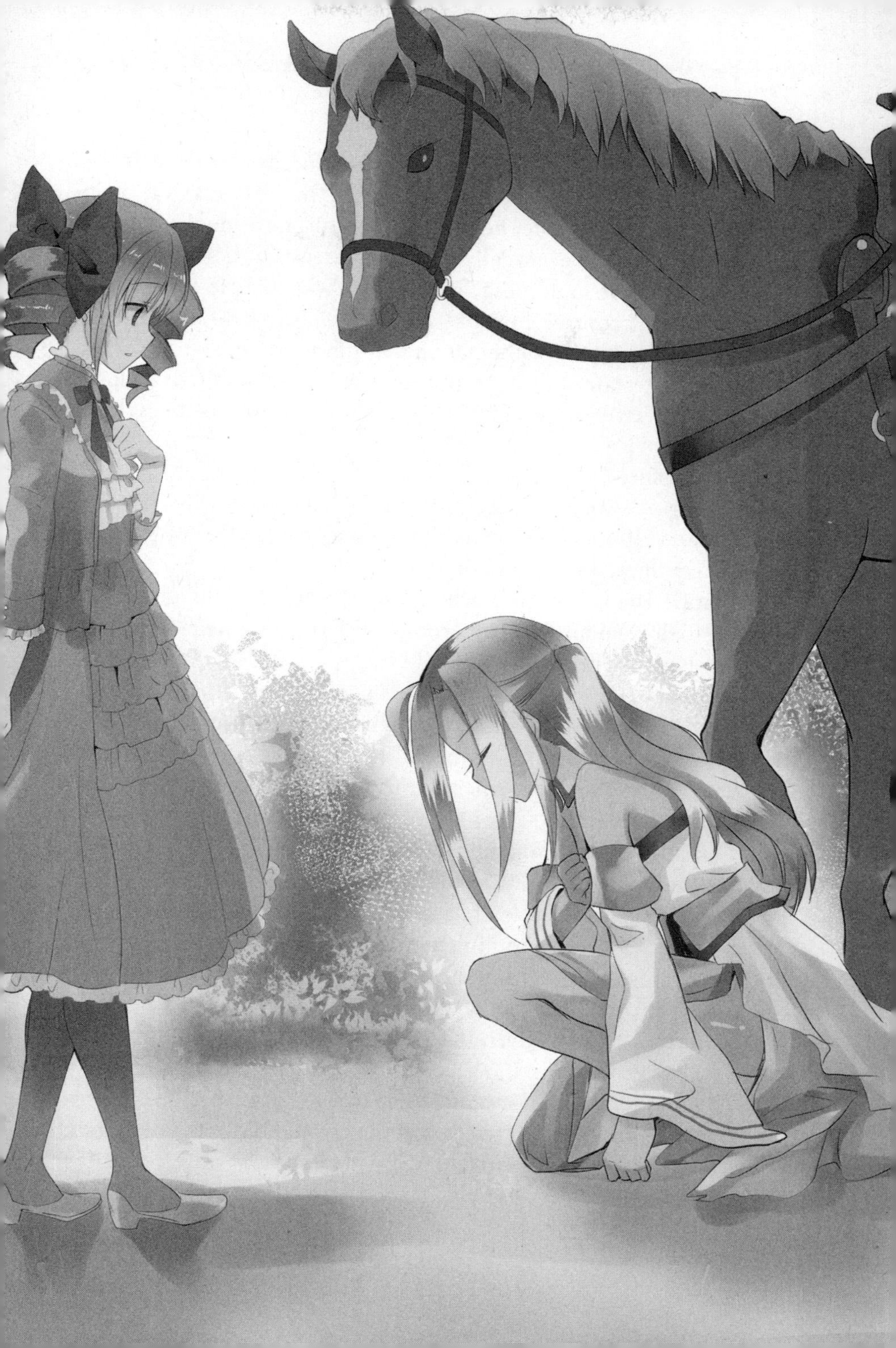

Searching her memory for information about the house, Euphemia confirmed the girl's story. All who had lived in the mansion were members of Lain's bloodline. After her death, they must have fought over who would succeed her and eventually wiped themselves out.

"Anyway, I have something I need to do. I was going to go on a journey, but I couldn't control the horse very well..." The girl trailed off.

"Shall I help you?" Euphemia offered immediately. For some reason, she held a certain reverence for this child. The rest of Lain's bloodline must have left her alone for the same reason, even while fighting each other.

"Are you sure?"

"Of course. I would be happy to." Euphemia's goal had been to find her people and rebuild their village, but it no longer felt that urgent. Her desire to help the girl was far stronger.

"Hurray! Thank you so much! To be honest, I had no idea what I was going to do. Having an adult around will be a huge help!"

"May I ask your name?"

"Ah! That's right! I don't even have a name! What should I do?!"

It seemed an odd thing for her to not have noticed before, but Euphemia supposed it hadn't mattered much while she was alone.

"It will be pretty inconvenient for us to talk if I don't have a name! Hmm, what would make sense? Mist...fog...drizzle...okay, how about Risley?" Listing off some random words about the weather, she somehow seemed to find a "name" that she liked. "Nice to meet you!"

The newly named Risley began to struggle to mount the horse. Apparently, she had been planning to ride it on her journey without even knowing how to get herself into the saddle.

"Where are you planning on going?"

"To the capital! I was given a message that said if I was going to leave home, I should go there first."

Euphemia considered how long a trip to the capital would take from their current location. At the very least, they would be on the road for a few days. If the girl was planning on taking a horse and riding off without any preparations, she was being far too reckless.

"Understood. Let us return to the house for a bit and gather the supplies that we'll need."

If her memories were correct, there would be plenty of supplies and even a carriage on the estate.

"Oh, yes, that's right! Of course we need to prepare!" Risley clapped enthusiastically, accepting the suggestion at once.

It seemed Euphemia was going to have her hands quite full with this girl.

ACT 2

Chapter 12 — I'm Not So Rude as to Complain to the Person Who Saved Me

Tomochika had figured there was no way she could sleep next to her classmate. But despite her doubts, she had indeed fallen asleep at some point during the night. When she woke up, she realized that Yogiri was clinging to her. With a start, she lurched back to wakefulness in a sort of panic.

While she had a general grasp of the situation, her understanding didn't reach past the fact that Yogiri's face was buried in her chest, a realization that left her feeling anything but calm. She knew plenty of useful techniques to use against opponents who were grabbing her, so she could certainly extricate herself from Yogiri in a way that would be extraordinarily painful for him. In fact, her first instinct was to do just that, but she quickly reconsidered.

Yogiri was still asleep. In short, he was holding her unconsciously. There was no way he was doing it with malicious or improper intent. He had just felt something soft and snuggled up to it. Realizing this, Tomochika hesitated to do anything violent. Seeing his face in the dim light of the room, he looked as harmless as ever, making her initial impulse to cause a scene seem like total overkill. On top of that, she got the impression that he was sleeping so deeply because of the constant use of his power, which pretty much meant that he was exhausted from taking care of her. If this could give him some semblance of peace, then she could deal with it.

As she considered things, she turned to look away and screamed. A face was peering at her through the wall. In response to her surprise, the face called out to her.
It is me! There is no need to be so alarmed!
"Mokomoko? Have you been sitting in the wall all night?!"
Yes. Is something wrong?
Thanks to Tomochika's outburst, Yogiri opened his eyes with a grunt, prompting her to hurriedly jump away from him.
"Come on! Sticking halfway into the room like that is terrifying, especially when I forget that you're here!"
Yes, well, about that. I am indeed somewhat stuck.
"What do you mean by stuck?"
I told you earlier that this tower is trying to collect spirits, yes?
"Yeah, and you said it would be no problem for someone like you."
The walls and floors of the tower are used to absorb and collect the spirits. So after merging with the wall, the pull got quite a bit stronger. I figured I'd be able to get myself out at some point, but as time went by I began to realize that I am actually in a rather dangerous situation.
"Well, we were only together for a short time, but I won't forget you. You were a pretty unforgettable person, all things considered," Tomochika said, clapping her hands together in prayer along with her short eulogy. While the family spirit had been useful to an extent, it was annoying to have her around all the time, so the loss didn't bother her all that much.
I'd appreciate it if you didn't write me off so quickly!
"But there's nothing we can do, is there? If this place is absorbing ghosts, then that's that."
You still have the boy! Come on, you can help me somehow, can't you?!
Yogiri yawned, still half asleep. Tomochika turned to him and quickly explained the situation. In spite of her words, it would have made her feel a bit bad to leave Mokomoko behind like that.
"Is there anything you can do?"
"Hmm...I suppose I could try taking out whatever is collecting spirits. But there's probably a reason it's doing all that, so I'm not sure it's a great idea to just kill it off..." Yogiri looked at Mokomoko, and it didn't

Chapter 12 — I'm Not So Rude as to Complain to the Person Who Saved Me

take long for him to make up his mind. "Well, whatever. Mokomoko is more important than the people here, anyway."

"Can you do it?"

"It's not targeting me, so it's kind of hard to narrow down the thing responsible, but..." He pressed a hand to the wall. "I *can* feel it trying to absorb 'life' in general. Maybe I can manage it based on that."

A moment later, Mokomoko shot out into the center of the room.

Ohhhh! I thought I was going to die!

"Didn't you die a long time ago?" asked Tomochika.

You're awfully cold for someone talking to her own ancestor.

Yogiri's face was growing increasingly troubled. "Seems like things are getting kind of bad."

"What's wrong?"

"Well, not only did I kill that Dark God earlier, but now I've killed part of the tower as well. That can't be good. I feel like we should probably get out of here before someone complains."

"That sounds like a great idea. We didn't really mean to come here and get involved in the first place, so there's no reason for us to stay any longer than we have to."

Tomochika leaned over and looked out the window. The sun was just climbing over the horizon. It would be best if they finished up and left the tower by the end of the day.

◇◇◇

"Things seem pretty calm now, so I suppose we should talk about our goals here."

"You consider us lying in bed together to be a calm situation, huh?"

Tomochika seemed unhappy about something, but after having slept so well, Yogiri's head was clear. With no one else around, it seemed like the perfect time to discuss everything.

"Fine. What do you want to go over?"

"First, I want to confirm our main objective, which is to — at the very least — get the two of us back to our home world."

Truthfully, his main concern was getting Tomochika back,

regardless of whether or not he made it himself, but he didn't think she would react well to hearing that. "Our secondary objective is to figure out exactly how to accomplish that main goal."

"And that's why we're heading to the capital…to meet up with this Sage Sion person and ask her about it. That's the whole reason we're trying to track down our class. You said to get at least the two of us back home, but we'll take the others with us if we can, right?"

Their classmates were currently trying to accomplish the missions that the Sage had assigned to them. If they continued to clear those missions, Sion would eventually show herself again. She was the one who had brought their class over to this new world, so there was a chance she could tell them how to get back.

"I won't go out of my way to abandon them, but things might not work out even if we do find the others. That's why we're here in the first place."

"What do you mean?"

"There's no guarantee that we'll actually meet the Sage, or that she'll tell us what we want to know even if we do find her. She might not even know *how* to get us back in the first place. That's why it's important for us to get as much information about this world as we can. The Swordmaster seems like a pretty famous guy, so I thought he might have some clues for us."

Yogiri had been hoping to get some information from the old man, but all they had found there was a massacre under the guise of an unusual trial. He was beginning to think there was no point in them staying any longer.

"Oh, really? I thought we were mainly looking for a way out of the canyon."

"I've actually got an idea about that. I was looking down at the canyon while we were on the rooftop, and I've got a pretty good idea of the landscape now. What about you, Mokomoko?"

Indeed, especially since I can fly even higher. I have more or less determined a way for us to make our exit.

"Really? Was I the only one standing around like an idiot doing nothing up there?" Tomochika quickly changed the subject, trying to hide

Chapter 12 — I'm Not So Rude as to Complain to the Person Who Saved Me

her surprise. "Also, that Aggressor robot said that we could return home as long as we knew the coordinates of our home world, didn't it?"

In addition to the coordinates, we also need the necessary energy. Remember, that creature left a part of itself in its own world as an anchor, which allowed it to return home with a minimal expenditure of energy. But that is not an option for us. You can think of it like...this world exists at the bottom of a crevice. Falling into a crevice is easy, but climbing back out requires a significant amount of energy.

"When you say 'an anchor,' you mean like a ship's anchor, right? Like it's connected by some sort of string?" Tomochika asked. She was finding the whole concept a bit difficult to visualize.

Something along those lines. It is just a metaphor, but you can imagine the robot having a lifeline connecting it to its original world. Someone pulling on that line would draw it back home.

"Okay, so we need energy. That doesn't help us a whole lot," Yogiri mused. They didn't know how much was needed, or in what form it would have to be.

I believe this tower may hold some clues about that. I was not simply trapped in that wall doing nothing. I was also monitoring the flow of power around us.

"I don't know, it sounds like you're making that up right now."

Quiet, you! Thanks to my efforts, I was able to recognize that the souls of the dead are being collected in one specific location. They are likely being used to maintain the barrier around this place. I do not know what level of power this Dark God possesses, but maintaining a barrier capable of stopping time just to restrain it must require an enormous amount of energy.

"I'm not really up for killing people just to steal their energy," Yogiri replied, although knowing that one could collect and store energy in such a way could prove useful to them, so he mentally made note of it anyway.

"Yeah, that's going a bit too far."

"Our immediate objective is still to get to the capital and rendezvous with our class, so we do need to get to the bottom of this tower." He was beginning to think that getting stuck on trying to talk to the Swordmaster was merely a waste of time.

"So we're back to the obvious conclusion."

"I just want you to be ready. I'm going to kill anyone we come across who seems to be an enemy."

"And that's different from the usual how?"

"I normally only kill people when I absolutely have to," Yogiri argued, finding Tomochika's skeptical look a bit hurtful. "But in this tower, those aiming to be Knights are more than ready to kill anyone they encounter. Hesitating at all could mean death."

"Like I said, that's nothing new. If you're asking if I'm prepared for that, then yes. You using your power to protect me is the same as me killing them myself. I've known that from the start."

Don't look down on the daughter of a warrior's house! Mokomoko said firmly.

This time it was Yogiri's turn for blank amazement. It still surprised him that Tomochika would be so easily prepared to take other people's lives.

"Like I've said, I'm not going to complain about *how* somebody saves me. Although…I do think we should keep the killing to a minimum, if we can," she added, feeling the need to throw in that caveat.

After a short pause, Yogiri changed the subject, somewhat embarrassed by her total trust in him. "Actually, I'm getting kind of hungry. We haven't eaten anything since yesterday, have we?"

◇◇◇

"Umm, I feel like walking around and looking for someone without any clues at all is kind of pointless."

The sky above was just starting to grow light. Daimon Hanakawa was trudging along behind a confident Aoi. Despite having given her every last drop of information that he possessed about Yogiri Takatou, she had yet to release him. Her ship — which he could only think of as a flying saucer — had landed in the canyon, and they had walked from there.

Upon learning that her targets had trekked out into the canyon itself, Aoi's investigation of Hanabusa had come to a quick end. It hadn't been

Chapter 12 — I'm Not So Rude as to Complain to the Person Who Saved Me

too long since their quarries had left the city, so she knew they were out here somewhere. Unfortunately, the canyon was a large, maze-like region. Searching it from the air hadn't gotten them any closer to finding the pair of otherworlders.

"Don't worry about it. I can tell which places have high Fate scores, which basically means that important events are likely to happen there."

"Ah, so now you're just meta-gaming. Is something wrong with your head?!"

"Hey, who do you think you are, talking to her like that?" a voice called out from the sheath at Aoi's hip.

"Hahaha! Like I'm about to be threatened by a knife that can't even move itself!"

"Well, I guess it is kind of meta. I can see Fate itself. In short, if this world were a movie, I would be able to read the script."

"Like I said, if you can do all that, what need do you have of me at all?! Why did I have to come with you in the first place?!"

"It's not that simple. To keep the movie metaphor, there are multiple protagonists all in motion at the same time. Multiple scenarios are unfolding at once, so the script is fairly chaotic. It's not easy to see through it all, and depending on the situation, each scenario can change in complex ways over time. I can only see the things that are right in front of me at any given time...and we're here, by the way." She pointed at the sky. In the darkness of the early morning, the spot she had indicated seemed to be glowing.

An enormous dragon, cloaked in lightning, was floating in the air.

"What the hell is that?! It's obviously absurdly strong!" The moment he saw it, Hanakawa recognized that it was a being on an entirely different level. There was no way they could win against it. If it unleashed its breath at them, they'd be dead in an instant. Judging from its appearance, it probably had lightning-property attacks. There was no way he could dodge such an assault, and with his meager defenses he would be dead the moment it struck.

"We should run! Even *your* abilities can't beat that thing!"

From this distance, once they had the creature's attention, even fleeing would be impossible. And Hanakawa figured Aoi would have no way of fighting a winged opponent, anyway.

"Why do you think I can't beat it?"

"Your power doesn't work on primeval beings, does it?!"

Hanakawa had seen Aoi fight in the Forest of Beasts. There, she had used the same cheat-like powers as Rikuto, and then erased them. Her ability seemed to negate the powers of those who had received their Gifts from someone else. It was hard to believe it could also work against a monster that was naturally so strong.

"Ah, it seems you've misunderstood something. Enemies like this are easy," Aoi said casually. "There's no way something so big could actually fly, right?"

The dragon abruptly fell from the sky. Even confused and caught totally off guard, it somehow managed to catch the air with its wings and glide into the side of the cliff, barely avoiding the fall to the bottom of the canyon below.

"My ability is simple. Just World works by dragging others into my own internal world. In other words, it changes the world around me to match my personal beliefs."

"Like I said, that's ridiculously overpowered!" Hanakawa couldn't think of her ability as anything but preposterous. It seemed like the ultimate trump card, capable of doing anything at all.

"That's not true. I can't do anything that seems impossible to me, and those with high Fate levels aren't affected at all. In those cases, I need to allow Fate to guide me."

"I-Is that right? A-Anyway, it seems you've defeated this monstrosity." Hanakawa approached the dragon. It had somehow managed to claw its way up the cliff face and was now lying on the ground. Its head was large enough to swallow him in a single bite, but perhaps disoriented by its sudden fall, it simply lay there with its mouth open and its tongue sticking out.

"Hah, you're just nothing but a big, dumb lizard, aren't you?"

"I wouldn't get that close if I were you."

Without warning, the dragon suddenly leaped up, snapping its jaws

Chapter 12 — I'm Not So Rude as to Complain to the Person Who Saved Me

shut. Everything from Hanakawa's right elbow down disappeared in an instant, brutally bitten off.

Hanakawa screamed, but he was more than accustomed to such injuries. His experience surviving numerous battlegrounds as a Healer wasn't an exaggeration. Within moments, his right arm had been restored and he had jumped away from the dragon.

"As you said, it's a big lizard. That's still plenty dangerous, don't you think?"

"Can't you do something about it with your power?!"

"Of course not. It makes perfect sense for there to be a reptile of this size. There's no way I can deny its existence."

"Then what are we going to do?!"

"We'll just have to fight it normally. I'm pretty strong, so it shouldn't be a problem," Aoi said as she drew her knife.

Was she planning on fighting the dragon with a tiny knife like that? It seemed crazy to Hanakawa, but he had not yet had a chance to see the reason for her confidence.

But before Aoi had even appeared to attack, the dragon's head was torn clean off.

"What just…?! Did you do something?"

"No. But this isn't good. In fact, this might be the worst possible situation for me."

Something was now standing where the dragon's head had been, blood gushing out in a river around it. It had a strange but vaguely humanoid appearance. Its blood-soaked body was covered in a lustrous black metal, with spikes and blades sticking out of every joint. It was hard to believe that someone could fit inside that slender body, meaning it was likely not a suit of armor.

"The Hedgehog…" Aoi muttered.

It was one of the beings the Sages referred to as Aggressors.

Chapter 13 — Horizontally Challenged

The creature facing them was like an incarnation of murderous intent. The blades that covered its body served no purpose other than to wreak mass carnage. Hanakawa couldn't take his eyes off its sinister yet somehow beautiful form. Clearly, staring at it like an idiot was little help, but he was absolutely sure that the moment he looked away, it would take his head.

"Now matter how you look at it, this is nothing but a murder machine! How are we supposed to fight something like this?! But wait... I have a Sage with me! Such an opponent should be no...wait, where did you go, Miss Aoi?!" As he continued to stare at the enemy, Hanakawa realized that Aoi was no longer standing beside him.

"I wonder why it attacked the dragon? If it's simply killing anything it can find, why didn't it attack me or the pig?" the Sage wondered aloud.

"Hey, why are you behind me?! And how can you so callously refer to me that way?!"

"You seemed like the appropriate size for a good hiding spot."

"That's your attempt at a euphemism for calling me fat, isn't it? Like saying I'm horizontally challenged or something!"

Aoi was hiding behind Hanakawa, but there was no way he'd be *that* useful as a shield. The Aggressor could cut through him like he was nothing but paper.

"It looks like it has eyes on its face, doesn't it? If I can get out of its line of sight, that might help a bit."

"I'm not sure about that! They look more like sensors that can take in its entire surroundings!"

While it was definitely a strange-looking being, its figure seemed to be roughly based on that of a human. Two red lights were blinking like eyes on its face. They may have been nothing more than decoration, but the creature also had what looked like ears and a nose. And while there was no obvious mouth, there seemed to be a thin line on its face where one should be, so it wouldn't have been surprising if something resembling lips suddenly opened up.

"Even if that's true, it doesn't look like it's interested in killing us. If it wanted to, we'd probably be dead already," Aoi observed.

Looking at its feet, they could see deep gouge marks in the dirt. It was just a guess, but the marks had likely been made when it landed, meaning it must have leaped from another cliff to get there and killed the dragon as it touched down. Such movements were generally much faster than the eye could follow, so it wasn't surprising that neither Aoi nor Hanakawa had seen it happen.

"Isn't there anything you can do?! Shouldn't your power be able to help us out here? Like with the dragon, just say 'There's no way a robot like this could exist'!"

"Unfortunately, I can't help but feel that it does seem possible."

"Is your power good for anything at all?!"

"Yeah, sorry, there are definitely limitations."

"W-Well, if we just stand here doing nothing, that should be okay, right?" It was possible that any movement would draw unwanted attention. Trying to maintain the current situation was best, or at least that's what Hanakawa told himself.

"Seems that way. It kind of looks like it's confused or something."

"You think so? Well, now that you mention it, I see what you mean..." The creature was leaning forward slightly, standing perfectly still, drenched in the dragon's blood. It seemed to be lost in thought, as if trying to figure out why it had actually killed the dragon in the first place. "How long should we stay here like this?"

"Until it leaves, I guess?"

She was right. There was really nothing they could do but stand still and see what happened. As Hanakawa resolved himself to a lengthy wait, the creature finally moved.

Its movements were terrifyingly quiet and entirely lacking in any sort of hesitation. Even after it had taken a few steps, Hanakawa couldn't tell when it had even moved, despite the fact that he had been watching it the whole time.

It looked like its only target had been the dragon after all. Standing over the disembodied head, it sank a hand into the reptilian skull, the blade-like limb pushing deep as if the bone beneath offered no resistance.

"What is it doing?" Hanakawa whispered.

"Well, the dragon is obviously dead, so it can't be trying to finish it off. It looks like it's perhaps trying to extract information from its brain?"

"But if that's the case, there are two more brains right here!"

In reality, they had no idea what meaning, if any, there was to the robot's actions. But when it pulled its arm free and turned its red eyes on them, Hanakawa was sure that he was going to die.

"Boobs! If I'm going to die anyway, please let me touch them! I'm not that interested in tomboys, but at this rate I'll take anything!"

"You must be joking."

"Uh, then...I'll try begging! Everyone understands that, right?!"

In a panic, he dropped to his knees and put his forehead to the ground. But he could only bear to look away from the source of his fear for so long. He soon lifted his head back up to look at the monster once more, only to find that it was gone.

"Huh?"

"It left."

"Why would it do that? Wait, do you think this is one of those moments where you think you're safe and it suddenly attacks you from behind?!" He looked around desperately, then checked the sky, and then glanced down the edge of the nearby cliff. There was no sign of the nightmare machine anywhere. "Are we...safe?"

"For now. Considering the Fate level of this area, I don't think it's likely that either of us will die here."

"You were awfully scared of that thing too, though, weren't you?!"

Whether she was avoiding the question or had genuinely not been concerned, Aoi ignored him and pointed upwards and ahead. "For just an instant, I saw a huge tower over there."

"Where? I don't see anything." All that Hanakawa could make out in the dawning sky were traces of faint, wispy clouds.

"It was just for a moment. But in that split second, I could see the thing heading straight for it. Either way, we're going to follow."

"Are you insane?! We're lucky to be walking away with our lives!"

"I thought we might trigger some sort of flag when that dragon saw us, but the monster went ahead and killed it, so now this is our only clue."

"Nooooo! Let me go home!"

Aoi reached down to where Hanakawa was crouched on the ground and grabbed the collar of his shirt. He was helpless to stop her from dragging him along with her.

◇◇◇

"Someone is messing with us, aren't they?"

"It's getting kind of annoying," Yogiri agreed.

Another dead end. A metal chest was sitting on the floor in front of the two teens. It was just big enough to comfortably carry, with a half-cylinder lid that made it look exactly like a classic treasure chest. As both of them were gamers of a sort, they hadn't been able to help getting their hopes up. However, the interior held only a single gold coin.

"Is this seriously part of the trial?"

"There was probably supposed to be a key or something inside."

They were on the fiftieth level of the tower now. The rooftop had been floor one hundred, and they had fought Teresa on floor ninety-nine. They had slept on floor ninety-eight, and from there, the stairs had taken them straight down. They were currently in a battle zone, so there was a risk of being attacked at any moment, but for the time being, they were alone.

"I'm not really on the Swordmaster's side, and I'm not at all interested in this trial that we've been roped into, but don't you feel a little bad about doing it this way?" asked Tomochika.

Chapter 13 — Horizontally Challenged

It was crazy that they were proceeding so quickly. Along the way there had been plenty of locked rooms, trapped corridors, and trick doors. One would have expected them to search for hidden keys or solve a variety of puzzles to continue at each stage, but Yogiri wasted no time on any of that, simply killing every obstacle in their path.

Luckily, the correct route wasn't difficult to figure out. As such, they had managed to get quite far by basically walking in a straight line.

"Do you want to stop and explore?"

"Not especially. But if this were a game, we'd be doing it all wrong, wouldn't we?"

To be more specific, if this were a game, they would have been flat-out cheating. As someone who enjoyed such games, Tomochika couldn't help but feel a little guilty. Yogiri didn't seem particularly sympathetic to this viewpoint, however, so she decided to change the subject. "You know, now that I think about it, you can just open any door or chest you want to, right? You'd be a pretty good thief."

"I'd never do that. I'm only resorting to this right now because we have to get to the bottom quickly," he replied, his feelings clearly a little hurt.

Tomochika couldn't help but find the way that he sulked to be kind of cute. She remembered a conversation that they'd had after first getting off the bus, when they were discussing how to access the luggage compartment. "I seem to remember you asking me if I was any good at lockpicking not too long ago."

"You being able to pick locks is totally different from me using my powers to rob people."

"I'm not so sure about that...but whatever, it's fine. Let's just keep going?" Refocusing on the task ahead, she turned around to leave.

"You guys seem pretty cheerful," a voice called out from behind them. A man was slowly walking down the narrow hallway to where they stood. At first glance, he looked like a beastkin, but they soon realized that it was actually a human wearing an animal pelt. The beast-like appearance was likely reflected in his fighting style as well, if the enormous claws strapped to his hands were any indication. "I've been watching you two for a while. Looks like you've got some sort of master key. Hand it over and I'll let the girl —"

"Die."

The man immediately collapsed.

"He didn't look like someone who would make a good Knight anyway, did he?"

"All the people who've come at us looking for a fight were pretty bizarre," Yogiri observed. Although he wasn't taking any chances, he was also trying to take Tomochika's request to hold back — if he could — into account. He made a point to wait a few moments to see what someone was going to do before killing them.

"It makes you wonder what the 'divine' part of the Divine King's name really means. There's nothing about the people here that strikes me as particularly holy," mused Tomochika, sinking into thought.

All those who had attacked them so far had been little more than oddly-dressed thugs. Maybe as long as a Knight could kill the Dark God's spawn, his or her personal character didn't matter much, but even so, the selection process looked like it needed a lot of work.

Yogiri was crouched down by the body, fishing through the man's pockets. "I heard that a long time ago, people who were a bit off in the head were thought to be holy. Oh, hey, this guy had a map. It's got an awful lot of blood on it, so he probably took it from someone else."

"I thought you were against robbery."

"This is just part of the trial."

Aside from the bundle of paper, it didn't seem like the fur-clad man had anything of value on him. Taking the map, Yogiri led Tomochika back down the hallway in the direction they had come from. The narrow corridor eventually branched into a four-way intersection. As expected, the smaller, less important-looking path hadn't been the correct one. The larger, more open passageways seemed to be the intended routes. The corridor immediately in front of them was the one they had tried first, with a wider hall off to their left.

As Tomochika moved towards the larger hallway, something dropped down from the ceiling in front of her. A man wearing a dark blue outfit lay motionless on the floor.

"And now we seem to have found a ninja. Why are all of these weirdos trying to become Knights?!"

Chapter 13 — Horizontally Challenged

Well, perhaps someone who looks so obviously like a ninja is merely doing it for the fashion statement.

Yogiri glanced over. "I couldn't see him until he fell, but it seems he was hiding on the ceiling."

Scattered around the fallen man were a number of sharpened sticks that Tomochika recognized as stick shurikens.

"Ugh. Why did he attack us in the first place? All you have to do is get to the bottom of this stupid tower, right? Why would they bother fighting each other at all?"

If the ninja had merely been hiding, Yogiri wouldn't even have noticed him up there. The fact that the guy had been planning to ambush them is what had allowed him to be killed.

"Maybe stealing keys from each other is part of the process. And looking at the map, the farther we go, the less room we'll have to move around. That means fewer treasure chests and more chances of running into others. It was probably made that way on purpose."

"And what's going on with the whole points thing?"

"Some of the guys that attacked us were telling us to give them our points, so maybe you can take them from someone else if you kill them."

"But we're at, like, five points right now, aren't we?"

They had come across a magic doll earlier and asked her about their current points. Yogiri had picked up four of those one-point plates, so the numbers did add up, but they clearly weren't getting anything from the people he had been killing off along the way.

"You probably do get points for killing. I guess that's why we're supposed to fight each other. But if they don't realize that I'm the one who killed our opponents, they're not going to give me points for it."

"Ahh, they just see them falling over so they don't know that you're responsible."

"Yeah, from the outside, there's no way for them to see the cause and effect. I don't care that much about the points, anyway. We just need to reach the first floor."

The two of them continued onwards, coming to a large door at the end of the hall. It appeared to be locked, but of course that was no problem for Yogiri. Beyond was a rather large room, on the other side of which was another big door. Judging from their experiences so far, this next door would lead to a staircase that took them down to the next floor.

Tomochika stepped forward to open it. "Looks like we've made it halfway. We've been moving pretty fast, don't you think?"

A strange voice suddenly rang out, catching them off guard. "Too fast, I'd say. It's not right for you to cheat like that."

"Where the hell did he come from?!"

There was a man standing in the middle of the room. They had seen him on the roof, clad entirely in gold. He wore a golden circlet, a golden robe, and plenty of matching jewelry. Decorated from head to toe, he looked like the spitting image of a fantasy mage.

"I'm the one who created this tower, so I can appear anywhere I want to."

"Sounds like you're cheating far more than us, then!" she reflexively snapped back.

"Of course it's cheating, but I can't overlook what you two are doing any longer. Can't you understand how it feels for the person who set up all these puzzles to watch people walk through them without even trying?" the man lamented, gesturing wildly. Although he was inarguably overdoing it, the exaggerated theatrics seemed strangely appropriate, especially combined with his outrageous outfit.

"We have no interest in becoming Knights. We just want to get out of the tower. Is there something wrong with that?"

"Of course there is," the mage replied with a smile.

"Why?"

If this guy didn't want them destroying the tower, he should have just teleported them to the outside. Yogiri figured that would solve all of their problems, but the guy didn't seem to be interested in an easy resolution.

"This tower exists to maintain the barrier. In short, it's essential for keeping the Dark God sealed away. Of course, it's not so weak that destroying the tower will utterly destroy the barrier itself, but damage to the tower is still problematic."

"All right. If you let us leave then I won't destroy it anymore."

Chapter 13 — Horizontally Challenged

"Why would I believe you? How do I know you aren't being manipulated by the foul thing's spawn?"

"Man, this guy is a pain," Yogiri muttered, scratching his head. He had no idea how to convince him.

"After waking up for the first time in a thousand years, the first thing I see is you wreaking havoc in my tower. I hope you can understand my frustration. But it is what it is. I'm not like the Great Sage, so I won't waste your time with complaints."

"Sounds like you've been complaining plenty to me." Tomochika was starting to share Yogiri's feeling of irritation.

"My name is Eglacia. I'm known as the High Wizard. I will give you the choice of —"

"Die."

High Wizard Eglacia immediately collapsed.

"Wait, wait, wait, *what are you doing*?! Don't you think that guy might have been kind of important?!"

"Who cares? I got him before he got us."

Totally uninterested in the man's personal history or status, Yogiri turned and made his way to the exit.

"What choices was he going to offer, though?! Maybe one of them wouldn't have involved having to kill each other."

"No, he was planning to kill us either way."

While she wasn't entirely satisfied with that response, Tomochika *had* said that she was fully prepared to kill anyone they came across. She couldn't complain much about his abrupt way of handling things.

Leaving her frustrations behind, she quickly ran to catch up with her companion.

Chapter 14 — I Figured if It Had Already Happened Anyway, I Might As Well Enjoy It

The tower was in chaos.

To be precise, the artificial spirits that controlled the tower were in a panic at the state of affairs unfolding before them.

First was the breaking of the Soul Paths. The tower collected the energies known as "mana" and "spirit," and used them to maintain the barrier. Those energies ran through a complicated network of pathways that had been built into the tower. But in defiance of all reason, a hub within that network of pathways had been destroyed.

Besides the fact that they were in a location resilient enough to effectively be called indestructible, the pathways were designed to repair themselves if they were damaged in any way. And yet, without warning, the hub had completely failed.

Of course, that disaster alone wasn't enough to allow for the Dark God's resurrection. The barrier that sealed him away was the final fortress standing in defense of humanity, so naturally there were numerous safeguards in place. Although the situation was certainly unprecedented, backup pathways existed to allow the tower to continue functioning unhindered.

But it was impossible to ignore that something had happened. The barrier around the tower had failed. The outage had only lasted for a moment, but they couldn't be sure that no one had noticed it. There were numerous cults and surviving spawn of the Dark God who were always watching carefully for any opening that would allow them to resurrect their master. The chance that they had noticed the barrier's brief failure was high. But the area beyond the barrier was outside of the tower's jurisdiction. The tower's only concern was to maintain the seal, so as long as that remained in place, no thought was given to anything else.

The tower had resumed its normal operations quickly, but not long after, another issue arose: one of the door mechanisms had failed.

Although this new problem wasn't connected to the barrier itself, and the mechanism ran strictly on surplus energy that the tower held, it wasn't something that should have broken.

Then, one after another, more doors, traps, and various other mechanisms began to fail. Searching for the source of the anomaly, the tower located its quarry immediately: a boy and a girl. Wherever the pair went, parts of the tower failed. Recognizing that those two had some sort of connection to the damage occurring wasn't much of a leap.

So the tower decided to kill them. And once it made that decision, a number of the artificial spirits controlling the building suddenly vanished. Thus, chaos.

The tower quickly lost track of what it was trying to do. It was forced to run a diagnostic scan on itself, during which it located these very same abnormalities all over again. Noting that the source of those problems was a pair of humans, it again attempted to remove them, prompting yet another spiral into chaos.

Piece by piece, the tower was dying.

◇◇◇

"Congratulations, Number 97. You have reached one hundred points," the magic doll announced to Rick.

As he'd expected, defeating the participants who had chosen to challenge him had allowed him to claim their points. Rick had begun with no intention of taking anyone else's life, but no matter what he did, enemies had come for him. While defending himself, his score had continued to grow.

Chapter 14 — I Figured if It Had Already Happened Anyway, I Might As Well Enjoy It

He was now in a safe zone on the fifth floor. The first floor was only a short distance away, but he couldn't let his guard down. After all, if someone were to defeat Rick at this point, it would be enough for them to pass the trial. Of course, you couldn't tell how many points someone had just by looking at them, but it wasn't hard to guess that an applicant who had reached the lowest levels of the tower would have amassed plenty of points by then. The fighting would only get more intense on the last few floors.

Rick gathered his wits and continued his descent. The beginning of the fourth floor was already a battle zone. Dodging an attack that came at him from behind the door, he instinctively cut down the source. These kinds of ambushes had been plentiful on his journey towards the bottom. There was no way that such an attack would succeed against him at this stage.

Quickly finishing off his attacker, he moved on. Before him was a room which, according to his map, was not a section that was necessary to pass through. But he could hear the sounds of combat coming from within. Curious, he approached the door, where he heard some familiar voices from the other side.

"I'm sick of this! Please, just let me go!"

"Dammit! What are you doing? Just kill me already!"

"Just do it! Someone like him should be easy for you!"

Inside the room was a strange scene. Two men were fighting within a cage of fire. Some distance away, a woman was watching the match. The fire spanned several meters on each side, but had no gaps to allow anyone through.

Rick recognized two of the people in the room. The woman was Frederica and one of the men fighting at the center was Lynel.

"Who are you?" Frederica asked as she noticed Rick enter the room.

"My name is Rick. Do you not remember me standing with Lynel on the rooftop?"

"Oh, right, you were there, weren't you? You're pretty lucky. I just made it to a hundred points a little while ago," she said, as if to suggest that she would have killed him on the spot otherwise.

"I am also satisfied with my total points, so I have no intention of fighting you. But what are you doing here?"

"Ah, this guy was being such a pushover; he was so scared to do anything on his own. He made it all the way here without getting any points, so I'm helping him out."

"You're...helping him?"

"Something wrong with that?"

"No, not at all."

Lynel was wearing armor and holding a sword, but they looked all wrong on him. His opponent also wore armor, but he looked much more like a proper Knight. The fight itself was difficult to watch. The area inside the cage was incredibly hot, if the combatants being drenched in sweat was any indication. Lynel was uninjured but his opponent seemed to be on his last legs.

The long, drawn out fight was likely a result of the difference in their equipment and skill levels. Lynel's armor was strong enough to deflect his opponent's attacks, while his weapon cut through the other man's armor with ease. In contrast, his opponent was clearly more skilled. He was more than able to dodge Lynel's weak attacks and riposte with precision.

In the end, Lynel would eventually win. But perhaps because of his personality, he couldn't seem to finish his opponent off.

"Ugh, this is so annoying to watch! You have one minute! If you don't finish by then, I'll roast you both!"

The flaming cage around them flared up, making the room even hotter. That seemed to be the last straw for Lynel's opponent, who began to waver on his feet, unable to take the higher temperature. A haphazard swing from Lynel finally landed, cutting cleanly through the man's torso and killing him instantly.

"Man, what a waste of time!" snapped Frederica.

The fiery cage vanished and the room immediately began to cool. Lynel staggered over to Rick, collapsing in front of him. "Ah, nice to see you again," he gasped.

"Are you okay?"

"Yes...after rolling the *gacha* ten times, I actually managed to get some decent gear! That rarity guarantee is an absolute life saver!" He seemed strangely energetic.

"This guy looked pretty weak. I bet he only had around ten points. Hurry up and check!" Frederica pushed her "friend" forward.

"Shall I accompany you, Lynel?"

"Oh, please! Please do!"

Rick was wary of the way Frederica was talking. Certainly, she appeared to be helping him gather points. But she was dangerous. If left alone with Lynel, he wouldn't be surprised if she killed him eventually.

With that in mind, Rick joined them for the final stretch.

◇◇◇

"Uhh, maybe I'm just being overly self-conscious, but doesn't it seem like they're all targeting me?" Tomochika asked, looking down at the recently deceased man wearing nothing but black cloth and a skull mask.

He had attacked them with some sort of vulgar declaration, and that had been the last of him. Mokomoko had warned them at the start to be especially careful of this guy, but in the end, they hadn't had time to see any of his abilities.

"You're kind of right. They seem to be fond of telling me to 'leave the girl behind.'"

They had reached the third floor of the tower. In what they figured was a corridor heading to the second floor, they found numerous bodies scattered around them. It had become a rather common sight.

"Right? But why are guys like this trying to become 'holy' Knights in the first place?!"

You could say the same about most warriors. It's hard to say that the Swordmaster himself is a man of virtue. They all seem like fairly vulgar people to me.

As they made their way through the tower, the amount of space on each floor had shrunk, bringing them into contact with more of the other participants. As such, the two of them were being ambushed with increasing frequency. Of course, none of their attackers had any idea how strong other participants might be, so they had no way of knowing what would actually happen if they chose to fight. It would have been smarter for them to be more cautious, but for some reason, almost everyone they had come across had been extremely eager to do battle.

So Yogiri had killed every single one of them.

If they were willing to talk, he let them, and if he could avoid fighting them, he did. But in the end, they still ended up with heaps of bodies surrounding them at every turn. Each of those people had underestimated them, attacking without stopping to listen.

"I guess these guys put too much trust in their Stats."

Tomochika shrugged. "To be fair, we don't look all that strong, do we?"

"But if they had any brains, they'd at least be curious about how we got this far in spite of seeming so weak. They must have all been idiots."

How blunt. But I suppose it's true that their lack of imagination killed them.

Tomochika finally gave in and asked the question that had been on her mind for a while. "I know it's kind of weird for me to ask this, but am I really that attractive? They all seem to become obsessed with me and attack us right away."

Ever since they had come to this world, everyone they met seemed to be targeting her for one reason or another.

"I mean that in, like, an objective sense. With what's going on here. I've never considered myself all that impressive, but maybe my acting that way is part of what's causing problems. Or maybe it's just that in a weird situation like this, where people are told to kill each other, it brings out the worst in them."

Tomochika recalled stories from back home of animals being pushed to the brink, which awakened their protective instincts. Perhaps it wasn't that she was particularly attractive, but rather an instinctive response on the parts of others.

"Yeah, as far as being attractive, I'd say you're pretty cute. You've got a great figure, so I can understand why they'd all be after you."

Tomochika jerked to a stop at the shameless, point-blank compliment. Yogiri stared at her, confused by her reaction.

"Uh, it's not like *I'm* going to attack you or anything. Asaka told me I'm not ever allowed to force people."

"Does that mean you *would* attack me if I was okay with it?"

"Why would someone even need to attack you if you were okay with it? I mean, obviously there would be no reason for someone to hesitate either."

"I-I mean...I guess...but wait! When we were in Hanabusa and you pushed me over to protect me from the Sage, I seem to remember you being more than happy to plant your face in my chest!"

"That was just an accident. But since it happened, at the time, I figured I might as well enjoy it."

"You seemed awfully proactive about it to me!"

This is the first time I've seen someone so honest about being a lucky pervert, Mokomoko commented, crossing her arms as she floated in the air beside them, seeming strangely amused by it all. *I'm also impressed that one of my descendants is so capable of handling these romcom-esque developments while surrounded by dead bodies. You are certainly not lacking in boldness.*

"A-Anyway, enough chit-chat, let's go!" Tomochika said quickly, stepping around the cadavers as she walked purposefully down the hallway.

Yogiri immediately followed, coming up alongside her. The door that they eventually reached seemed like a sign that they were on the right path. Beyond was yet another staircase, which they descended without hesitation.

As they opened the door that led to the second floor, they were greeted by a white hallway, marking the first safe zone they had seen in a while. On the right side of the corridor was a reception desk, behind which sat another of the magic dolls they had been encountering throughout the tower.

"Congratulations on reaching the second floor. Would you like to take a rest?"

"Aren't we pretty much finished now?" Tomochika asked. "And don't we need to reach the bottom by three o'clock?" Checking her watch, she saw that it was now two o'clock. It seemed odd to be concerned about passing the test at this point, but she figured it was better to finish within the time limit if they could.

"That's right. There aren't many people who would stop to rest on the second floor. But beyond this zone is the final part of the trial. Don't you think that taking a break and having a meal will help you perform better?"

"You seem awfully desperate for some reason," Tomochika commented. While the puppets all looked identical, they seemed to have different personalities. "Are you lonely here?"

"Shut up! Fine, whatever! Just go! Oh, first let me review your points for you. Number 98, five points. Number 99, one point."

"We didn't even have to ask..."

Yogiri must have been Number 98, making Tomochika Number 99. Their numbers were probably based on the order in which they had entered the tower.

"Wait! What's the point of getting all the way down here with so few points?! What were you thinking?! You need one hundred of them to get to the first floor! Wait...that's so strange. There are many rooms where you have to kill others to pass through, so there's no way you could get so far with so few points to show for it..."

"Well, time to go." Yogiri immediately made to leave, with Tomochika close behind. They both figured that a continuation of the conversation would only cause more problems and unnecessary delays.

After walking for a while longer, they passed through another door into a gray hallway, which split off into three directions. They didn't have a map of the lower floors, and all three pathways looked identical. Without any clues about which option to take, Yogiri picked the middle one and on they went.

Tomochika felt that she was beginning to understand him. Actively picking a direction was too much work, so he had just decided to avoid any choice at all and simply walked straight ahead.

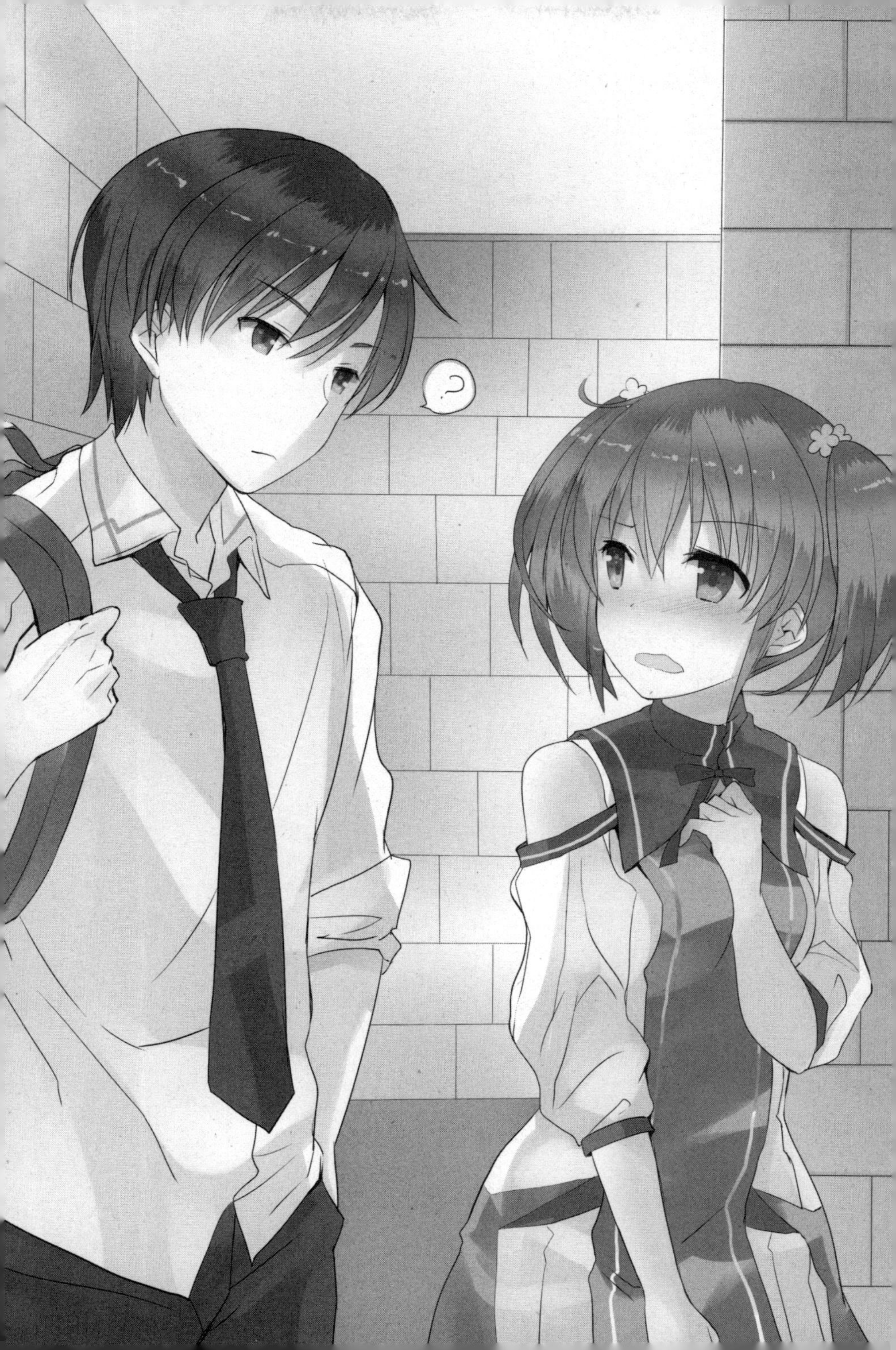

Chapter 15 — What Makes You Think That Talking Will Work This Time?!

The room in front of Theodisia was like nothing she had seen on the upper floors of the tower. It was circular, with a diameter of twenty meters, and the floor was covered with dirt. It was the second floor, so the soil must have been brought up there intentionally. There were stairs leading to seats that had been set up around the room, making it look like some sort of arena. The exit was directly across from where she had entered, presumably leading down to the first floor and thus the place where their final scores would be checked, but the door was being blocked by a man with three girls.

Theodisia doubted her eyes. The man was sitting on a kind of throne, with the girls surrounding and fawning over him. At first, she couldn't believe the stupidity of the scene before her, but she quickly got over it.

Looking around for others, she saw a number of people sitting in the stands, but realized upon closer inspection that they were actually dead bodies that had been discarded like garbage. One of the magic dolls that managed the tower was standing among them. The only living beings were the four positioned in front of the exit.

"If you made it this far, you must be pretty strong. And you've probably got a good number of points by now, right?" the man on the throne called out as Theodisia approached.

Although she felt it was pretty idiotic to be sitting on a throne in the middle of an arena, if he was able to prepare such a scene within the tower, he couldn't be just another run-of-the-mill participant. The white, fur-lined jacket that he wore was almost painfully bright, without a single speck of dirt on it. Those ordinary, unsullied civilian's clothes spoke volumes about his inherent strength.

"Let me guess," Theodisia replied, "you thought waiting here would be faster?"

He must have felt that running around the tower collecting points himself was a waste of time. Instead, he had chosen to wait near the end, ambushing those who had already done the hard work. Considering the layout of the room, it seemed like a strategy that the tower wholeheartedly supported.

"Exactly. I've already got all the points I need for myself. I just need a few more for these girls here, but...a woman, huh? I don't really like killing women..." The guy looked her up and down, as if appraising her.

Theodisia was a perfectly plain-looking woman. Her skin was pale and she was rather tall but not especially curvy. Given that plus her dirty clothing, she wasn't particularly impressive to look at. She was well aware that her appearance wasn't suited to the tastes of most men.

"Well, it's not like I'll be killing you directly, so I guess it's all right." He appeared to have no problem bending his own rules. Or maybe he had just decided that she didn't count as enough of a woman. "I'll have you fight her. This is Shiro."

At the man's urging, one of the girls who had been wrapped around him timidly stepped forward. She was a beastkin, with red eyes and a pair of long ears sprouting from her soft white hair. She seemed anything but confident as she walked into the arena. Her rabbit-like features and bright white clothing lent her a uniquely monocolored appearance.

"Um...could you not just fight her for me and then give me the points?" she asked the man behind her.

"Of course not."

"O-Okay, how about you get her close to death, and I just finish her off?" The rabbit girl was trembling, but her words seemed anything but shy.

Chapter 15 — What Makes You Think That Talking Will Work This Time?!

"I don't know. Hey, you, would that be allowed?" the man asked the magic doll in the stands.

"Well, this is a trial to measure your combat ability. Being able to handle an opponent in direct combat is crucial, but if you only step in to finish someone off, you would not receive any points for it."

"Well, there you have it." The man shrugged and looked back at Theodisia. "So you can relax over there. It looks like it'll just be one on one."

"I still feel somewhat outnumbered," Theodisia answered. After all, if she defeated the first girl, the next one would attack her immediately. She would have to defeat them all in order to get through.

"If you can beat this one, I'll let you pass," the man said.

She couldn't tell if he was being sincere or not, but if they planned on fighting her one at a time, at least she had a chance. And if she found an opening, she could try to kill the other three beforehand as well.

Theodisia drew a short single-edged sword from her cloak.

"What's the rush? Aren't you going to at least tell us your name?"

She felt no desire to answer him. There was little point in getting to know someone you were about to kill, and she didn't feel like sharing her own details either.

"Come on, at least say something like 'Introduce yourself before asking someone else's name.' How miserable are you? Well, I'll introduce myself anyway. I'm Masaki Kazuno. To be frank, I'm not interested in this Divine King or Swordmaster stuff at all."

Theodisia focused on Shiro, ignoring Masaki entirely. Perhaps because she was a rabbit beastkin, the girl was still trembling. She looked every bit the amateur. If it was just an act to throw others off their guard, it was certainly impressive.

"That's right. It's going to be hard if you don't even have a weapon."

Masaki threw a longsword to Shiro. The rabbit girl screamed, with an exaggerated dodge to get out of the way of the blade.

"Hey! Don't throw things at me like that!"

Timidly, she retrieved the sword from where it was sticking into the ground. Holding a weapon didn't seem to boost her confidence, and even the way she was holding it made her look like more of a danger to herself than anyone else.

"Why is it so heavy?! Do I really need it? I feel like I'd be better off without it."

"Becoming a Knight means becoming one of the Swordmaster's subordinates. So show that you can at least look like a swordsman."

Theodisia ignored Shiro's pathetic attempt at taking a combat stance. Masaki stood up, leaning against the wall and crossing his arms as the other girls continued to fawn over him. He maintained the appearance of a casual observer, but the chair he'd been sitting on had disappeared. And she knew that he had *not* been holding the sword he'd thrown until the moment he threw it.

"You…are you working with the Sages?" That was her first guess, given he seemed to have a highly unusual power. There were plenty of strong people in the world, but many of them got their abilities from the Sages, who were quite happy to dole out their powers to anyone and everyone around them.

"I've got nothing to do with the Sages or the Swordmasters. I just got too strong, so I ran out of things to do. I came here 'cause it looked fun."

If he was an enemy of the Swordmasters, there was no need to fight him. If she let him go, it might even help her reach her goal, but it looked like things weren't going to be that easy. First, she would have to defeat the rabbit girl.

Theodisia steeled herself. A one-on-one fight in an arena that offered no place to hide. There weren't many tactics that one could employ here. The first to strike would likely win.

She swung her blade in an arc that couldn't possibly have reached her target. Even so, the move cut apart the arena, the shockwave created by her blade carving a straight line through the dirt floor towards her opponent. Unable to respond in time, Shiro took the blow head-on.

"Owwww! What was that for?! Give me a warning if you're going to attack!"

Somehow, the rabbit girl was totally unharmed. Although she had taken the hit straight on and been sent flying, she climbed back to her feet, rubbing her forehead like it had been nothing more than a hard tap.

Chapter 15 — What Makes You Think That Talking Will Work This Time?!

Theodisia hadn't been going easy on her, nor had she let her guard down. Her intent had been to settle the match with a single blow, but she had failed to so much as scratch her opponent. It looked like brute force wasn't going to work.

"Shiro, you get it now, right?" Masaki called out. "Her attacks aren't anything to be afraid of. There's no need to be so scared."

"Oh, you mean, I might actually be able to win?"

"Of course you can win. Don't you remember how many stats bonus seeds I gave you?"

"Okay, then, here I go!"

Shiro closed the gap between them, rushing forward on unstable footing. As she raised the sword above her head, Theodisia struck her horizontally. Once again, the beastkin was unharmed. Her clothes had been sliced through but her body remained intact.

Ignoring Theodisia's attack, Shiro brought her sword down. It was a swing that clearly came from a novice and the blade wasn't even straight. Additionally, no magic at all was used in the swing, so it didn't present the slightest threat. Even so, Theodisia dodged much farther back than was necessary. With barely any resistance, the sword cut into the ground, burying itself deep.

"Hey! Stop dodging!"

The strength of her blow was incredible. Theodisia's own attacks were useless, and if she took one hit from the girl, it would be over. This was going to be a hell of an uphill battle.

◇◇◇

At Mokomoko's warning that someone was already inside, Yogiri and Tomochika cracked the door open to take a peek. There were five people in the chamber, two of whom were currently fighting. One was a woman with black hair and dirty clothes, who gave the impression of an experienced warrior. She was dancing around the room at a bewildering speed, launching repeated precision attacks. The other was a girl with flowing white hair and long, rabbit-like ears. She was practically naked, swinging her sword around unsteadily.

"This is the first time I've seen two people actually fighting each other with swords since we got here," Tomochika remarked. Their opponents thus far had all favored rather eccentric gear, so it was a refreshing sight, in a way.

However, something other than the fight itself had caught Yogiri's attention.

"She's a bunny girl! Look, she even has a fluffy round tail."

The rabbit girl's clothes were in tatters. Her backside was basically entirely visible, with its white, bunny-like puff of a tail in full view.

"That's what caught your attention?! Can you please stop staring?"

The rabbit was swinging her enormous sword around recklessly. It seemed too heavy for her, as every time she swung it, her whole body was taken along for the ride.

Naturally, such haphazard attacks had no chance of landing, so the cloaked woman was freely moving into her blindspots before unleashing her own blows. Even Yogiri could easily notice the difference in their abilities.

But the strangest part was that even with such an obvious skill gap between them, the fight showed no sign of ending. No matter how many times she was struck, the rabbit girl seemed to take no damage at all, so she was simply ignoring the attacks as she hopped around. The woman in the cloak, who possessed actual skill, seemed to be struggling far more.

"Even if she's naked, she's still just a rabbit, so I don't think it's that big of a deal."

"Come on, she's a human except for the ears and tail, right?!"

"You think so? I don't mean to be discriminatory or anything, but once they've got animal parts, they stop being human. Or at the very least, they stop being attractive."

"But she's still got boobs, doesn't she? Look how big they are!"

"Having boobs doesn't mean much. I mean, they're fine on their own, but once attached to a rabbit, they kind of lose their appeal."

"Are you serious? Just look at her, she's nice-looking, isn't she?!"

"Sure, but sticking random animal parts on her still ruins it."

"I guess you had a pretty weak reaction to that cat girl we saw a while back, too."

Chapter 15 — What Makes You Think That Talking Will Work This Time?!

Putting the boy's tastes aside for now, what do you plan on doing here? Mokomoko seemed to be getting impatient.

"This has nothing to do with us. All we want to do is go past, right?"

"That's true, but we can't really get through the room while they're duking it out like this, can we? And you're not just going to kill them, right?"

The rabbit girl was still swinging her sword wildly, while the cloaked woman was dancing around, striking back with her own shorter blade. If that had been all there was to the fight, they could have snuck around the edges of the arena, but occasionally, the combatant's clashes would unleash shockwaves throughout the room. There were no safe places to hide, making it seem like reaching the other door safely could be dangerous.

"Why would I kill someone for standing in my way? We can just wait a bit."

While Yogiri wouldn't hesitate to kill anyone who threatened them, they had no way of knowing yet whether these people were actually their enemies. Of course they were in the way, but he had no interest in killing those who weren't planning to harm them.

It doesn't look like they'll end this any time soon. The woman with the cloak is rather impressive, but her attacks aren't having any effect, even though she's been aiming at the rabbit girl's vitals and her blows have been landing. Even hitting her straight in the eyes isn't doing anything! Oh, and even getting her between the legs did nothing.

The cloaked woman slid between the rabbit girl's legs, driving her sword upward as she passed beneath her. She seemed to be looking for a spot where her attacks would get through. But even that vulnerable place wasn't so much as scratched.

As the cloaked woman opened up some distance between the beastkin and herself, the man at the back of the room called out to her. "Would you take this seriously already? It will never end at this rate. You're not using that much power on your disguise, are you?"

"Well, if you've already figured it out, then there's no point in keeping it hidden."

In an instant, the atmosphere surrounding her changed. While she had seemed plenty terrifying before, Yogiri could feel her intensity suddenly jump up several levels. And it wasn't only her personal vibe that changed, but her appearance, too. Her black hair turned silver and her pale skin darkened.

"To think you were hiding that you were a half-demon," the man chuckled.

Without a word, the woman swung her sword even harder than before. The rabbit girl screamed as her right arm dropped to the floor.

"Masaki! It hurts! It really hurts!" Despite her cries, the beastkin didn't seem extremely bothered by what should have been a critical injury.

"Now that I've shown my true form, it's only a matter of time. I'll have to push through before that time runs out!"

As if to try and finish things all at once, the woman swung her sword with even more strength. Darkness enveloped the blade, more than doubling the weapon's size. She sliced the hazy weapon through the air again, releasing all of the power that it held as she did. The shockwave from the blade became a shadow, tearing across the floor.

Such an attack would easily slice the rabbit girl in two — or so Yogiri had thought. But it didn't happen. Instead, the rabbit girl vanished, leaving nothing but her sword behind.

It was hard to say whether her reaction had been a trained response or just a coincidence, but the cloaked woman barely managed to block the beastkin's punch with the side of her blade. Although it sent her staggering back several steps, she had managed to avoid taking the blow directly.

Yet in that instant, the two of them had traded places. After having lost an arm and abandoning her sword, the rabbit girl began to move faster than the eye could follow.

"Looks like it's still going to go on for a while," Tomochika grumbled.

"It does. At this point, maybe we should try to talk our way through."

He wouldn't simply kill the strangers, but standing around doing nothing wasn't going to get them anywhere either.

"And what makes you think that talking will work this time?"

Ignoring Tomochika's retort, Yogiri opened the door the rest of the

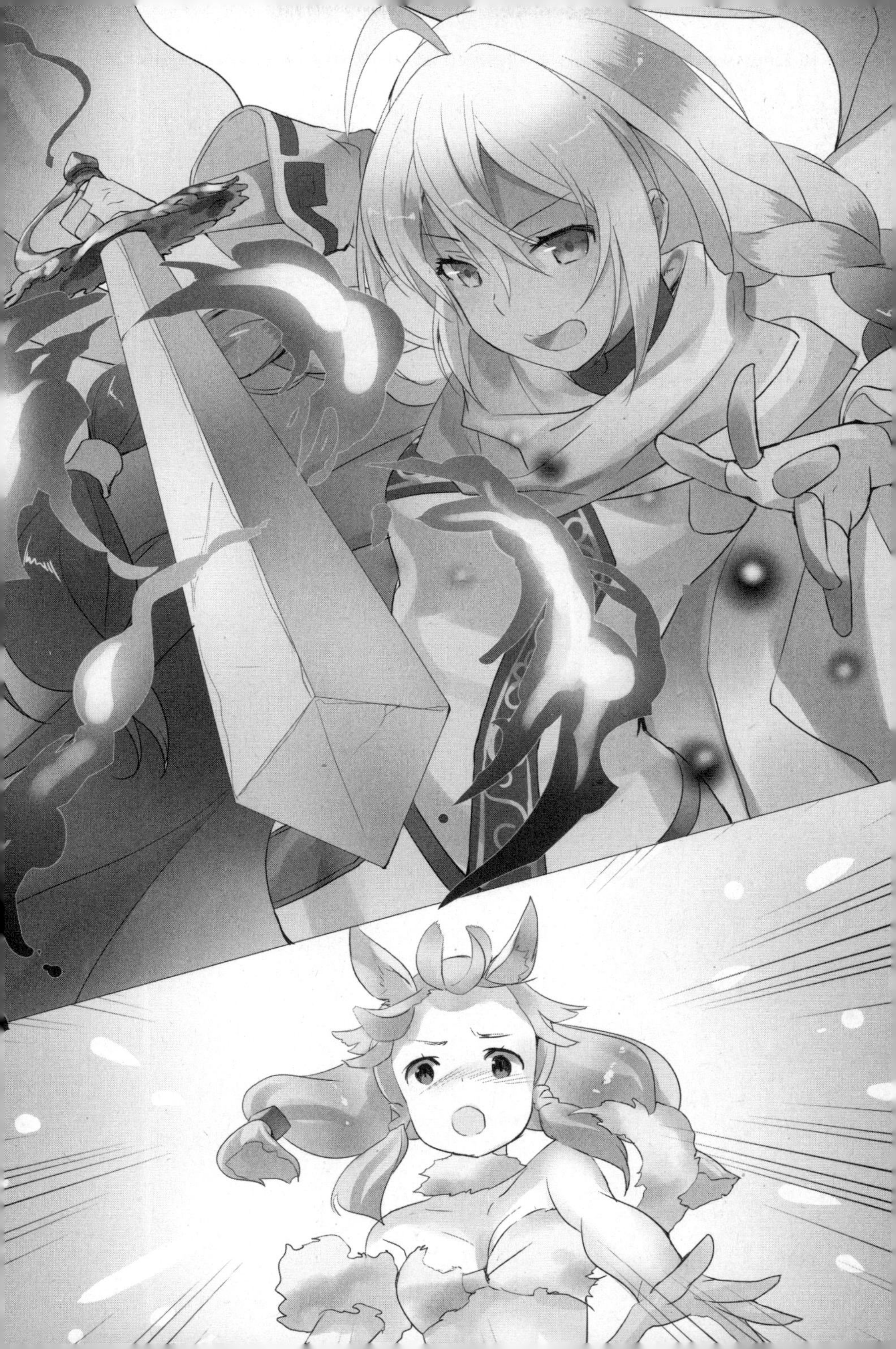

way and stepped inside. "Excuse me, do you mind if we pass through?" he asked, raising his voice so that everyone in the room could hear him.

Tomochika grabbed him from behind, trying to shake some sense into him. "Takatou, could you try to read the atmosphere a bit?! There's no way they'll let you pass! They're literally in a life-or-death struggle over there!"

Abruptly, everyone inside the room froze, their eyes moving to glare at the intruders.

Chapter 16 — You Picked a Fight With the Wrong Guy

The five people in the room turned to look at Yogiri at once. In the middle of the arena were the rabbit girl, dressed entirely in white, and the silver-haired, dark skinned woman who had been fighting her. Looking on from the edge of the chamber was a man in a white jacket, a woman in a tidy military uniform, and a young girl wearing a dress.

All of them had stopped what they were doing and were staring at Yogiri in shock, as if his appearance was some sort of inexplicable event.

"How did you get in here?" the man asked, as if he couldn't believe what he was seeing.

Yogiri decided to answer the stupid question as directly as possible. "Didn't you see me just open the door?"

"Ah, is that what happened? I guess I was an idiot. I forgot to take into account how strong the tower itself is. So, basically, you guys totally ignored the door I made and just broke in through one of the walls." The man had apparently come up with his own explanation already.

Now that he mentioned it, though, Yogiri realized where everyone's confusion was coming from. The door leading to the room was visibly different from the others they had passed by earlier. Of course, he hadn't cared, since it had opened just like any other door in the tower once he applied his power. A door's function was to limit the ways in and out of a room, so it made sense that if you killed it, that function would cease.

"Well, it doesn't really matter. Like I said, we're just planning to pass through. It seems like your fight has stopped for a moment, so now is perfect," Yogiri replied, casually walking forward. Tomochika stuck as close to him as she could.

"Hey, hey, hey. Hold on a second."

Astonished by the newcomer's brazen attitude, the man held up a hand and Yogiri complied.

"What? You guys are fighting that one in the cloak, right? So it shouldn't be a problem if we just go on through. We won't get in your way. It would probably be more of a nuisance if we stood around and watched you, right?"

"No, I'm going to need you two to stick around. We're here to collect points, and my apprentices still require quite a few. Between her and the two of you, we should have as much as we need. It's perfect."

Yogiri nodded to himself, finally understanding the situation. Since everyone had to come through here on their way out, it made sense to camp out and wait for them. "In that case, fighting us wouldn't be worthwhile. We only have six points between us."

"That's all the more reason for you to fight!" the man cried, as if worried on their behalf. "Are you serious? Hey, how many points do they have?" he asked the magic doll in the stands.

"I can't simply tell you other people's points," the puppet responded.

"You can tell him. I don't care," Yogiri said.

"Well, if they give their permission then it's fine. Number 98 has five po-po-po-po-po-po-po…" The magic doll began to shout in total gibberish. After a few moments, its voice suddenly cut off, and with its mouth and eyes still wide open, it collapsed to the floor.

"There you go. Something seems off, but like she said, I have five points."

"That didn't answer anything! Hey, what's wrong?!" the man shouted at the fallen puppet, but it didn't respond.

"We were never interested in becoming Knights anyway, we just kind of got wrapped up in all this by accident. So we didn't pay much attention to the whole collecting points thing in the first place. So…can you just let us go through?" Yogiri asked again.

Chapter 16 — You Picked a Fight With the Wrong Guy

"Of course, letting you through would be simple. I know this is a trial, but I could force my way through these sealed doors if I wanted to. I could even break straight through the floor. There are plenty of ways to get down to ground level, but this is a game where you're meant to collect points. Sticking to the rules is part of the fun. I'm not going to let you cheat."

"What about you?" Yogiri asked the other woman.

"I don't care what you do. I already have my points, so I have no need to fight you."

He had thought they might be put off by him interrupting their fight, but it seemed the woman didn't feel that way at all. She had clearly been at some sort of disadvantage, so maybe she was grateful for the chance to stop and catch her breath.

"Okay, what am I supposed to do, then?" Yogiri muttered, starting to get fed up with the situation.

The fighting in the room was currently on pause, so it would be easy for them to cross over to the other side of the arena. He certainly had no intention of fighting anyone for points. But the man seemed to have no intention of letting them through, either. It was starting to look like they wouldn't be able to settle this very peacefully.

"To be honest, things have worked out quite well. Now we can do a three-on-three," the man suggested.

"Even though we have no points?"

"I don't care about that anymore. Something weird is going on here, but this is a great opportunity regardless. After this, my group can go on ahead." He urged the two girls beside him forward. "The rabbit over there is Shiro. The bigger one here is Geralda, and the smaller one is Ema. They are all my apprentices. I brought them here as part of their training. If you can beat them, I'll let you pass, and I'll even let you become my students as well."

Geralda, in the military uniform, and Ema, the small girl wearing a dress, stepped forward to stand beside Shiro. At some point, the silver-haired woman had moved to Yogiri's side, so just as the man had intended, it had turned into a three-versus-three setup.

"I feel like there are some issues with your negotiation skills. What did you just get us into?" Tomochika asked.

"It was kind of unavoidable. He seems like the kind of guy that's too full of himself to listen to what other people have to say."

"You should have known that just by looking at him!" she replied before turning to the silver-haired woman to apologize. "Oh, umm, sorry for making things all weird like this."

"Don't worry about it," their new "teammate" replied. "It seems like you two are the ones in the most trouble here, after all. If those girls are as strong as the rabbit, then we have no way of winning. And I don't quite believe this guy will let us go even if we do win."

"That's right," the man said in response to her conjecture. "Shiro is the weakest of the three. She's pretty tough, but new to fighting. Ema, however, is an expert swordsman, and Geralda is proficient with magic. Honestly, I'm not especially concerned about whether or not I'll even have to let you pass. Aside from Shiro, these girls are seasoned apprentices that I have personally trained. If they fight in earnest, this will be over in an instant."

"What do you mean, 'aside from Shiro'?! I'm strong too!"

"First of all, would you hurry up and put your arm back on? Obviously, you have no talent whatsoever with a sword, so go ahead and fight without it this time."

"Master, what did you mean just now? It sounds like you intend for us to not fight at full strength," Geralda, the uniformed woman asked.

"I'm not ordering you to hold back or anything, but if you go all out, there won't even be ashes left when you're done. Read the situation and fight accordingly. Oh, and the cloaked woman actually looks pretty good now that she's ditched her disguise, so you can leave her alive. Plus that other girl looks Japanese. It's been a while since I've had a Japanese beauty, so we'll keep her too."

"Master, your bad side is starting to show," Ema complained. "Anyway, you're saying we should only kill the boy? Personally, I kind of like him."

"Good-looking guys have to die. That's how I've always done things."

"Understood. But I should warn you that keeping the girls unharmed will probably be impossible," warned Geralda.

"What, are you jealous or something? Well, as long as they're alive, we'll manage, so I'll leave it to you."

Having finished the discussion, the man crossed his arms, leaning back against the wall. He was fully confident in his party's success, content to kick back and watch things unfold.

"What should we do?" Tomochika asked, bewildered by the sudden change in the situation.

"The same thing we've been doing this whole time, I guess?"

If the man had told his girls not to kill them, they may have been able to end things in some other way. But the moment they began to radiate killing intent, Yogiri had only one way to respond.

"Die."

The three women fell to their knees before simultaneously collapsing forward.

"So, we can go now, right? That's what you promised."

Not understanding what she had just witnessed, the silver-haired woman was still on guard. She stared at their fallen enemies intently, waiting to see what they had up their sleeves. Meanwhile, the man was gaping at them too, his jaw just about on the floor. It must have been an entirely unexpected, unbelievable outcome for him. He looked as if his mind had simply gone blank.

Yogiri casually began walking forward. Tomochika pushed down her growing frustration that these people kept throwing themselves at Yogiri in spite of his best efforts to keep from killing anyone, and followed close behind him once again. When they reached the exit, Yogiri kicked the door open without a problem. Yanked out of his stupor by the sound of the door giving way, the man, who had been leaning against the wall in shock, finally managed to move.

A pitch-black shadow rapidly washed over the entire chamber. It was the first time in a while that Yogiri had seen such a clear, pure form of killing intent.

"Liar," he said with annoyance as he released his power at the man.

◇◇◇

Geralda had originally tracked down Masaki with the intention of killing him. After Masaki had defeated a Demon Lord, he had taken up residence in its castle and had come to be seen as a Demon Lord himself.

Truthfully, he had just been bored. He figured if he waited, some idiot Hero who thought it was their job to kill Demon Lords would come along and fight him. And eventually, Geralda had shown up. After he had easily defeated her, and she had learned that he wasn't a Demon Lord after all, her admiration for his abilities led her to ask to be taken on as his apprentice.

Masaki had liked the sound of that. Fighting things himself meant an easy, obvious win, and that got old fast. But training students to fight in his stead sounded interesting.

It had ended up being a good way to stave off boredom, so he began to take on more students. He traveled the world, searching for those with natural talent. The first one he had found was Ema. Although still young, her skills had exceeded Geralda's. But being too strong was also boring in its own way, so he decided to train someone who was rather weak as well. He had looked for the weakest-looking woman from the weakest possible race, the rabbit people, and had ended up with Shiro.

It turned out to be an excellent way to pass the time. The three women each had their own distinct personalities, so they responded to his instruction differently, and he had begun to take great pleasure in watching them grow.

Yet those three were now lying motionless on the floor. It had taken Masaki a moment to understand what that meant. At first, he thought they were just messing around. He had told them not to go all out, and figured they were simply taking it to some sort of absurd extreme. But as he silently chided them, he realized that they weren't moving at all. So, using his artificial eye, he checked their conditions.

All three of them were dead. It had all happened so fast, he couldn't understand how it had even occurred. But hearing the sound of the door behind him being kicked open, he had returned to his senses.

These three strangers had done something. He couldn't think of any other explanation. With the boy who had killed his students right in front of him, he went blind with rage.

Chapter 16 — You Picked a Fight With the Wrong Guy

And then time stopped.

It was a state that Masaki called Command Mode. It wasn't like he could move around freely while time was stopped, but it allowed him to think of his next move at his own pace.

"Monad! Explain the situation!"

"Oh! It's been a while since you've called me out!"

Monad was the second thing that Masaki had created with his powers: a tool used for analysis. It wasn't like it was omniscient, but with access to a tremendous amount of information pertaining to this world, it was capable of producing the optimal solution to any situation.

However, Masaki had never before come across any serious trouble, even while fighting blindly and without help, so he rarely ever used his creation.

"Forget the greetings! Tell me what's going on!"

"Hmm...ah, my condolences. Your students have died. The one responsible is that boy, Yogiri Takatou. He's Japanese, just like you. It looks like he was summoned here by the Sages."

"He wasn't reincarnated by a goddess?"

"No. The administrative power that you stole from the goddess won't work on him."

"Who the hell is he?! What did he do?!"

Monad looked through the records of everything that Yogiri had said since he'd come to this world, eventually finding something of note. "I have no idea who he is. According to his own explanation, he has an Instant Death ability of some kind."

"Like hell! You think I'd make a mistake like that?! We took every precaution — they were completely immune to Instant Death magic!"

"If you say so."

"Goddammit! Whatever! It's a pain in the ass, but I can always get more students. For now, I'm just going to have to kill this guy." He didn't know how the kid's ability worked, but once he had decided on his next course of action while in Command Mode, whatever he chose to do would happen at once when time started moving again. Masaki was as capable of causing "instant death" as the next person.

143

"Hey, hey, hey. You said they could pass if they won, right? That's awfully petty of you."

"Wait a second. What's gotten into you? Something seems wrong." Monad had always been pretty rough in the way that it talked, but it had never spoken out of turn before.

"Seems like you've misunderstood something. You didn't *create* my personality. You wanted omniscience, and as a preexisting intelligence that's as close to omniscient as one can be, I was simply roped in and bound to the object you designed. I figure this is the last conversation we'll have, so I decided to let loose a bit."

"What are you talking about?!"

"You picked a fight with the wrong guy. And you could have been so happy if you'd just used your powers to enjoy living!"

"What the hell are you saying?! In a second, he's going to be completely incinerated and it will all be over! I could even erase this whole tower if I chose to!"

"Ahahahahaha! There won't be a next second! Never again! It's already over! Yogiri Takatou has unleashed his ability! Nothing you do will make it in time! If you don't believe me, test it out yourself. Do whatever you like!"

"Th-Then I need some sort of defense! That's why you're here, right?! You can predict the future so that I can bend and twist it to my benefit!"

"Whether you can see the future or not, there's nothing you can do about it now, so what does it matter? Ah! There is one thing!"

"Tell me!"

"Just stay like this! You probably can't keep it up forever, but from your perspective, you could probably last in Command Mode for about three years!"

Despair began to creep into his mind. Slowly but surely, Masaki was starting to understand the situation.

"No way...wait! Why do I have to die?!"

"Everyone dies eventually, right?"

"But I'm supposed to be different! I even killed a god! I took its power! That makes me a god! I'm supposed to be immortal! There's no way I can die here and now!"

Chapter 16 — You Picked a Fight With the Wrong Guy

"If that god was supposed to be immortal, how did you kill it in the first place? Did you ever think of that? Let me say this as clearly as I can: Yogiri Takatou is a being that surpasses human understanding. There is nothing that someone like you can do. If he uses his power, it doesn't matter who or what his target is…death is the only outcome. But who cares? You don't have to believe what I'm saying. Hurry up and pick a command. Don't worry, his way of killing is surprisingly gentle!"

As absurd as it sounded, Masaki couldn't ignore what Monad was telling him. He had always believed himself to be a perfect being. And the tool that he had created was telling him he was going to die. If he denied that declaration, it would be the same as denying his own perfection — a fatal blow to his self-image.

Masaki was in anguish. He had as much time as he needed, but it didn't take long before he lost the ability to think clearly at all.

◇◇◇

The man fell to the ground with a thud. Yogiri must have used his power, but Tomochika didn't bother to ask why. If Yogiri had killed him, it meant the man had intended to harm them.

"Wait, doesn't he look different somehow? It's like his face has changed." Tomochika cocked her head to the side as she looked down at the guy's unmoving form. She felt like he had looked a little cooler before, but he suddenly looked rather old.

"No idea. I don't remember what his face looked like in the first place." Yogiri wasn't interested in the details. Without even looking back, he proceeded onwards.

"P-Please, wait!" The silver-haired woman ran up beside them and pointed at the bodies. "Are you the one who did this?"

"Yeah."

"Then, please! I know it's incredibly presumptuous, but would you be willing to help me?" she pleaded, bowing her head deeply.

"Huh? Uhh…?" Yogiri just wanted to go on ahead, but now he hesitated. He seemed to have a weak spot for people begging him for help. He turned to look at Tomochika with a troubled expression.

"Hey, don't look at me. I suppose there's no harm in hearing her out, though."

She was all for getting out of the tower as quickly as possible, but she didn't want the guilt of ignoring someone's request any more than he did.

Chapter 17 — This Feels an Awful Lot Like a Last Boss

Having Mokomoko keep an eye on their surroundings, the trio moved to settle into the arena seats.

"First of all, my name is Theodisia." The woman wore a somewhat shabby cloak. Her silver hair and dark skin lent her a unique kind of beauty, while the way that she carried herself gave the impression of a skilled and confident fighter.

"I'm Yogiri Takatou, and this is Tomochika Dannoura. We're on our way to the capital, but we ended up getting caught up in this trial by accident."

"Is that true, though?" murmured Tomochika. "I mean, to be fair, we kind of stuck our heads in on our own..." They had only gone to the tower at the request of the dragon girl, Atila, but Tomochika figured they'd had plenty of opportunities to walk away.

"So, what exactly do you want from us? It's got nothing to do with the trial, right?" Within the trial, other participants were only opponents to be fought. Even if they temporarily worked together, it wasn't the kind of setting where you could rely on others for help.

"You two seem to be foreigners. You may have come across gossip about us, but the people here refer to my kind as half-demons. Do you know much about us?"

"No, we basically know nothing about this world. Even if it seems like common knowledge, it would help if you could break it down for us."

"It has become something of a disparaging term in this world, but my people are a unique tribe here. As a general term, the name 'half-demon' is fine. The main characteristics of my kind are silver hair and dark skin. And, more importantly, we all possess an enormous amount of magical energy."

"Does that mean you can use really strong magic? I saw that black stuff haloing your sword earlier."

"That was just a combat technique," Theodisia said, as if the distinction should have been obvious.

"How exactly is hardcore magic considered a 'combat technique'?!" It was so different from the sword techniques that Tomochika was familiar with that she couldn't help but be skeptical. She was going to have to ask Mokomoko about it later.

"At any rate, I have no real talent for magic. Most of my people are like that, so such a store of magical energy is unfortunately a useless treasure to the tribe. However, it is still a treasure, and there are those who would seek to take it from us. Those who need large amounts of magical energy to fulfill their goals find us to be a useful resource."

"You think the Swordmaster is one of those people?" Yogiri asked.

For a moment, Tomochika was confused by the leap in his logic. But if Theodisia was asking them for help, and it wasn't related to the trial, she must have had some other reason for coming to the tower. According to what she had told them, her people were being hunted by others. It wasn't hard for Yogiri to guess that the Swordmaster could be one of those taking them captive.

"That is correct. My people have been abducted and are trapped within this place. I am here searching for information about my lost sister, Euphemia."

Yogiri felt like he had heard that name before, but he couldn't quite remember where. "From your wording, it sounds like some of your people are here, but you're not sure about your sister?"

"Yes, I have a general idea of where my people are. They are still a ways below us, likely underground. But I can't tell exactly *who* they are."

"So, you want us to help you set them free?"

"Precisely. Now that my disguise is gone, I won't be able to move around the tower freely. It is only a matter of time before I myself am captured and meet the same fate as them. But if I had your power on my side..." She trailed off, as if realizing how selfish her request sounded.

"First of all, I feel like the fact that your disguise is gone isn't a huge problem," Yogiri noted. "I don't think they're looking that closely at what's happening in the tower anymore." He had destroyed so many things since arriving that it seemed like the surveillance system was no longer functioning properly.

"Can't you just put the disguise back on?" asked Tomochika. She figured if that was possible, the whole problem would be solved.

"No, the disguise was a spell that a friend of mine placed on me. My own power was fueling the disguise, but I can't recast it myself."

"Hmm, that's too bad, then. But if they are capturing people just for being half-demons, I guess I'll come and complain right alongside you," said Yogiri.

"Does that mean you'll help?" Theodisia wasn't sure why he had agreed, but the way he had responded made it sound like it was obvious that he would help her.

"Yeah. You don't mind, right?" he asked Tomochika, clearly not wanting to leave her out of the decision. "Even though it might take us a little longer to get out of the tower."

"Well, she doesn't seem like a bad person. Though to be honest, I thought something like this would be too much of a bother for you."

"What makes you say that?" Yogiri asked, pouting slightly. "If someone asks for help, you should help them, right?"

"Now that you mention it, I guess I've never seen you turn someone down, have I? Of course, since most people attack us instantly, it hasn't come up all that much."

Yogiri had saved Tomochika shortly after they had come to this world. At first glance, he seemed to lack the motivation to do anything, as if it was all too much for him to bother with, but thinking back on it, that attitude didn't truly line up with his actions thus far.

"Perhaps it's strange for me to say this, since I asked you to help me in the first place, but working with me means becoming an enemy of the Swordmaster. Are you sure you're okay with that?" Theodisia asked, still bewildered.

Her original objective had been to sneak into the tower under the guise of being an applicant for the Knights, search for her people, and then sneak back out with them. But now that her disguise had been blown, that plan had effectively failed. The only thing she could try was a desperate all-out attack, which inevitably meant fighting the Swordmaster himself.

"I think I've already sort of made an enemy out of him. I destroyed an awful lot of his tower."

"I've been wondering how we'd deal with it if they ask us to pay them back for all the damage we've done…" Tomochika mused, airing a concern that she'd been feeling for a while. At this point, it was hard to imagine the Swordmaster would be willing to politely speak with them.

"B-But, still! There's nothing in it for you! Even if you help me, you gain nothing! Do you realize how much of a risk it is to be an enemy of the Swordmaster?!" Theodisia must not have expected to receive his help so easily. For her, the Swordmaster was an overwhelming threat, so it was unthinkable that someone would so casually position themselves against him.

"Well, even if there's nothing in it for us, you seem like you really need the help."

"That's right. Even when you saved me, there was nothing much in it for you…wait, that was just for my boobs, though!"

Tomochika looked at Theodisia's chest. It was hard to tell through the cloak, but it seemed fairly prominent.

"My chest? Ah! If all you desire in return is my body, that is a cheap price to pay. Do with it as you will."

"Hey, we don't need any of that clichéd nonsense here! You're not interested in her body in the first place, are you? Are you?!"

"Yeah, I have my own tastes."

Yogiri denied it, but Tomochika couldn't help but worry that he seemed like the kind of guy to jump at any attention from a woman.

"Putting that aside for now," he continued, "I can't just take everything you're saying at face value. I'll decide what to do once I've seen the whole situation. Is that fair?" There was still the possibility that Theodisia's goals were evil, or that the Swordmaster had complex and justifiable reasons for his actions. It was impossible to judge the old man as being in the wrong just from Theodisia's words alone.

"I have no other option, which is why I asked you in the first place. Whatever you decide, I will not complain."

"Then I guess for now our objective is to rescue your friends and get out of the tower. We'll head towards the basement, and if anyone tries to stop us, we'll try to talk our way through first."

Tomochika often found herself forgetting that Yogiri didn't just kill people on a whim. As a rule, he only used his power in self-defense. It was pure coincidence that his only way of protecting himself was to kill others.

"Okay, but I can't imagine we'll be able to talk our way past anyone," Tomochika replied.

Theodisia had requested Yogiri's help to defeat the Swordmaster. That was likely an easy task for him. Swordmaster or not, the moment he showed any intention of attacking, Yogiri would kill him. No matter how important he was to this world, Yogiri wouldn't care.

"Well, it would be nice if he *was* willing to talk things over with us..."

But Tomochika had already given up on that.

◇◇◇

Having finished their conversation, the three of them left the arena. After descending the stairs, they immediately came upon the door to the first floor. Before they entered, Theodisia drew her hood up, hiding her face and hair. Although likely a meaningless precaution, she figured it was better than doing nothing at all.

It was almost three o'clock. They had just managed to finish within the time limit.

Opening the door, they were greeted by the sight of a familiar room. It was a large, circular reception room, with the entrance to the elevator at its center. There were a dozen or so people gathered in a circle, watching something intently.

"Oh, Rick and Lynel are here. It looks like they made it," breathed Tomochika, relieved.

It was the two companions they had started out with. They seemed to have met up again somewhere along the way. The girl who had unleashed her magic at the barrier from the top of the tower, Frederica, was also with them, so they had probably all joined together.

Lynel was wearing what looked like rather high-grade armor. He had likely gotten it from using his star crystals to roll the *gacha*, but seeing him like that made Tomochika feel uneasy. She couldn't help but wonder how many of those star crystals it had cost him.

None of them seemed to notice the new arrivals, so the three of them joined the circle to see what everyone else was looking at.

The first thing they saw was the Swordmaster unleash a high roundhouse kick.

"Where's the sword? How is this 'swordsmanship'?!" Tomochika blurted out.

He had kicked the swordsman in black — the same one who had complained to them when they'd first arrived in the forest.

I knew of a family of swordsmen who were quite skilled with upper roundhouse kicks once.

"What's the point of calling yourself a 'Swordmaster' if you don't actually use a sword?"

Well, I suppose that just means he doesn't even need a sword for something like this.

"Umm, what's going on?" Tomochika asked Rick.

"Miss Dannoura! I'm glad to see you are well."

"Yeah, I'm doing great. So, what's happening here?"

"The man in black challenged the Swordmaster to a fight."

The black-clad man in question was now lying on the ground. He was probably unconscious, but it was hard to tell from where they were standing.

"Is this part of the trial?"

"The Swordmaster said that if anyone can defeat him, they can skip

Chapter 17 — This Feels an Awful Lot Like a Last Boss

over becoming a Knight and go straight to being a Swordmaster. So yes, you could say that it's part of the trial, but as you can see, I doubt that anyone else will take up the challenge."

"Now, how about the rest of you?" the Swordmaster asked, looking around the circle. He showed no sign of his previous fight having been any sort of effort for him. No one stepped forward to answer the challenge. "All right then, the side show is over. It is now three o'clock, so it looks like seventeen of you have passed," he said, noticing that Yogiri's group had arrived.

Yogiri counted the people around him. It appeared the black-robed swordsman on the ground had been included in the tally.

"With that, you are now all Knights of the Divine King. I'll leave the explanation of what rights and obligations that entails to the dolls."

As he spoke, a group of magic puppets entered from a side chamber just off the main room. Their behavior was rather odd considering they were meant to be providing guidance and information. They ran forward with wild expressions. The Swordmaster's face grew suspicious as he watched them approach.

"Swordmaster! The tower has gone silent! We cannot ascertain its current condition!"

"Swordmaster! According to our observations, there is something wrong with the seal! The first barrier may soon fail!"

"Swordmaster! A fluctuation has been detected in the outer parts of the second barrier! The prediction of when the spawn will break through has changed —"

The last doll was interrupted by the sound of an explosion shaking the tower. The tremors were bad enough that standing became difficult, and Yogiri instinctively crouched down to regain his footing. Tomochika was also caught off guard by the sudden shaking, but managed to keep her balance.

Their surroundings had suddenly grown bright, prompting Yogiri to look upwards. He could see the sun hanging in a blue sky. The upper parts of the tower had been cleanly stripped away.

"Hm. I thought that destroying the tower would erase the barrier, but it seems like things might be a bit more difficult."

A powerful voice resonated in the space around them. It didn't take long before everyone gathered had located the source...there was no way any of them could miss the overwhelming aura of pure evil that its owner projected.

The speaker glared down at them from the sky where the tower had been moments before. It was dark, beautiful, and sinister. Aside from its six wings, it looked more or less human.

"I thought you weren't supposed to show up for three more days," the Swordmaster said with a fearless laugh. "Well, whatever. This is your first job as Holy Knights, everyone. Defeat that thing. If you fail, humanity will be wiped out."

"Right, let's go find a way underground," said Yogiri. Clearly, the Swordmaster wouldn't have time to worry about the half-demons if he was dealing with a monster.

"Hold on! Are you seriously just going to leave that thing to wreak havoc?!" Tomochika cried. "It feels an awful lot like a final boss, don't you think?!"

"That's none of my business. If I kill it, the Swordmaster might take an interest in me, so having these guys fight it for us is more convenient."

Though Tomochika was still unconvinced, Yogiri began to scan the room around them. The elevator in the center stood out the most, but there were a number of doors along the outer walls. One of those likely led underground.

"I agree. We don't have time to deal with this thing, and it's a good distraction," Theodisia nodded.

The three of them ran for the nearest door.

Chapter 18 — I Don't Know What Will Happen if I Kill Space Itself

The tower appeared out of nowhere. It was the same structure that she had caught a brief glimpse of before, and this time it was definitely not an illusion. There was no denying the reality of it as it stood tall before them.

"To think we missed such a thing..." Hanakawa muttered.

He and Aoi were perched on a high cliff, having followed the path of the bladed monster in the direction of the structure that Aoi had seen. The tower, which had suddenly popped into view before them, stood out for not only its size but the fact that it was the only artificial structure in the canyon. Aoi figured it was about five hundred meters tall.

"It looks like they had some kind of illusion around it. The fact that they were able to hide something so big means that it must have been pretty impressive magic. This area is under the control of the Swordmaster, though, so we Sages rarely have a reason to come here."

"Swordmasters are the ones who train Heroes, right?" Hanakawa asked.

"Heroes are more like those who failed to become Swordmasters. From the rumors I've heard, they gather people for a selection process to become Knights of the Divine King. Those who have talent later become Swordmaster candidates and are trained by the Swordmaster personally.

Those who don't are cut off and become Heroes. It's pretty similar to what Sages do in the end."

"Ah, now that you mention it, I seem to recall being told to attempt to become a Sage..."

"By who?"

"Sion, I believe her name was."

"Ahh, my condolences then." She had thought of Hanakawa as little more than a fat kid who didn't know how to take care of himself, but suddenly she was overcome by a strong feeling of pity for him.

"Hold on! Why are you looking at me like an insect whose wings have been ripped off?!"

"Sion is very much all or nothing in her methods. She has no interest in actually training people. She much prefers driving them to the edge to see if any of them miraculously survive, even if she could get better results by helping them to grow slowly. So you'll probably run into a bit of a rough patch sooner or later."

"I feel that things are sufficiently rough already! Perhaps you would be willing to help me, since I've come this far with you? We've been traveling together all this time, so you've grown a little attached to me, right? Maybe you're even starting to think I'm a little cute? Like a kind of Stockholm Syndrome thing?"

Aoi took a good look at Hanakawa, but she felt absolutely nothing for him. "Sorry, we're not allowed to intervene when it comes to Sage candidates."

"Then please send me back! I'll do my best to become a Sage!"

"It's okay. Staying with me will be pretty good training."

"Now I just feel like I'm going to die either way! Really, we've got one foot in the grave here! Why are we chasing that monster?!"

"We're just heading to a place where it looks like something will happen. But don't worry, I don't have any intention of fighting that thing. My target is Yogiri Takatou, so we'll be avoiding the Aggressor."

"But like I said, if you are merely targeting Takatou, what need do you have of me?!"

"Oh, I guess I never properly explained that part. Think of it like Nobunaga Oda."

Chapter 18 — I Don't Know What Will Happen if I Kill Space Itself

"What is that supposed to mean?"

"You don't know who Nobunaga Oda is?"

"Please, don't insult me. Of course I know of the Demon King of the Sixth Heaven!"

"People like him, who have high Fate levels, rarely die. Even when he was attacked by Zenjuubou Sugitani, or when he pretended to be a common foot soldier and fought on the front lines, or when he recklessly attacked Okehazama, he just didn't die. From his opponents' perspectives, it must have seemed like he was cheating somehow. But in the end, someone still managed to find a way to kill him."

"You mean the Honnoji Incident?"

"Exactly. To kill someone who is protected by Fate, you need to use that Fate against them. Trying to kill them randomly is impossible. You need to create a situation where killing them will be suitably dramatic, where it'll cause a huge uproar. Fate tends towards the most interesting outcome. So you need to fashion a scenario where him dying makes a more interesting story than him continuing to live."

"This is supposed to be about why you brought me with you, right?"

"Of course. Reuniting with a classmate is rather dramatic, don't you think?"

"But wouldn't it be easier if you just used your power to counteract his? That seems much easier to me."

"I don't have enough information on him yet, and it's not safe to rely entirely on my ability. In the end, the fight will be decided by Fate. The best I can do is try to create a situation where Fate will push things in a direction that works for me." Truthfully, she didn't have much in the way of expectations for Hanakawa, but it was worth a shot. "Anyway, I just figured that you might be useful somehow —"

Before she could finish her sentence, a sound like an explosion filled the air.

"Umm...it looks like the tower has disappeared again. Did they put the barrier back up?" Hanakawa asked, knowing full well that probably wasn't the case.

"Looks like someone blew it up," Aoi answered.

The tower appeared to have been cleanly wiped from the landscape.

And not just the tower — the surrounding canyon and forest had similarly vanished. In their place was a dangerous-looking individual, floating in the air. He fired something into the ground, and everything along the projectile's path was annihilated.

"That's ridiculous! That thing is strong enough to change the landscape!" Hanakawa screamed in a shrill voice.

"Well, this is a problem. If Yogiri Takatou was in that tower, there's no way we can confirm whether he's dead or alive." For someone in her line of work, having a target die on their own without her knowing about it was extremely annoying. "Well, if that was enough to kill him, then I wouldn't be needed in the first place, right?"

Grabbing Hanakawa as he tried to run away, she dragged him along to where the tower had once stood.

◇◇◇

"Huh? Where are they going?!" Lynel hesitated as he saw Yogiri, Tomochika, and another woman run off at full speed. He wasn't sure whether he should also run away or if it would be better to stand and fight.

"Lynel! This isn't the time to be worried about the others!" Rick shouted, bringing him back to his senses. Running away wasn't really possible anyway. Their opponent was someone who could destroy a one-hundred-floor tower in an instant — there wasn't anywhere safe to escape to. And more importantly, the creature floating in the air was certainly one of the Dark God's spawn. If they didn't do something to stop it here, it would destroy the barrier, unleash its master upon the world, and bring about the end of humanity.

"We don't need cowards like them anyway! If these things are clawing their way past the barrier for us, that just makes things easier. This time I'll show you my true strength!" Frederica brandished her staff, once again full of confidence. Though her abilities far exceeded those of an ordinary person, she was particularly skilled with magic, possessing an amount of magical energy that was easily ten thousand times greater than the average mage's. In fact, as far as he knew, she was the strongest

Chapter 18 — I Don't Know What Will Happen if I Kill Space Itself

mage in existence, so as pathetic as it made him feel, Lynel found himself instinctively hiding behind her.

"You realize that's not actually the Dark God, right? It's just one of its spawn."

"Of course I know that! Dealing with its underlings should be easy!"

"Lynel, please get ready to use one of your stones," Rick said calmly, drawing his sword. Those around them who had also just become Knights took up fighting stances of their own.

The creature floating in the air slowly descended, landing in front of the Swordmaster. It looked basically human, with the only real difference being the three pairs of black wings that sprouted from its back. But the tremendous aura of evil it exuded made it clear that this was no ordinary person. It was a life form on an entirely different level, far above humanity.

"How does one remove the barrier? If you tell me, I won't kill you." The way it spoke would be enough to make a weaker person fall to their knees before it. There was magic in its voice — a magic that was resisted by one of the rings that Lynel was wearing, which protected him from mind control.

"How kind of you to say that after destroying my tower," the Swordmaster replied. As expected, he wasn't the least bit cowed by the spawn's imposing presence.

"I'd assumed that destroying the tower would have a high likelihood of dispelling the barrier. But since it didn't work, I'll need to find another way."

Accepting the Swordmaster's response as a refusal, the spawn pointed a finger at one of the gathered Knights. For an instant, the tip of its finger glowed, then a thin bolt of black lightning shot forth and punched a hole through the man's forehead, killing him instantly.

"There is no need to rush. I will kill you one by one so that you have plenty of time to change your minds."

"Don't make light of us!" another man shouted, jumping into the space between the Swordmaster and the spawn. He immediately split himself into six clones, each of them slashing at the creature simultaneously, striking all at once from six different directions. It was an absolutely unavoidable, inarguably fatal attack, but the creature didn't attempt to dodge it in the slightest. Instead, it flicked a hand outward in irritation as the six blades struck home. The assault failed to make so much as a mark, accomplishing nothing but the addition of six new corpses around the creature, each cut in half at the waist.

"Huh. I thought those were illusions or something, but I guess they were real bodies," Lynel remarked.

"You seem awfully calm about the whole situation," Frederica replied, impressed by his composure.

The Swordmaster leaped backwards, distancing himself from the spawn. Perhaps still waiting for the right opportunity, he had yet to draw his weapon.

"I'd be more than happy if there was no barrier!" Frederica shouted, lifting her staff into the air as its tip began to glow. The glowing light strengthened and eventually detached from the staff, leaving an enormous ball of light floating through the air.

"Um...i-is this really the time to be saying such things?" stammered Lynel. "A-And isn't that orb getting a little too big?!" It was now even larger than the ball of fire she had unleashed at the top of the tower. The light continued to grow, reaching a size that wouldn't have fit inside the tower if the building had still existed above them.

"Full throttle, full power! No restraint!"

"But, um, won't we be hit by that too?"

Lynel's worries amounted to nothing, however. The sphere of burning light that blocked out the entire sky above them suddenly shrank, the air around it wavering in the heat. The enormous magical energy in the sphere had been compressed to its utmost limit, but it was hard to tell what result the impact would have once she unleashed it. Lynel felt his whole body begin to tremble as he was struck with a terrible premonition.

Luckily, the spawn hadn't taken notice of her yet. It was simply focused on killing the new Knights around it one by one.

"Take this!" Frederica swung the staff downwards, pointing it at the spawn. The sphere of light, condensed to the size of a fist, flew at the

Chapter 18 — I Don't Know What Will Happen if I Kill Space Itself

creature at a terrifying speed. Without even sparing it a glance, the spawn swung around and snatched it out of the air.

Frederica froze. Her mind couldn't keep up with the reality unfolding before her. This was the best she had to offer, an attack with all of her power behind it, and yet the spawn had crushed it in a single hand without any apparent thought or effort.

"That was quite impressive for a human. If it had hit, it might even have left a burn," a young boy remarked, standing in front of Frederica. He had appeared there at some point, unnoticed, casually standing with his hands behind his head and a big smile on his face. "But if you can't get past the Dimensional Wall, nothing you do will matter."

"Dammit!" Frederica instinctively swung her staff at the boy, who casually stopped it with one hand. Lynel couldn't believe it — that hadn't just been an ordinary strike either. Lynel had seen that same attack shatter the head of a dragon, and yet it was being blocked by one of the child's small hands.

"Too bad. Looks like you're not strong enough to fight us yet. You don't even see what just happened, do you?"

"What are you talking about?!" Frederica yelled, falling back as she tried and failed to pull her staff away. With a great wrench, she fell hard onto her backside. But while she had never let go of the staff, neither had the boy. Her right arm had been split in half at the elbow.

"Girls like sweet things, right? So I decided to try making you into a dessert. What do you think?"

"N-No! What's happening?!" Frederica's right arm had turned brown, taking on a solid, rough texture that resembled some sort of baked good. Taking a bite from the hand that was still holding the staff, the boy made a showing of spilling crumbs all over.

Watching the child eat her own hand, Frederica lost the will to fight, prompting Rick to attack in her stead. The boy made an exaggerated leap backwards, dodging out of the way.

"Yeah, you can still fight. That sword and armor are pretty impressive. I don't know where you got them, but it looks like they could work against us."

"Lynel! Please take care of Frederica!" Rick shouted, snapping the stunned Lynel back to his senses.

"Uh, right! Got it!"

"Swordmaster!" A magic doll appeared, giving its report far too late. "Another unique-type monster has appeared!"

"What a rude thing to call someone," the boy complained. "We have names too, you know. I'm Lute, and that fellow with the wings is Orgain. Well, we won't know each other for much longer, but it's nice to meet you," he offered politely.

"This is bad. This is the first time that two have broken out at once," the Swordmaster said, distress clear on his face. There were times in the past where such spawn, unique enough to have their own names, had made it past the barrier. But there had never been more than one at a time.

"Lynel! What do I do? What do I do?! I can't heal it! I'm still just a dessert!" Frederica was going crazy. She had never been so much as hurt since being born into this world. And now, the first time she had ever lost at something, the result was her right arm being turned into some sort of confection. Her panic was understandable. And despite the fact that she was plenty skilled at healing magic, no matter how hard she tried, her arm wouldn't return to normal.

Meanwhile, Orgain was taking his time wounding the people around him one by one. It was as if he wasn't planning to kill them until they had been sufficiently terrified. Lute was laughing, dodging around Rick's attacks as he mocked him. And their last ray of hope, the Swordmaster, was still standing there doing absolutely nothing. Crouched in a combat stance, his hands were on the hilt of his sword, so it looked like he was planning something, but as of yet, he wasn't helping at all.

Lynel could do nothing but watch. He was entirely powerless. From the beginning, he had never had any real talent. The only reason he had made it this far was because of Frederica and the others. With barely any star crystals left, it was doubtful that he could summon anything useful for such a fight either. And even if he died and came back, there was hardly any point in trying again considering the enemies before him. There was nothing he could do but give up.

As he gave a weak, defeated laugh, he noticed something blinking at the edge of his vision. Another message from the goddess. Willing to take anything he could get, he opened the message.

【Announcement】 Ultra Rare Guarantee Once More!

It was the ultimate Hail Mary, but Lynel had no choice. He decided to put all his hopes on one last roll.

◇◇◇

While all of this was going on above, Yogiri, Tomochika, and Theodisia were descending the stairs to the depths of the tower's basement. They had found a staircase in the first room they'd checked out, so there hadn't been any need for them to keep searching, but a new problem had arisen — the staircase was showing no sign of coming to an end, seemingly continuing downwards forever.

It was especially strange since the tower was on the edge of a cliff. From the direction the stairs descended, they should have long since exited through the side of that cliff. Since they couldn't just sit around feeling stunned by the strangeness of the situation, they went onwards for a while longer, but no matter how far down they walked, there was no sign of the descent coming to an end.

When they turned around to climb back up, they reached the top of the staircase almost immediately.

"Um, I guess there's some sort of spell in place here, too," Yogiri said as they began down the staircase again.

If there is a barrier that influences time, perhaps one that influences space is not so far-fetched, Mokomoko mused. *Maybe they have extended the distance from here to the basement infinitely.*

"If the control room for the barrier is down this way, it makes sense that it would be protected," Theodisia added. Apparently, being a half-demon allowed her to see Mokomoko just as Yogiri and Tomochika could. And she was right; a trial was being held within the tower, after all. It wouldn't do to have random passersby wandering into a restricted area like that.

"Can you feel your friends down there?" Yogiri asked.

"There's no mistake. Their presence has grown much stronger. This is certainly the right direction."

So the barrier isn't obstructing her senses, then. An odd development.

"I'm not sure, but it is quite possible that this barrier was set up by my own people."

I see. I knew that the tower was absorbing souls to power the barrier, but it also has a population of half-demons to power the tower itself, as well as the independent barriers set up throughout the area.

"That's cool and all," Tomochika interjected in a bored voice, "but what are we supposed to do about it?" It seemed the conversation was going a bit over her head.

"Getting down there is our objective right now, so we need to find a way. I'm just not sure how we can get around this."

"Oh, well why don't you just kill it? You know, kill the barrier or whatever," she suggested.

Yogiri stopped for a moment, considering whether or not such a thing was actually feasible. "Hm, that's kind of challenging. What would I actually be killing?"

"Uhh...I don't know, the infinite space?"

"I have no idea what that means."

"Oh, right, but killing ice and doors makes perfect sense!"

"Well, for example, if the barrier was trying to keep me trapped, that would be enough of a threat for me to perceive it. But all it's doing is stopping us from going forward, and it's not like we'll die if we don't get down there."

To kill something, Yogiri had to be able to sense it. But space itself was a bit too abstract to target. Even if he couldn't perceive something, he could respond to anything that offered any sort of threat against his life, but that simply didn't apply here.

"I'm not sure what killing space itself would do, so unless we're desperate, I feel like it's probably not a good idea." In the worst-case scenario, it could destroy the entire world, so that was something he preferred to avoid.

Chapter 18 — I Don't Know What Will Happen if I Kill Space Itself

"What about the way that you saved Mokomoko? You stopped the tower from absorbing the spirits, right? Can't you break it like that?"

"But in this case, the source of the barrier might be Theodisia's friends, remember? If that's the case, and I destroy the source of the barrier, the people we're trying to save would be dead, so it would all be for nothing."

It may be possible for me to pass through alone since I don't have a physical body, Mokomoko suggested. Since the ghost had been following the other three, she had also been wrapped up in the space-distorting effects of the magic. *It appears that her companions can be sensed through this illusion, or whatever it may be. As such, I will venture forward on my own. If I can find the source of the barrier, I will create a path back to Theodisia, which the boy can follow to disable it.*

"All right," Tomochika shrugged, "I have no idea what you're talking about anymore, but go for it."

Very well. Hmm, what's this? Mokomoko tilted her head to the side.

"What's wrong?"

I feel vibrations.

"I don't feel anything."

It's more like a shaking that can only be felt in the mind.

"I'm not sure what that means..."

An ear-splitting roar filled the air, cutting Tomochika off. At the same time, space itself seemed to shift around them. It was like a line ran vertically down through the region around the staircase, causing it to shift slightly. It lasted for only a moment, but when things returned to normal, the stairs before them had changed. Rather than leading straight down as they had before, they now followed a gentle curve, twisting out of sight. The true form of the passageway had been revealed, showing a large spiral staircase heading down below the tower.

The barrier is gone? Just like that? What happened?

"We really don't have the time to worry about it, so let's just go." As Yogiri made to continue on down, a gust of wind blew past them. Tomochika suddenly grabbed on to his arm, trembling. "Hey, what's wrong?"

"I saw something…something black just went past us, all covered in blades…"

Whatever Tomochika had seen, it hadn't cared one way or the other about them. Yogiri turned around, but there were no traces of anything having actually passed through. Whatever it was, it had gone straight to the surface.

Chapter 19 — Your Luck Really Is the Worst of the Worst

Using the star crystals, Lynel could summon a new companion. It was something he had tried many times before, but he normally got small animals like squirrels and mice. The best results he had seen were dogs or wolves. On rare occasions, a person would be summoned, but they would be a normal villager with no combat abilities at all. For Lynel, relying on such a summoning was a final, desperate gamble.

Even if it had an Ultra Rare guarantee, that didn't change anything. After all, the last Ultra Rare guarantee had got him a beautiful but powerless clone of the goddess. The chances of the same thing happening again were fairly high. So the number of star crystals required carried only the barest trace of hope for him. Five stones had been needed last time, but this time it was ten. The larger quantity should have meant a stronger effect, otherwise there would have been no point in the difference. This time, maybe his Ultra Rare guarantee would get him a warrior with real skill, someone who could smash through this otherwise hopeless situation. If that were even possible, it was worth spending the last of his star crystals.

But he also had another thought. If he wanted to survive, even for a little longer, he should hold on to them. Using them to revive himself was the most effective option. With only one stone, he could recover from any injury and overcome his terrible luck. And for someone with luck like Lynel's, that was invaluable.

Lynel looked down at Frederica who was curled up on the ground. Her transformation had occurred from the shoulder down, likely so that her arm would come off more easily. Luckily, that meant that her life wasn't in danger, but even so, she could hardly accomplish much in that state.

If they waited there helplessly, they would eventually die.

This isn't the time to hesitate! Lynel chided himself.

Drawing the last of the star crystals from his pocket, he held them in both hands as he prayed. Trying to imagine the most powerful being that he could, he rolled the *gacha*.

The stones immediately vanished, a brilliant light appearing in the space before him. Glittering stars filled the air, dancing around him. He immediately felt that something had gone wrong — this was the exact same thing that had happened last time. He tried to convince himself that it was simply the standard process for an Ultra Rare summon. The light gathered in one spot, taking on the form of a person.

Lynel was dumbfounded. It was a woman. She wore gorgeous clothing and flashy jewelry, yet none of it drew the focus away from her curvaceous figure. In her right hand was an enormous ornate sword, and in her left was a wheel of some sort, clearly imbued with divine power but its exact function was unclear.

In addition to the weapons in her hands, axes, spears, swords, and shields floated in the air around her as if to protect her. Flowers and stars began to grow and glitter in the surrounding space, and a gentle breeze enveloped the area. The sound of praises being sung filled the air, voices overflowing with joy but coming from no visible source.

It was truly a figure that looked like it deserved the title of Ultra Rare, but Lynel couldn't hide his disappointment. Because this woman was, unmistakably, the same goddess who had brought him to this world. In other words, he had gotten the exact same result as last time.

"Hey! What's that look for? You seem like you're disappointed to see me!" the goddess complained, noting the despair clearly written on Lynel's face.

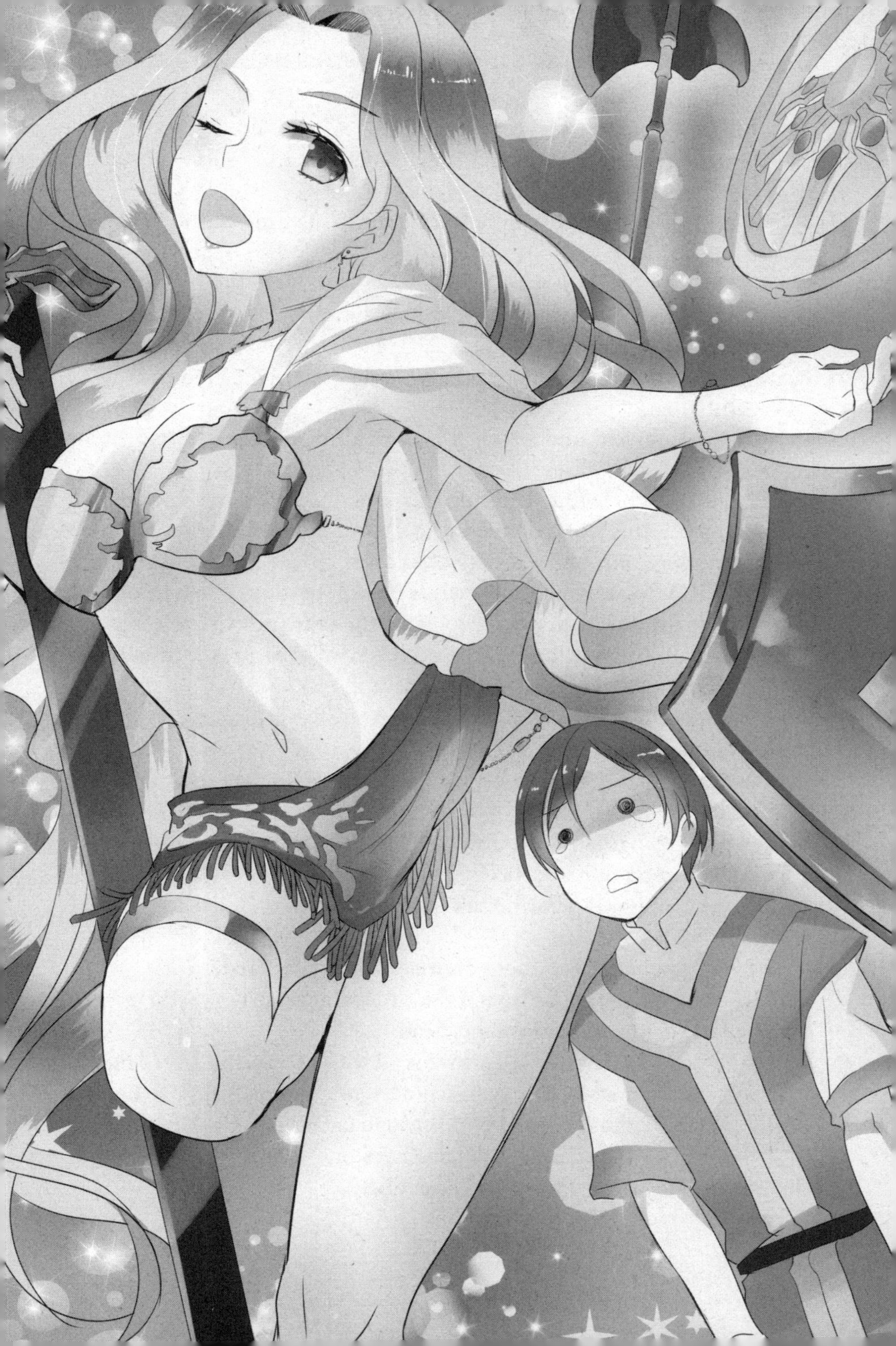

"I mean, you're just going to say something like 'Sorry, I used all my power on the graphics again,' right?!"

"Ah, don't worry, this time is different. This time I came with my actual body."

"Wait, uhh, that means…"

"This time I can use all of my divine authority! Spawn of the Dark God? Please. Something like that is so far below me as to be wholly irrelevant. Even calling them small fry gives them too much credit!"

"Oh! Then…"

"Yes. Go ahead and watch. I'll have all of this cleaned up in an instant!"

Lynel felt relief wash over him. It seemed like everything would be okay. After all, this was a goddess. No matter how strong the monsters were, they were only the servants of a fallen "god." There was nothing they could do but prostrate themselves before the glory of a true deity.

The goddess walked calmly towards the spawn. As if just realizing that someone different had appeared, the two creatures immediately stopped fighting and turned towards her.

"Lynel, this is…" Sensing the lull in the chaos, Rick made his way to his companion's side.

"I did it! It's the goddess! I managed to summon the goddess! Everything is okay now!"

"I don't recognize her, but she certainly has an overwhelming presence. With her on our side, maybe…"

Lynel could see Rick's shoulders relax. He too could tell how powerful the goddess was.

Lynel grinned. "She might even be able to heal Frederica!"

The goddess stood before Orgain, the winged spawn, who in turn dropped to his knees, lowering his head.

"Oh! Look at that! She'll finish this all without even having to fight!"

Lynel was moved. Things had never gone so smoothly for him in his life. To think that he could pull through at this point, when the continued existence of humanity itself had been on the line, made him think that maybe his luck wasn't so bad after all.

But his luck really was the worst.

Chapter 19 — Your Luck Really Is the Worst of the Worst

"Lady Vahanato, what brings you to a place like this?"

Something wasn't right. The way the Dark God's spawn were acting was totally wrong for a confrontation with a goddess of justice. At first, it looked like Orgain had recognized how outclassed he was and was begging for mercy. But now it looked more like the thing was happily greeting someone close to his own master.

"Oh! Miss Vahanato is here! What's up? The barrier should be coming down quite soon." Acting like an excited puppy, Lute leaped towards the goddess, whose name Lynel hadn't even known until then.

"Ummm...what's going on here?" he asked hesitantly.

"Let's just say, the moment you laid eyes on me, your luck was the absolute worst of the worst."

"Then, when you said you'd clean everything up, you meant..."

"Wiping out humanity could be called cleaning up, right?"

At Vahanato's indifferent response, Lynel could feel himself striking the rocky bottom of the pit of despair. It would have been far better if he had simply failed to do anything at all.

Instead, he had brought forth an even greater disaster. Go figure.

◇◇◇

Reaching the bottom of the stairs, Tomochika's group entered a room in the basement. It was in terrible condition. Though it was made of stone, the walls, floor, and ceiling were covered with scars. It looked to Tomochika like it had been done intentionally, the deep gouges giving the appearance of someone having tried to cut their way through. It almost looked like someone had stormed into an empty room, carved up the walls for no apparent reason, and then left. The only thing that stood out was an opening along one wall.

"Looks like it keeps going," Yogiri observed. The opening was like a window, offering a view of the canyon and the barrier that imprisoned the Dark God, but there was no point in heading that way. Their best bet was the door on the far side of the room. It was closed, but Yogiri opened it easily. There had likely been some sort of powerful seal on it, but in the end it was just another door, and disabling it was child's play to him.

Yogiri led the group inside. It was dark; the room had no windows.

"Leave it to me. I can at least use enough magic to make some light." After she muttered some sort of incantation, a ball of light appeared over Theodisia's palm.

"You say you're no good at magic, but that seems pretty impressive to me," said Tomochika.

The ball of light, about the size of a fist, rose up and stopped at the ceiling. As Theodisia stepped into the room, the orb moved to follow her, staying directly over her head. Inside the chamber were a number of large glass cylinders, all destroyed in the same manner as the walls of the previous room. It was as if everything inside the room had been sliced apart.

Yogiri stopped Tomochika as she tried to step inside. "Wait there for a second, Dannoura."

"What's wrong?"

"You don't want to see this."

If it had just been a bunch of mutilated bodies, he wouldn't have stopped her.

I recommend you do as he says, Mokomoko added.

With both of them advising her to stay outside, Tomochika decided to comply.

"Can you tell if your friends are here?"

"Probably, here…" Theodisia pointed at one of the glass tubes. The glass had been shattered, but the broken fragments had kept in at least some of the fluid. People were floating within, their dark skin and silver hair betraying them as half-demons. But they were badly mutated, hardly shaped like people anymore. All of the cylinders in the room held the same macabre contents.

Theodisia carefully inspected all of the tubes, then turned to the others. "I know it's terrible for me to feel relief despite seeing my people like this, but…"

"Your sister isn't here, then?"

As deformed as they were, the bodies were still identifiable, so she would have known if one was her sibling.

"No. But what can I do? Could your power put them out of their misery?"

Some of her people looked like they were dead, killed by a monster of some kind, but plenty of them were still actively writhing in pain.

"I don't think that's a good idea. Not if you believe in any sort of afterlife for them."

"I suppose you're right. Leaving them to an outsider would be unacceptable." Theodisia drew her sword, prompting Yogiri to step out of the room. A little while later, she rejoined them in the corridor.

"So, what do we do now?" Tomochika asked meekly, her demeanor indicating that she had guessed what had happened inside.

"First, let's get back to the surface and see what's going on," Yogiri suggested.

"That's right! That thing looked like a final boss! Maybe the Swordmaster has already beaten it, though."

"What should we do about that Swordmaster, anyway?" Yogiri asked, somewhat upset by the scene he had witnessed. He had no idea what circumstances had led to the Swordmaster's heinous actions. Perhaps it truly was a necessary sacrifice to keep the world safe. But no matter the reason, stepping on the dignity of others that way was something he couldn't accept.

"I was taught to always ensure that a grudge never survives to linger. But this is not a vendetta that I can entrust to others, and I couldn't hope to defeat a Swordmaster on my own, so in this case I will set aside my desire for vengeance."

"All right," Yogiri nodded. In his current state of mind, if she had asked him to help her, he probably would have agreed. But if he killed someone just because he didn't agree with their actions, it would be overstepping his bounds. And once he crossed that line once, there would be no going back.

Well, it won't be an issue if the Swordmaster tries to kill me next, Yogiri thought to himself.

◇◇◇

With the arrival of the goddess, the battle had fallen into a lull. Of course, there were still those who were foolhardy enough to attack without knowing who their enemy was, but in front of the goddess's majesty, even they had been stilled.

"Kneel."

With that one word, invested with the authority of a powerful deity, everyone in the area dropped to their knees. The only ones who were able to resist were Rick, Lynel, and the Swordmaster. In short, they were the only ones left who could still fight, meaning that any chance at a coordinated defense had effectively been removed. Luckily, the goddess's exchange with the spawn had continued for a while, and she had yet to turn her attention back to them.

As Lynel stood dumbstruck at the disaster he had brought forth, the Swordmaster approached.

"U-Umm…"

"I'm not going to blame you. And I don't expect you to do anything about it, either."

Lynel struggled to come up with an excuse in response, but the Swordmaster had already moved on, turning to their other companion.

"This is the worst possible situation imaginable, but there is still something that we can do. First, let me give you the qualifications to be a Swordmaster."

"M-Me?!" Rick gasped, shocked by the suggestion.

"After me, you are the only one left here who has a chance. And so that we're clear, there can only be one Swordmaster at a time. In short, if I die, you'll immediately become the next Swordmaster. It's not just a title, but you'll figure that out when the time comes. And I don't plan on dying so easily myself."

"So what should we do?"

"There's a possibility that we can take them while they're sitting around chatting. At the moment, I'm absorbing all of the power that the tower holds. If I can take in enough of that power, I'll be able to face down even a goddess. This was one of many measures that we took when planning for a fight against the Dark God, after all."

Chapter 19 — Your Luck Really Is the Worst of the Worst

Rick steeled himself. "In other words, you want us to buy you time. All right, it seems we have no other choice."

At that point, Lynel realized they were expecting him to contribute nothing at all. It was true that there was little he could do. But he was the one who had made the situation downright catastrophic. He couldn't just sit around and wait for others to act. If he killed himself...

Lynel's Random Walk ability would allow him to redo everything. But his savepoint was at the top of the tower. The spawn of the Dark God would still come, and even without summoning the goddess, he would still die. So Lynel thought of what he could do here and now.

"U-Umm! Goddess! Could I talk to you for a moment?"

The goddess was the one who had brought him to this world in the first place. He wasn't some random stranger to her. If they needed to buy time, he might be able to get her talking.

"How can I help you?" Vahanato replied, clearly in a pleasant mood.

"I, uhh, really don't know what's going on here. Could you explain it to me, please? I summoned you, right? So why are you getting along so well with the people who are trying to kill me?"

"Ah, I suppose it makes sense that you would be curious! But I don't know, should I tell you?"

"Please do! I need to understand!"

"Of course you do. It must be terribly confusing for you. Well, we've been together for quite a while, so you dying without knowing what's going on would be kind of sad, wouldn't it? All right, I'll explain."

With surprising ease, the goddess had agreed.

Chapter 20 — Aren't You, Like, a Perfect Example of an Enemy of the World?

"Now then, where should I start? Well, my ultimate objective was to bring Lord Albagarma home after he went missing."

The moment he heard that name, a shiver ran down Lynel's back. It must have been the name of the Dark God, a name so taboo it had passed out of human memory.

"My darling just up and disappeared one day! That was a habit of his, though, so I figured it was nothing special. But no matter how long I waited, this time, he never came back."

"Um, does that mean you two are married?" He really didn't care one way or another, but asked as if it were of deep interest to him. If he was going to buy some time, he needed to extend the conversation for as long as possible. Luckily, the Dark God's spawn were quietly waiting while they talked.

"Ah, sorry, did I make us sound too close?"

"No. While your positions may be different, there is still a relationship between you two. Please don't concern yourself with the semantics," Orgain answered reverently, still kneeling.

"Hmm, maybe something like 'concubine' would be more accurate? Well, unlike humans, it's not something that is legally monitored, so as long as both parties have consented, it's fine. Maybe it was a bit more than that, though. My darling was always so quick to grow embarrassed."

"I see," Lynel said, desperate to fill the space with empty words.

"I thought something must have gone wrong, so I went looking for him. I heard that he had traveled to another world, so I sent messengers to many worlds and eventually discovered that he was likely here. I started focusing my efforts on this world, but I couldn't directly intervene, so it was rather difficult. The best I could do was gather small pieces of information from the humans that I reincarnated here. Putting it all together was quite challenging." Vahanato spoke as if she had been wanting to complain about the pain of that struggle to someone for a long time.

"Uhh, aren't you intervening directly right now though?"

"No, this is a fairly roundabout method. I had to add the star crystal expansion to the world's system myself. Then I had to set you up as a person from this world so that you could avoid conflicting with the local system. That allowed me to operate as a manager of the bonus content that's available to you, so I could send you all of those messages. And now, using the front of being someone that you've summoned, I can finally take direct action. Now that I know for sure that my darling is here, I can ensure that the seal is lifted. I can't get involved this way over and over, so I had to wait for the perfect moment!

"Anyway! After analyzing my stores of information, I found that he was locked away somewhere in this very world, and that he was being held here by the Swordmaster, so I decided to get rid of the old coot. But then I hit another snag. No matter who I sent, no one could beat him!"

Vahanato paused to glare at the Swordmaster. Lynel didn't know how long she had been sending messengers to this world, but she had likely been working at it for millennia. It wasn't hard to believe that she was starting to lose her patience.

"Since this silly human had taken humanity's entire fate on his shoulders, his Fate level was absurdly high! No matter how much stronger the people I sent against him were, they simply never won."

"Umm, can I ask a question?"

"What is it?"

"Did those people you sent not use Random Walk? I would expect them to eventually win if they could just keep trying over and over."

"Ah, that wouldn't work. Powerful warriors with especially high Fate

Chapter 20 — Aren't You, Like, a Perfect Example of an Enemy of the World?

levels can't keep coming back to life to try again. That would be pretty lame, don't you think? So that's an ability that only garbage-tier mooks can use."

"Garbage-tier..." Lynel felt his heart drop.

"Oh, but it's not like I'm making fun of you. In the end, it was thanks to you and your awful luck that things worked out so well. No one I sent could stand against the Swordmaster. Trying to fight him made them an enemy of humanity, and Swordmasters totally outclass such enemies. So I changed my whole strategy. What if I sent someone to be an ally of humanity instead? Someone who was so unlucky that they'd die immediately if left alone?"

"Wait, you mean..."

"That's right! If someone with luck as awful as yours was on humanity's side, then humanity would be wiped out! In short, such ill fortune would give rise to a rebirth of the Dark God."

"But wait, I die so often! There's no way I'd survive long enough for a plan like that —"

Lynel stopped short as the realization hit him. That was why he had been given Random Walk and all of those star crystals.

"Well, obviously I needed some way to keep you alive even with your terrible luck. I knew that Fate would definitely try to have you killed. If it failed to accomplish that over and over, it would start to try harder and harder to make it happen. In the end, the cycle would build up to a calamity on a level that would threaten the world itself. And so here we are!

"I'm not sure of the exact chain of events that led to the barrier being so close to failing, but your luck is so awful that terrible things have just been piling up on top of each other until the situation ended up like this!"

"You've got to be joking..." Lynel had fallen to his knees. He had always known that his luck was abysmal, but he had never thought it *so* bad that it would bring about the destruction of humankind. "S-So, if I kill myself here..."

"Feel free, but at this point, you'll just die. This is the specific future that I've been looking for. Now that we're here, I made sure to take away your power, just in case. But if you're going to die regardless, why not wait until you see my darling first?"

"I don't understand! From my perspective, I go back when I die and try again, but to everyone else, I just die, don't I? Why bother taking away my power if it can't actually change anything?"

"Well, this is just something that gods do. We can keep rolling the dice until we get the results we're looking for, and once we have those results, we can make that particular future inevitable. To be fair, I have a feeling that trying to explain this sensation to a human is a wasted effort."

Lynel had intended to keep her talking for as long as possible, but at this point, he had lost the will to continue. Although in reality he could hardly be held responsible, he certainly felt like it was all his fault — that his very existence would bring about the end of the world. And even if he died now, nothing would change that.

As Lynel dropped his head, he heard the sound of something landing nearby. Slowly, he lifted his head back up and was greeted by a scene that seemed to be taken straight out of hell. An army of terrifying monsters was now filling the area around them. They had suddenly begun to arrive at the remains of the tower in droves.

"The outer parts of the barrier have collapsed. I thought we were almost done here, but I suppose I should have known it wouldn't be *that* easy," Lute remarked.

"After coming all this way, I can hardly sit around and do nothing, can I? I'll go take a look," Vahanato offered, pressing a hand to her forehead in thought. It was an all too human quirk.

After staying like that for some time, she suddenly burst out laughing. It looked like she was trying to hold it in, but she couldn't help laughing so hard that tears flowed from her eyes as she looked over at Lynel.

"Wow, your luck is so hilariously bad, I can't help but laugh! The man who first created the barrier was here. He could have repaired all of this in an instant."

Lynel was confused. He had no idea what was so funny about that.

"Fate must have brought him here, knowing that something like this would happen. But he's dead! I don't even know what happened to him! There was also a godslayer here. An awfully vile person, in my opinion. If I wasn't careful, he could definitely have killed me, but he's dead

Chapter 20 — Aren't You, Like, a Perfect Example of an Enemy of the World?

too! You really are amazing. I never dreamed that things would go this well. Aren't you, like, a perfect example of an enemy of the world at this point?"

Lynel could only stare at her, utterly speechless.

"So, what about the barrier?" Lute asked, clearly growing tired of waiting.

"Right, right. It's in a terrible state, and the core is plainly visible."

The goddess tossed aside the sword in her hand, and it floated back to join the collection of weapons hovering behind her. She then extended her right hand forward, and it disappeared as the air around it rippled like water. She fiddled around inside the distortion as if searching for something for a few moments, then pulled her hand back out. She was now holding a pulsing purple-red mass. A number of tubes were sprouting from it, each oozing a filthy black liquid. Based on the conversation, Lynel assumed that it was the core of the barrier.

"Why did you bring it *here*? Just destroy it."

"But then the barrier would simply disappear. Don't you feel bad for the people who've been protecting it for so long? I want them to be around to see the moment my darling returns to power."

Lynel looked towards Rick and the Swordmaster at his side. Despair was clear on both of their faces. The Swordmaster had said that if he was able to absorb the power from the tower, he could do something to stop their enemies. But would he be able to say the same thing now that the Dark God's entire army was standing before him? And no matter how much power he had built up, the core of the barrier was already in their opponent's hands. In short, the moment the goddess had appeared, they had already lost the fight.

"By the way, what do we do about the Divine King? She managed to fight our lord in some capacity. Don't you think she'll be pretty strong?" Lute asked.

"She used a tremendous number of sacrifices to match him for only a single instant. Once the barrier is gone, she'll have nothing left," Orgain answered, unconcerned.

"But that woman was facing down my darling for over a thousand years. Doesn't it look like they're hugging? That annoys me a bit, so I'll have to make her pay. Make sure to capture her alive. Ah, you lot are in the way, so please move. These humans won't be able to see the grand finale with you blocking their view."

At Vahanato's command, the gathered spawn immediately dispersed. The goddess then waved the wheel she was gripping in her left hand. With that one motion, the remainder of the first floor of the tower was obliterated, revealing the canyon beyond and the barrier surrounding it. The goddess and the two humanoid spawn walked to the edge of what had once been the tower, where they could better see the Dark God's prison.

"Look, look!" Vahanato urged Lynel and his companions. "You can't see anything from there, can you? Come a little closer."

It was an inappropriate invitation, yet hardly one they could refuse, so Lynel, Rick, and the Swordmaster did as they were told. They all looked equally demoralized in the face of such a hopeless situation.

Peering over the edge of the tower, they could clearly see the canyon. At the center of the large spherical space that had been carved into it, two figures were floating in the air.

The Dark God, dressed in black.

The Divine King, dressed in white.

Facing each other as if in the middle of an embrace, they were perfectly still.

◇◇◇

When Tomochika and the others finally made it back up the stairs, there was no longer a room there. A wide open space greeted them instead.

"I'm thinking that things got a lot worse while we were gone," Tomochika murmured.

It was like a scene out of hell itself. Monsters that could be described as nothing less than demons were crowded around them. To make things even stranger, the creatures were all shaking with laughter, their voices painful on the ears. The evil aura that they gave off was strong enough to be palpable, making the area look strangely darker to Tomochika's eyes.

Chapter 20 — Aren't You, Like, a Perfect Example of an Enemy of the World?

Looking around, she soon found the central figure of the chaos. A beautiful woman who stood out from the crowd was standing at the edge of the cliff. Though she looked like neither a monster nor one of the Dark God's spawn, it was easy enough to guess that she was the driving force behind the current situation.

The humanoid monsters around the woman were kneeling reverently before her. One of them was the winged spawn that Tomochika had pegged as the final boss. They must have been the highest ranking members of the demonic horde.

Facing the army of monsters were the Swordmaster, Rick, and Lynel. They were the last three standing. All of the other Knights had been killed, heavily wounded, or were kneeling there motionless. No matter how she looked at it, she couldn't help but feel like they had lost.

However, the situation seemed to have come to a pause for the moment. Everyone was staring intently at the center of the barrier, waiting for the beast within to make his move.

"Well, this has totally spiraled out of control," Tomochika muttered idly. She had no idea what the best way of handling the situation might be.

"It certainly does look like the beginning of the apocalypse," Theodisia remarked frankly. "I can't imagine being able to defeat even a single one of these creatures, let alone all of them."

"Speaking of which, what happened to that other monster you saw, Dannoura?" Yogiri asked.

"Oh, right. That was a while ago, so it should have made it up here by now..." She scanned the crowd but couldn't see it anywhere.

"Now! An age has passed and the seal shall be undone! This is the time of my darling's revival!" the woman declared, her voice somewhat lacking in regalness but otherwise clearly filling the area. Lifting some sort of gross-looking mass high above her head, she crushed it between her fingers in a dramatic display.

A sound like a heartbeat pulsed out from it.

The space around the Dark God throbbed and distorted. The air wavered and appeared to crack. Thin, delicate fissures spidered across the spherical gouge in the canyon, like it was encased in a globe of glass. The cracks spread with terrifying speed, and before long, the space burst outwards with a brilliant flash.

The barrier had been destroyed. Time, frozen so long within it, had started to move again.

"Hahahaha! Ah, my darling! I've missed you so much! Please wait, I'll be down there in a moment!" the woman shouted with a trance-like ecstasy.

At the same time, the lady dressed in white, who had been at the center of the barrier for ages untold, flew towards them, landing beside the Swordmaster. Based on Rick's story, she must have been the Divine King.

The Dark God, however, teetered for a moment and then pitched forward.

"What…?"

Tomochika couldn't tell whose voice was yelling, but almost anyone present could have been shouting the same thing. The Dark God was falling, brought straight down to the ground by nothing more than gravity. As it fell out of sight, Tomochika heard the splash of something hitting water, and assumed the body had fallen into the river that ran through the canyon.

Everyone had gone dead silent.

"Sorry, I guess," Yogiri apologized.

Chapter 21 — Was There Actually a Reason for Us to Get This Close to You?!

While most of the people present were frozen, awestruck, there were a few who were spurred to immediate action.

The first was Theodisia — as she couldn't care less about the barrier or the Dark God, the incident left her unfazed. Seeing a chance that she knew wouldn't come again, she didn't hesitate. The moment she stepped onto the scene, she drew her sword and swung it with a horizontal slash. The shockwave that it unleashed promptly separated the Swordmaster from his head.

The next to move was the monster of blades that Tomochika had seen on their way to the lower levels.

◇◇◇

The goddess Vahanato stared speechlessly at the scene before her. Watching from the air as the Dark God Albagarma fell like a stone, she had a clear view of him hitting the water below. Her mind had gone completely blank. She couldn't believe what she was seeing…couldn't accept the truth of the situation.

She was finally brought back to her senses by the shock of a long black blade punching through her chest.

"What…?" She turned her head to see the source of the attack.

Behind her stood a creature covered entirely in blades. One of those blades, sprouting from the creature's elbow, was currently embedded in her back. The sight simply confused her further. What in the world was happening? Her body as a goddess should have been entirely impervious to harm. It was unbelievable that another life form could even scratch her.

The creature's glowing red eyes stared straight into hers. As she tried to decipher some sort of intent from its hellish gaze, her thinking was sent into further disarray when the monster punched its fingers into her head.

A god couldn't die from something as minor as having its brain destroyed. But now that Vahanato had taken on a physical form, the majority of her thought processes relied on that brain — and with it destroyed, there was no way she could think coherently enough to formulate a plan to counter-attack.

She could tell that the monster was searching for something inside her head, felt its fingers wriggling around in her skull. Soon after, its thoughts seemed to flow into her.

This creature was responsible for destroying most of the barrier. It had been trapped by the barrier's defensive systems, but had managed to escape by simply destroying everything in sight. Having wasted most of its energy on that escape, it had waited, hiding until Vahanato had shown an opening.

Not you, a thought flowed into her mind, clearly disappointed.

She knew that something had been targeting Lynel. She hadn't figured out what it was or why, but now it was painfully clear. This monster was searching for gods. Following the faint traces of her presence on Lynel, it had actually been tracking *her* the whole time.

The creature smoothly withdrew its blades from Vahanato's body. Having lost interest in her, it didn't even feel the need to finish her off. Letting the goddess fall to the ground, the monster leaped away.

◇◇◇

Once the Swordmaster's head fell to the ground, and some bizarre monster stabbed the gaudily clad woman before abruptly disappearing, the frozen atmosphere lifted and everyone finally began to move.

Chapter 21 — Was There Actually a Reason for Us to Get This Close to You?!

"My lord!" the winged creature cried, leaping off the cliff, followed closely by a number of its fellow spawn.

"Uhh, what exactly is happening?" Tomochika asked, having difficulty keeping up with the rapidly unfolding events occurring in front of her. She turned to look at the woman who had killed the Swordmaster.

"I figured now was a good time to catch him off guard," Theodisia said indifferently.

"Jeez, was that really your first thought in a situation like this? That's kind of scary." Her way of thinking was somewhat reminiscent of Yogiri's. But as she had said, the Swordmaster had been totally defenseless just then. Theodisia's ability to grasp that and jump at the opportunity showed an impressive amount of nerve. "So, what happened over there?"

"That's the thing you saw on the way to the basement, huh?" Yogiri commented. "No wonder you were freaked out. It looked like it was made entirely of blades."

The monster had used those blades, which sprouted from every part of its body, to stab through the woman with ease. After piercing her back and head, it had seemed to lose interest, leaving her where she was and disappearing.

"I wonder if we could just walk on out of here," said Yogiri, unfazed as always. "If we're stealthy about it, I doubt anyone would notice."

The whole place was still in chaos, so there was certainly a chance they could slip past the crowd. As they considered their options, the winged spawn returned, both he and the Dark God he was now carrying soaked through with river water. The creature lay his master on the ground, but the Dark God remained perfectly still.

"My lord! Please awaken! What is wrong?!" Orgain's voice was ragged. No matter how it shouted or shook the body, the fallen beast failed to answer. "Haha...hahahahaha...I see...sacrifices...our lord is a god who demands sacrifice..." the monster began to mumble with a faraway look.

"I'm getting a bad feeling about this..." Tomochika muttered. According to what Rick had told them, the Dark God was a being who granted wishes in exchange for sacrifices.

"No doubt your power has waned after being sealed away for so many long years," Orgain continued. "The answer is clear — I shall offer up all of humanity as a sacrifice to you!" As the winged spawn stood, the others gathered around it began to whip themselves into a frenzy.

Moments before, they had been stunned and at a loss. Now, a clear objective had been placed before them, cutting through their confusion. With humans standing right there, ready to be sacrificed, it wasn't any surprise that they would immediately turn to venting their fury through violence.

With a horrible cry, the massed monsters turned gazes brimming with wicked intent towards the frail humans around them. The looks in their eyes made it clear that they didn't intend to kill them quickly. They would draw as much agony, hatred, and terror from them as possible first, all as part of a sacrifice to their god. That overriding impulse dominated their thoughts entirely.

"There are an awful lot of them," Yogiri observed. "This seems kind of dangerous. Could you two try to stay a little closer to me?"

"Like this?" Tomochika asked, stepping up and grabbing his arm. Theodisia followed suit, clinging to his other arm.

The spawn burst into action. As one, they rushed forward to overwhelm the gathered humans as if trying to create hell on earth.

"Die."

Yogiri unleashed his power and the entire horde dropped, leaving them once again surrounded by a mountain of corpses. The only figures still standing were those who at least looked human.

"Hey, was there *actually* a reason for us to get this close to you?!"

"Well, it would be dangerous to risk getting separated in a situation like this, right? It's easy for me to respond to danger pointed at me, so it's more convenient if we're all in the same place."

Tomochika had her doubts. She couldn't help but remember Yogiri's story about "enjoying the situation while he had the chance."

But her classmate just shrugged. "Anyway, let's get out of the tower. It seems like sticking around is going to cause us more problems."

"Not that this counts as much of a tower anymore..."

There were still plenty of problems piled up in front of them, but

Chapter 21 — Was There Actually a Reason for Us to Get This Close to You?!

with the Dark God and his spawn dead, the other issues were probably minor at best, or so Tomochika tried to convince herself.

"Sir Takatou, do you think it's okay to leave her as she is?" Theodisia asked, pointing at the woman in gaudy clothing.

"She doesn't have any intention of killing anyone, and she seems human enough to me, so I don't see a reason to kill her."

"If you say so," their companion conceded.

Of course, no matter what Yogiri thought her to be, it didn't matter to the woman herself. Though her chest had been impaled and her head smashed, she was now standing again, her injuries healed. She stood with hollow eyes, not looking at anything in particular, having clearly lost her mind.

With a shrill, mad laugh, she waved her hands around. As she did, the weapons floating behind her began to glow, firing beams of light in all directions. Those beams sliced through the nearby mountains, tore apart the tower rubble, and flash-boiled the river at the bottom of the canyon. Everything in their path was completely annihilated.

Tomochika was taken aback. "That's just ridiculous...what is she even doing?!"

The surviving Knights hurriedly tried to get out of the way. The woman wasn't aiming at anything in particular, but anyone who was so much as grazed by those streaks of light was instantly erased from the scene.

"Miss Vahanato, what's wrong?! Dammit, has she gone crazy?!" a young boy shouted.

Why was a boy like that here, of all places, and who was that woman? Tomochika was curious, but more than anything, she was worried about the safety of the people she actually knew. She chanced a look around.

"Where are Lynel and the others?"

It was hard to see anything through the flying chunks of rock and clouds of dust being kicked up by the destruction, but it seemed like the Divine King was blocking those deadly rays of light, having created a wall of her own light as a barrier.

"Wait, aren't there a few more people here than there should be right now?"

Lynel, Rick, Frederica, the Divine King, and the Swordmaster's body were all accounted for. But at some point, two more people had joined the group.

◇◇◇

"I'm sick of this! Let me go home!" Hanakawa shrieked.
They had finally reached the tower, only to be greeted by a storm of destruction that defied description. Beams of light were being fired wildly from a single point, vaporizing anyone and anything that they touched. At this rate, the entire canyon, never mind the tower, was going to be obliterated.
"It's fine, we won't be killed by something like this. You've seen action movies, right? The main character never gets hit during the firefight. It's the same thing. Dying to some stray shot wouldn't be an interesting enough development."
"I believe your perception of what constitutes a firefight is a bit too broad!"
"Whether it's lethal beams of light or bullets, it's still something that kills you if it touches you." Aoi somehow understood that they would be fine here. She was absolutely sure that she wouldn't die. Pulling Hanakawa along behind her, she made her way to the source of the commotion. It was more than probable that Yogiri Takatou would be there.
Heading toward the area that seemed to promise the most exciting storyline, they found a woman dressed all in white creating a wall of solid light to block the rays of destruction.
Hiding behind that wall were a tall, lanky fellow, a knightly-looking man clad in silver armor, and a girl whose right arm had turned into some sort of baked dessert. While the tall guy and the girl were crouched low to the ground, trembling in fear, the knight stood with his sword drawn, looking nonplussed.
"Is one of those guys Yogiri Takatou?" asked Aoi. "Doesn't look like it."
Both of the men seemed to be natives of this world. As a person of Japanese origin, her target would have a very different appearance. For

Chapter 21 — Was There Actually a Reason for Us to Get This Close to You?!

that same reason, the woman likely wasn't Tomochika Dannoura either. There was also a body beside them, lying beheaded on the ground, but it was an old man. There was no one who looked like a high school student.

"Who are you? Perhaps an acquaintance of Takatou?" the knight asked, shock clear in his voice. It must have been unthinkable for a pair of random people to show up in the middle of such a dangerous and chaotic situation.

"My name is Aoi. I'm not, but this pig knows him."

"We're not *really* acquaintances or anything!" Hanakawa protested.

Aoi shrugged. "Well, whatever. Do you know where Takatou is right now?"

"I don't believe this is the time for that!" Ignoring her, the knight turned back to the center of the destruction.

"I guess you're right. From Fate's perspective, nothing else can happen until this whole thing is resolved."

It certainly wasn't the type of scenario where they could relax and talk. Aoi took stock of the hellish scene. Reading the flow of Fate around them, the situation before her — and the solution to it — became immediately clear.

"Hey, did you know that you're a Swordmaster now?"

The knight once again looked at Aoi. "What? Oh, yes, the Swordmaster did say something about that!"

"Then problem solved. Go kill the goddess and it'll all be over."

"But to face such an opponent without a plan..."

"Don't worry, she's completely lost her mind. She's firing those things off randomly, so if you just keep an eye on the weapons floating around her, you'll be able to dodge them, no problem. With the power of a Swordmaster, it should be quite easy for you. Her chest and head are already injured, so aim for one of those areas with your sword. Killing a goddess would normally be impossible, but if you hit her with the Holy Sword Awz before she's fully healed, you can finish her off."

"How did you know about this sword?!" Despite his confusion, Aoi's knowledge of the weapon lent credibility to what she was saying, and after a moment, he seemed to let the matter go. It appeared he had resolved himself to act, as he began to take some practice swings with the blade. "Fine. Understood. The Divine King's power won't last much longer anyway, so sitting around doing nothing will certainly lead to our demise."

Steeling himself, the knight passed through the protective barrier of light. Dodging the goddess's lethal rays, he determinedly made his way towards her. Even for a Swordmaster, avoiding something that moved at the speed of light was impossible. If, however, he could read the movements of the weapons responsible for firing those objects, he would be able to manage. If the goddess had been sane and actively targeting him, there would have been no chance, but given her present condition, the knight easily made it to her side and plunged his sword into her chest.

The beams of light stopped, the weapons firing them abruptly clattering to the ground. Aoi confirmed to herself that the goddess was dead — according to Fate, that was a sensible outcome for the current scenario.

Now that the attacks had stopped, she looked around again. Yogiri Takatou should have been somewhere close by, but the dust kicked up by the goddess's attack had yet to settle. While that made it difficult to confirm anyone's identity, the fact that most of the people in the area were dead made the search much easier.

Not too far away, a lone figure was standing dumbstruck amidst the rubble, but whoever it was, they were too short. So her targets were most likely among the group of three at the far end of the tower.

"Hey, piggy, is that Yogiri Takatou over there?"

"Huh? Ah, it's hard to tell through all this dust, but I would recognize Tomochika's silhouette anywhere, so probably."

"Things get gross with you pretty quickly, don't they? All right, let's go."

"Umm, actually, I'm pretty sure if they see me, they'll kill me on the spot."

"If you don't intend to hurt them, they won't kill you, will they?"

Continuing to drag Hanakawa along behind her, Aoi made her way over to where Yogiri was standing. Once she had passed through the thickest part of the dust, she could see them clearly. Yogiri Takatou and Tomochika Dannoura. There was a half-demon woman with them.

Chapter 21 — Was There Actually a Reason for Us to Get This Close to You?!

The first thing she had to do was measure what kind of being Yogiri was. So Aoi activated her Hero Killer eyes — her ability to see Fate itself.

Immediately, her vision warped and twisted. Losing her sense of balance, she fell forward, unable to keep herself upright. A deep, wrenching pain in her gut brought forth a wave of nausea that she couldn't suppress.

Hanakawa was screaming again for some reason, but it sounded extremely far away. Propping herself up on the ground with both hands, she vomited. As pathetic as she must have looked, Aoi had long since lost the composure to care about keeping up appearances.

She needed to escape. That thought alone crowded out all else from her head.

Chapter 22 — I Might End Up Falling for You Anyway

She had to escape. She had to. She *had to.*

That was the only thought running through her mind. But no matter how much she wanted to, her body wouldn't move. Now that she had witnessed it for herself, her mind couldn't focus on anything else, fear of that one thing dominating her thoughts.

It was a dead end. The inevitable destination of all fates, beyond which there was nothing. The end of all things in human form. An embodiment of nonexistence that would overcome all others, something that no one could ever hope to surpass. Before this *thing*, the machinations of Fate were nothing more than a crude joke.

The idea of fighting such a thing was absurd. When she had first heard that it could kill with only a thought, she had figured that was ridiculous, an obvious exaggeration. She had assumed that the difference in skill level had simply been so steep that it had merely looked that way to bystanders. There had to be some sort of trick behind it, and by analyzing that ability, she knew she could come up with a way of countering it. As long as she had access to her own powers, she would be able to find a solution.

How naive she had been. Far, far too naive. She understood now just by looking at it. With a simple wish, this thing could kill anyone. No manner of object or phenomenon could survive its final choice. There were no countermeasures that could be taken. That was the kind of creature it was.

At that moment, Aoi realized the goddess's attacks hadn't come close to touching Yogiri. Even in her madness, she had instinctively understood that she should be afraid of it...that if she'd attacked that being, she would have died.

Sion...what the hell did you do?!

It was impossible to believe that such a creature could exist. It was hard to put it into words, this phenomenon like a great calamity or a curse. It was impossible for such a thing to hold a personality, to act like an ordinary person. And even if its existence *were* possible, there was no way someone like Sion would be able to summon it.

This was the worst situation imaginable. Sion — no, the Sages in general — had been far too simpleminded and arrogant. Why had they believed that only beings far weaker than themselves would be summoned? Why had they assumed that just because it had worked out that way so far, that's how it would always be?

Aoi stared down at the ground, which was now covered with her own vomit. She didn't feel like she could ever raise her head again. Even if Yogiri let her live, she felt that she would go insane. And really, that would be fine. What she was truly afraid of was what she would do once she had lost her sanity. If by some freak chance she attacked *him*, she would die in the truest sense of the word. This was the first time she had ever dreaded her own certainty in the existence of the soul.

She had to do something. First, she had to calm down. If she did nothing but cower here in fear, she obviously wouldn't be able to escape, nor could she kill herself before he got to her.

"Gahaha! As I said, I normally have no interest in tomboys, but seeing your usually calm and collected persona break down as you vomit and wet yourself so freely, I feel like I might end up falling for you anyway!"

As Aoi desperately tried to collect herself, Hanakawa's voice broke through the haze in her mind. He had been talking for a while, but now that she heard how absolutely stupid he was being, that ridiculousness somehow managed to help her calm down a little. And as

Chapter 22 — I Might End Up Falling for You Anyway

she did, she realized there was no reason to despair. She wasn't Yogiri's enemy yet. From his perspective, she was just some girl who'd shown up and started puking all over herself. She could still find a way out of this.

Taking hold of that faint hope, she lifted her face.

◇◇◇

"Hey, isn't that Hanakawa?"

"Oh, it is," Yogiri replied disinterestedly.

The moment that Tomochika and Yogiri noticed him, Hanakawa dropped onto his hands and knees. "I promise, I am not here because I wished to follow you! Miss Aoi forced me to come here against my will! Isn't that — wait, Miss Aoi?!"

Just as Tomochika was about to ask them what they were doing there, the girl with Hanakawa doubled over, falling to her knees as she became violently ill.

"Uhh, are you okay?" asked Tomochika. The girl seemed human enough, and the fact she was throwing up likely meant that she was not one of the Dark God's spawn.

"Fear not, I am in perfectly good health!" Hanakawa answered.

"Sorry, I couldn't care less about you," Tomochika retorted.

"I thought you could never disobey our instructions with that slave collar on. Aren't you supposed to be in the middle of a forest somewhere?" Yogiri asked. It occurred to him that Hanakawa wasn't even wearing the collar anymore.

The collar in question forced one to be entirely subservient to the first person they laid eyes on, so Hanakawa had placed it on himself while looking at Tomochika. Disgusted by the whole thing, she'd passed on control of their former classmate to Yogiri, who had told the sleazeball to go wait in the Forest of Beasts. If he was truly following those instructions, there was no way he could have left.

"Ah, well, that is..."

"So you were lying after all."

"No, I wasn't! At that point, I was very much under your control!

But I never said how long the effect would last. Please, you have to remember that much!"

"Well, I figured it would be something like that." Yogiri had doubted from the beginning that the collar would work forever. "So, what's going on here? Who is that?"

"This person brought me with her! Her name is Miss Aoi, but I suppose you should ask her yourself why she is here..." Still on his hands and knees, Hanakawa glanced over at the suffering girl beside him. "Gahaha! As I said, I normally have no interest in tomboys, but seeing your usually calm and collected persona break down as you vomit and wet yourself so freely, I feel like I might end up falling for you anyway! How does it feel to be looked down upon by someone as weak and pathetic as myself? Perhaps I'll make up a humiliating nickname for you as well!"

"Wow...this guy is still so gross..." Tomochika muttered, taking an unconscious step backwards.

"I don't care about Hanakawa, but something seems wrong with her," said Yogiri, stepping closer to the girl with a look of concern. As Tomochika made to follow him, the stranger suddenly raised her head.

"I-I'm okay!" she cried, stretching out a hand to stop them.

"Really? I can rub your back for you if you like."

"Please, there is no need for you to dirty yourself! I couldn't ask you to do something like that when I'm covered in filth like this. You don't have to worry about me!"

Tomochika narrowed her eyes. "She's awfully subservient, isn't she?"

"I'm okay, really," insisted Aoi. "It felt like my insides were being twisted and my brain was being fried for a moment, but now I'm fine! There is nothing for you to concern yourself with!"

"You don't look that okay to me...!"

"Honestly, I'm better! Please, I'm sorry; just don't get any closer! I'll even eat all this back up if you want me to!"

"I mean, if you're going to go that far, then I'll step back." Aoi's desperation had Tomochika more curious than ever, but she decided to honor the girl's wishes. The newcomer's face looked sickeningly pale, enough that it was worrying to look at her, but she truly didn't want them to come any closer.

Chapter 22 — I Might End Up Falling for You Anyway

"It's okay. I'm okay. I just need to rest for a bit."

"All right, we get it. You can calm down now."

"Yes, I am calm. I came here to deliver this pig to you. Since you are classmates!"

"Hm? That is the first I've heard of this, Aoi."

"Heh, don't make me kill you, pig. You followed me because you were stuck wandering the forest, separated from your classmates, right? You came with me hoping I would help you reunite with them."

"Uh, yes, I seem to remember that being the case. Somewhat." At the girl's vicious expression, Hanakawa immediately crumpled. It appeared he was now on a mission to reunite with his classmates.

"Perfect. As such, I am here to deliver him to you now."

"No, thanks, we're not interested," Yogiri immediately replied.

"Ah, understood. Then I will dispose of him immediately!"

"Could you not speak of me like I'm nothing more than a worthless book in a second-hand store?!"

"Now that I have delivered him to you, please excuse me!"

Crawling along the ground, the girl made her exit. While they were certainly worried about her, if she was going to reject their help so vehemently, there wasn't much they could do. After crawling a distance away, she seemed to recover enough to stand up and immediately sprinted towards the forest.

"Ah, uhh, what should I do now?" Hanakawa asked, puzzled by Aoi's sudden departure and the fact that she had run off without disposing of him first.

"You can go wait in the forest again," Yogiri answered bluntly.

"Not again! Please, have mercy on me!"

As Hanakawa began to wail, Rick and the others finally rejoined them.

◇◇◇

Rick, Lynel, Frederica, and the Divine King. Aside from Yogiri's group, those four seemed to be the only survivors. All of the other Knights had been killed by the goddess's free-for-all attack.

"There are a number of things I would like to ask, but first, you..." Rick turned to Theodisia with a stiff expression. From his perspective, she had just murdered the previous Swordmaster in cold blood. It was natural for him to be on his guard.

"I took my revenge on the old man for wrongs that he committed against my people. It is none of your concern."

"So you say, but I am now a Swordmaster. It is hard to argue that I have no connection to the situation."

"Since you only just became the Swordmaster, there is no connection. Or do you intend to continue the wicked acts of your predecessor?"

The atmosphere around them was taking on a dangerous tone. Sensing that things were about to escalate fast, Yogiri stepped in.

"I think it's best if you take a look underground yourself, Rick. If you still plan on avenging the old Swordmaster after that...well, frankly I'm on Theodisia's side, so you'll be facing me too."

Now that Rick had become the Swordmaster, Theodisia wouldn't stand a chance against him. But Yogiri wasn't interested in sitting back and watching her die.

"Sir Takatou, I apologize for my rudeness, but I am now a Swordmaster. Even though you bear the title of Knight, for someone powerless like yourself —"

"Cease this impoliteness," the Divine King interrupted.

"But surely we cannot allow the person who murdered the former Swordmaster to escape!"

"Don't let your new title go to your head. You don't stand a chance against this boy. After all, he was strong enough to slay the Dark God itself." Rick gasped in shock. "The same is true for the death of its spawn. Both were your work, were they not?" the Divine King asked, turning her gaze to Yogiri.

Given the certainty in her words, there was little point in trying to trick her or deny it. Reluctantly, Yogiri confessed. "I'm really sorry about that. I didn't mean to kill him, or to ruin all of this."

He and Tomochika were outsiders who had stepped into the middle of an encounter millennia in the making, and then thrown it all into

Chapter 22 — I Might End Up Falling for You Anyway

chaos. It was something he really should have left to the people of this world to settle.

"No, you have my thanks. In truth, there was a limit to how long we could keep the barrier in place. That strain was likely the cause for your companion's desire for revenge."

Rick looked around at the scene again. The Dark God, who had driven the ancient world to the edge of destruction, the source of all this calamity, lay dead, surrounded by the corpses of the twisted spawn it had birthed and who had worshiped it in turn. The young Swordmaster's expression grew even harder.

"Sir Takatou, exactly who are you?"

"I'm a high school student who was summoned here by the Sages."

"Oh, you're just a normal high school student now?!" Tomochika said with exaggerated surprise. But Yogiri had always wanted to think of himself that way — an ordinary teenager who just happened to have a strange power.

"Very well then," Rick relented. "I will set aside the issue of the previous Swordmaster's death for now. We must consider what comes next."

"Honestly, we ended up here by accident on our way to the capital, so that's where we're heading now," Yogiri replied.

"Ah, well in that case, I will accompany you. There is nothing more to be done here, so I may as well return home. I'm sure you will be going back as well, Lynel and Frederica?" Rick, it seemed, lived in the capital, and apparently his companions did too.

"I will need to search for more information, so I will likely head to the capital as well," Theodisia added, likely still wondering how to find her sister.

Tomochika decided to bring up something that had been bugging her for a while. "Theodisia, could you tell us your sister's name again?"

"Her name is Euphemia. Do you know anything about her?"

"I feel like I've heard it before...do you remember anything, Takatou?"

"I feel the same way, but I tend to forget anything that I don't actively try to remember."

201

"Even that much is helpful," said Theodisia. "Since you did not come here from the capital, please tell me which cities you visited along the way. I will go to those places in search of leads."

Tomochika quickly outlined their journey from their bus's arrival in the field to their time at the tower. When she finished, Theodisia decided to head for Hanabusa.

"I will also go to the capital. It has been more than a thousand years, has it not?" the Divine King mused. "Though it may now be abandoned, I should visit the temple first."

It seemed their decisions had been made, with most of them planning to take the same road.

"All right, can you please tell us the way?" Yogiri asked. "We have a general idea of how to get there, but if you have a map or something, that will help a lot."

"A map?" Rick frowned in thought. "A short distance away lies the camp of those who came here with me, and they should have a map. But... why don't you simply travel with us?"

"Y-Yes!" Hanakawa interjected, having added himself to the group at some point. "This is normally the point where one obtains a large number of companions, correct? So now we make our journey to the capital together! That's what should happen next!"

"No way. Dannoura and I are traveling alone," Yogiri proclaimed shamelessly.

Tomochika was at a loss for words.

◇◇◇

Having flat-out declined the offer to travel alongside the others, Yogiri and Tomochika returned to their truck. Though the goddess's rampage had destroyed the surrounding area, the vehicle itself was miraculously unharmed.

"Hey, wouldn't it have been easier to just stick with everyone else?"

"I don't like big groups of people. It gets to be too much of a pain."

"Yeah, that's understandable." Tomochika hadn't been especially excited about traveling with the others herself, so if Yogiri preferred that

Chapter 22 — I Might End Up Falling for You Anyway

it just be the two of them, that was fine with her. "Speaking of which, what happened to that dragon girl? Her name was Atila, right? Wasn't she supposed to take us to the capital?"

"We already know how to get there, so we should be fine. And now that the Swordmaster is dead, it would probably be hard to face her."

"That's true."

Additionally, having her guide them meant having to travel along with her. That went against Yogiri's wish to keep them as a party of two. Then again, while they had been traveling alone together for most of their journey, now that he had put it into words, Tomochika couldn't help but find it a little embarrassing.

As she hesitated, thinking things over, Yogiri made his way to the passenger seat as usual. With no desire to force him to drive, Tomochika took the wheel without complaint.

"All right, this time we're heading to the capital for real! So, which way should I go?"

I have more or less determined the correct route.

"Oh, Mokomoko is still here. I hadn't seen you for a while so I figured you'd finally passed on to the next life or something."

Come, now! I suppose I didn't end up being all that useful back there, but still...

"Anyway, we'll be leaving navigation entirely up to you. So, once again, let's go!"

"Hurray," Yogiri said, lifting a hand into the air with absolutely no energy at all. Though it was better than when he simply ignored everything in favor of his video games, he still seemed awfully sleepy.

Tomochika put her foot on the gas, and the truck slowly rocked into motion.

Chapter 23 — Interlude: Why Are You Using Such an Annoying Method?

"And now I've been left behind again!" Hanakawa wailed.

Yogiri had refused to let him travel with them. On top of that, he was a stranger to the others and Rick's group had felt no obligation to take him along either.

"W-Well...at least it seems this place is safe for now, so I guess I'll go look for somewhere a bit calmer..." Compared to ordinary people, Hanakawa had a considerable amount of power. His physical characteristics were significantly higher than most, and he had the ability to heal from any wound in an instant. As long as he kept his greed in check, he should be able to make it as some sort of discount Hero. If he found a desolate, faraway village, he could hunt the monsters lurking around it to curry favor with the locals. Even his dreams of building a harem weren't impossible.

"That's right. I was still a member of the party that took down a Demon Lord. Asking for a slight boost to my status isn't a very big deal! Well then, let's first investigate the basement of this tower. Takatou seemed entirely uninterested, so there may not be much in the way of rare items down there, but you never know."

Although he had been dragged there against his will, he had guessed what this place was from listening to the conversations around him. The tower must have been built to seal away the Dark God. That meant there might still be something left over that was worth looting. Hanakawa possessed a skill that let him carry an unlimited number of items; no amount of treasure would be a burden to him.

Just as he had decided to head down to the basement, he sensed someone behind him and turned around. A young boy was standing there, and although he looked totally exhausted, there was a mad light burning in his eyes.

Hanakawa immediately dropped to his hands and knees. Perhaps because he had done it so often, he slid into the position relatively smoothly. His instincts were screaming that while this creature looked like no more than a child, he was incredibly dangerous. Hanakawa would do everything in his power to obey him.

"Hey, what happened here?" As the boy stepped forward, the floor beneath his feet cracked and shattered. He must have been furious. All Hanakawa could do was pray that his anger wouldn't be directed at him personally.

"U-Umm…that's right! This was all done by a man named Yogiri Takatou! Everything, all of it, every single thing was his fault! That's the truth!"

This boy must have been one of the Dark God's spawn. Hanakawa had assumed that Yogiri wiped them all out, but apparently that wasn't the case. He had no idea what his former classmate had been thinking, but it may have been something as simple as this "boy" not directly intending to kill him at the time.

"Even Orgain's death?"

"Yes!"

"And all my companions?"

"Yes!"

"And my lord's death as well?"

"Yes, yes! All of it! It's all his fault! It had nothing to do with me; I just happened to be here by coincidence!" Hanakawa pleaded pitifully. Fighting was entirely out of the question, but even running away seemed impossible right now. There was nothing he could do but beg for mercy.

"That's a bit hard to believe."

"I realize that, but…!"

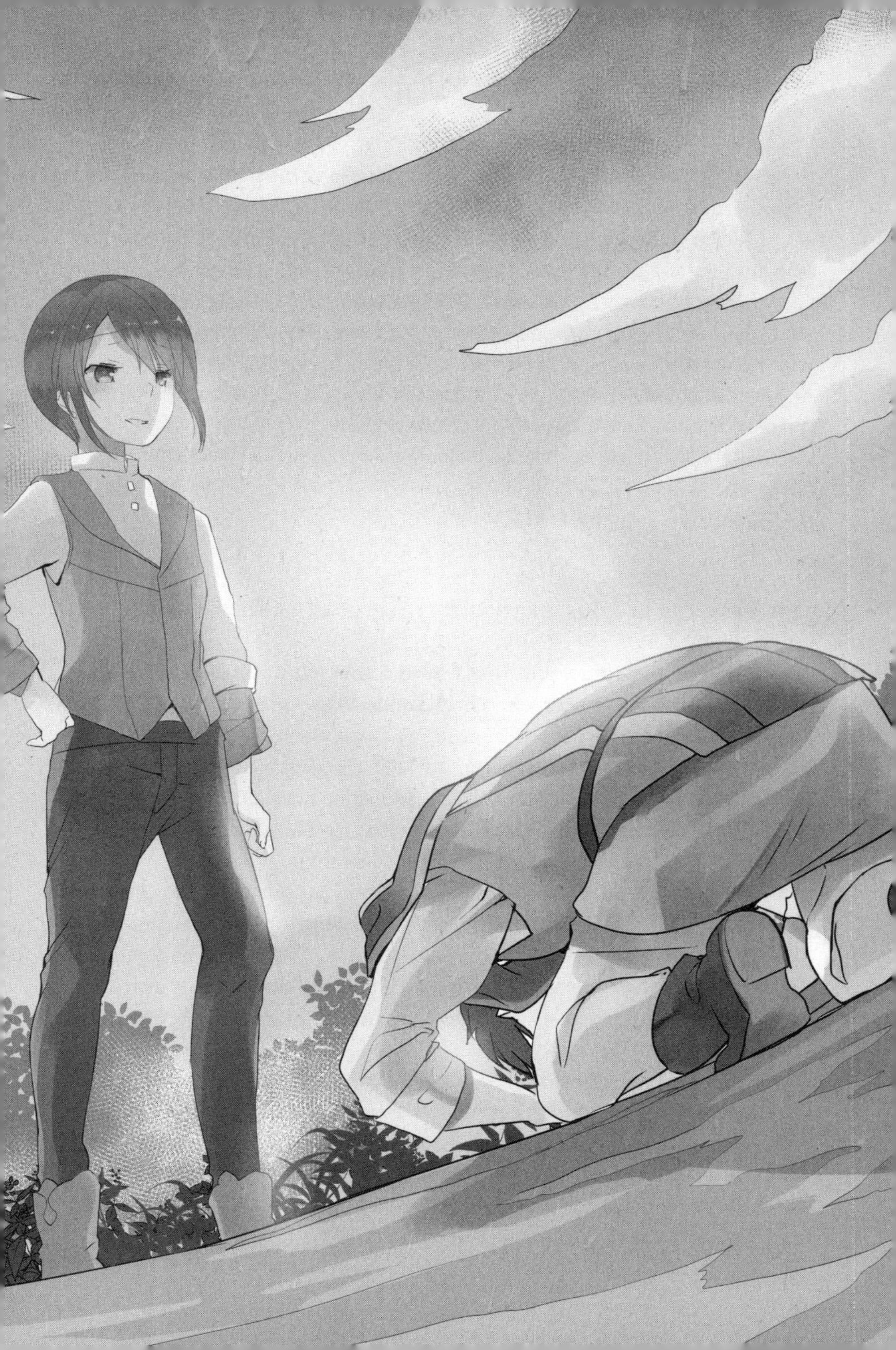

"Still, I don't understand exactly what's going on right now. Can you explain it more clearly?"

"Very well! Understood!" Hanakawa pressed his face into the ground.

First Rikuto with his harem, then Aoi running him ragged, and now this spawn of the Dark God seemed poised to do the same. But anything that happened twice could happen three times, or even four. As long as he was alive, there was still a chance. For now, Hanakawa would simply have to be obedient and see where things went.

There was a way out for him somehow. He decided to hold on to that hope.

◇◇◇

In a room in Sion's mansion, four Sages had gathered around a circular table.

"We've lost contact with Aoi," Sion reported.

At their last meeting, they had decided that one of the candidates Sion had summoned, Yogiri Takatou, was a problem. He had likely been involved in the disappearance of Lain and the death of Santarou. They didn't know for sure that he was responsible, but he was only a Sage candidate, and his death would hardly be a loss, so they had decided to get rid of him just in case.

Imagining that he might possess powers on par with those of the Sages, they had sent Aoi, who specialized in hunting rogue Sages, after him. If he was just some fool who had stumbled across an exceptional power, she was the perfect choice to deal with him. However, they hadn't heard a word from her since she'd left Hanabusa and headed for the canyon.

"Seriously, whether it's Lain or Aoi, I can't see either of them dying. We did see Santarou's body, so I agree, that one is hard to ignore," said Yoshifumi, a seedy-looking man whose leather pants and studded jacket made him look like a common thug, although he was indeed a Sage. In fact, he was the emperor of the land of Ent. Unlike most Sages, he directly ruled over the area under his jurisdiction.

Chapter 23 — Interlude: Why Are You Using Such an Annoying Method?

"There are signs of large-scale destruction in the canyon," Sion replied. "The landscape itself has completely changed. There were rumors that a Swordmaster lived there, but I find it hard to believe that Aoi would pick a fight with him. If she had, I doubt she would have made it out unscathed."

"But we have no idea where this Takatou guy is, right? So there's nothing we can do but leave it for now."

"Wait, you're the one who summoned him, aren't you, Sion?" The next to speak was Alice, a girl in a golden dress. Although she styled herself as a princess, unlike Yoshifumi, she wasn't actually connected to a royal house. Sion didn't understand it, but Alice adamantly insisted that she was a princess through and through. "Is this something you should be pushing off on others? I feel like you should take some responsibility and deal with it yourself."

"I suppose you're right. Luckily, we know the locations of the others who were summoned alongside him, so they may have had some contact with him. Very well, then. I will continue to share information about the case, but from now on, I'll take care of it personally."

Aoi failing — or encountering any difficulties at all — had totally defied Sion's expectations. Obviously, she had been completely wrong about this one candidate, but there was little she could do now other than solve the situation herself.

"Ahh, actually, we're starting to run quite low on Sages, aren't we?" Jumping into the conversation as if he had just remembered something was a blonde-haired, blue-eyed young man.

As his appearance suggested, he was not Japanese like the rest of them. His name was Van, the true grandson of the Great Sage. All of the current Sages referred to themselves as "Grandchildren of the Great Sage" but for those like Sion, it was only a title. Van had actually been born in this world, and had a true blood connection to their leader.

"Yes, that's why we've been summoning candidates repeatedly to try and fill in the gaps. It seems we aren't producing much in the way of results, though."

"But why are you using such an inefficient method? If you want more Sages, shouldn't it be an easy process?" Van stared at them with blank

209

amazement. He really believed that finding replacements was an easy task.

"It's not that simple. That's why we've been trying out so many different methods. Are you saying *you* can get us more Sages?"

"Sure, I'll give it a shot. I just need to find replacements for Lain and Santarou, right?"

"Actually, as many as you can find would be great. The recently invading Aggressors have been fairly strong, after all."

"All right, I'll try to find some, then."

At Van's light-hearted reply, Sion's expression grew troubled. If he could create viable Sages so easily, it would make the rest of them look like idiots for going through all the trouble of summoning candidates from other worlds. But at this point, they would just have to wait and see how he fared.

"Fine, I'll leave that to you two, then," Yoshifumi said. "But honestly, why do you even care? Why not just let the Aggressors do as they like if they aren't in your territory? Our job is to fight the Aggressors in the areas that are under our jurisdictions...the rest is none of our business, is it?"

It was a fair point, but if the number of Sages continued to decrease, eventually that burden would shift to the rest of them instead. It was best to deal with the issue as quickly as possible.

"Maybe so, but if we just let those areas be, the people there will be in trouble." Even if it was outside of their own territories, the people in the regions threatened by Aggressors would be left to die. They couldn't just ignore that.

"Yeah, about those empty areas..." Yoshifumi continued. "It was left kinda vague last time, so let's clear this up right now. I want Lain's territory."

"Excuse me, I also want Hanabusa!" Alice interjected, raising a hand energetically.

"Screw off, bitch. It's nowhere near your jurisdiction!"

"Oh really? That's rich coming from the guy who's stuck on an island! It's a whole ocean away from you!"

Hanabusa was the closest thing in this world to a modern Japanese city. Since the majority of Sages had come from Japan, it was a highly desirable location to them.

"And what's with that mook-like fashion you've got going on?" snorted Alice. "You look like such a small fry! Like you'll be wiped out within seconds of hitting the field!"

"The fact that you don't get it is exactly why you're a brainless tart! And what's with that floaty look you've got going? No princess in the world looks half as ridiculous as you do!"

"You wanna go a round?! My Imperial Guard isn't just for show, you know!"

"Bring it! My Four Heavenly Kings will crush you!"

"Ha! Four Heavenly Kings? I guess if the boss is a small fry, the underlings would be no exception! Sounds like they'll die quick!"

The mounting tension between Yoshifumi and Alice was showing no sign of easing.

"Very well," Sion interjected. "I will decide on a course of action here. Let's split Lain's territory between you. If we cut it in half, that should be fair, right? I'll let you two decide where the halfway point is."

Predictably, the resulting discussion immediately devolved into another heated argument.

"Well, please work it out yourselves later on."

Fed up with their antics, Sion forcibly removed them from the room. Aside from Sion herself, the Sages present at the meeting were merely illusions. As the owner of the room, Sion had the authority to cut off their transmissions at any time.

"I'll give you a shout if I manage to make some more Sages," Van stated before he too disappeared. He didn't seem to be at all interested in the matter of the unclaimed territories. She didn't know why he had even come to the meeting, but he had a tendency to drop in on a whim like that. It may have been nothing more than a way for him to kill time.

Seeing that the meeting had finished and that Sion was now alone, her attendant, Youichi, stepped inside. "If Sages are meant to do whatever they want, how did you end up saddled with managing the decreasing number of Sages and the unclaimed territories?"

"I guess that's just my nature. Grandfather told us to 'do as we will,' so that's what I'm doing. No matter what's going on, I always end up trying to bring some sort of order to it."

"So, what are you going to do about that Yogiri guy?"

"Let's see...we still don't have a good idea of what he actually is. You said he was maybe using some sort of Instant Death magic..."

"I talked to the lord of Hanabusa, but he didn't really understand what Yogiri was doing. The little information he was able to offer was totally useless. Why don't we try asking the other candidates from his class?"

"I'd prefer not to interfere with them beyond the bounds of their missions...ah! How about this?" Sion clapped her hands together as an idea came to her. "Let's summon someone who knows Yogiri from back in Japan!"

"Can you do that?"

"I still have the data from their transmigration left over, so I can probably narrow it down well enough. Let's give it a try."

Summoning magic was ordinarily an incredibly difficult task, but it was second nature for Sion. After all, she produced magical energy just by breathing, so she was always overflowing with power.

Sion stretched a hand outwards and a magic circle appeared on the table before her, linking that spot to the other world. It was like making a trap door that connected the two locations. The process created a tunnel leading from this world, which rested at the lowest possible energy potential, to another one higher up. All she had to do was wait for someone to fall into it.

She had set up the trap in a specific location based on the information she currently had about Yogiri Takatou, but the chances of actually snagging someone related to him were fairly low. There was a high probability that nothing would come of it, but she had the magical energy to spare, so there was no reason not to try.

"Wait, Sion, can't you just summon Yogiri himself? That would make getting rid of him awfully easy."

"Unilateral summoning is rather challenging for someone in the same world. This trans-world approach is possible due to the difference in energy needs between our worlds. Ah, we've got something."

Chapter 23 — Interlude: Why Are You Using Such an Annoying Method?

With the sound of a string being plucked, someone appeared on the table. It was a man in a white coat.

"Success?" Youichi asked.

"Who knows? We'll have to ask him and find out."

The man in the coat looked extremely bewildered. That was to be expected, though. From his point of view, the world around him had suddenly transformed, leaving him in a new and strange place.

"Hello. My name is Sion, a Sage. I am the one who summoned you here."

"Sage? Summoned? What are you talking about?" The man seemed to calm down slightly upon hearing her voice.

"I called you here to ask you about a boy named Yogiri Takatou."

The moment she said the name, the man began to panic, even more so than at the moment of his summoning.

"Summon — wait, is that why $A\Omega$ suddenly disappeared? Is this a different world? No, that's definitely possible. After all, we have no idea where he originally came from. If there are other worlds, then maybe that's where the source of his power is…but then the energy source would be…" Though he had been alarmed at first, he seemed to immediately accept his situation and began muttering excitedly to himself, pulling a cell phone from his pocket.

"Ahahahahaha!" The moment he looked at the screen of his phone, he began to laugh maniacally. "This *is* another world?!"

"That's right," Sion replied, taken aback by his bizarre reaction. Normally, she would have expected him to take longer to accept that fact, and to be more distressed when the realization hit.

"He's here! I've got his signal again! Of course, there's no way he could die! And you're the ones who brought him here?! In that case, you are our saviors! You've literally saved our world! On behalf of Japan — no, on behalf of all humanity, please accept my heartfelt thanks!"

"What do you mean?" Youichi asked with a frown. Though the man in the white coat didn't appear to be completely insane, they had no idea what he was rambling about.

"Of course, that just means *this* world is now in danger! Dammit! Why me? Why did I have to be brought here now that my own world is safe?! Look, the seal has even been removed! Do you have any idea what that means?!"

"AΩ, first gate release confirmed. Taking Level C precautions. Self-destruct sequence initiated. Warning. Please step at least five meters away. Beginning countdown. Ten...nine...eight..."

A machine-like voice was emanating from somewhere on the man.

"No, please, help me! I don't want to die! Please, return me to my world!"

Sion and Youichi watched, dumbstruck, as the countdown quickly reached zero.

The moment it did, the man's head exploded.

Pieces of skull and chunks of brain matter sprayed outward as his body slumped over on the table. Naturally, he died instantly.

"What the hell was that?!" Youichi mumbled, unable to comprehend what they had just seen.

"I have no idea...but I suppose summoning any others would be meaningless."

In truth, she hadn't been overly concerned with this Yogiri Takatou before, but Sion was now starting to get a very bad feeling about him.

MY INSTANT DEATH ABILITY IS SO OVERPOWERED, NO ONE IN THIS OTHER WORLD STANDS A CHANCE AGAINST ME!

Side Story

Side Story: The Agency

The village was not marked on any maps. Since long ago, its existence had been kept a secret. It was left out of all official records, and its residents were not included in any census. In effect, it was a town that didn't exist. But that didn't mean it was an undeveloped, stone-age settlement. It was impossible for the people who lived there to be completely disconnected from the outside world so it was known to the settlements around it as a bizarre place that shouldn't be dealt with.

As people are wont to gossip, there were those who took an interest in the village. No matter how well it was hidden, Japan was only so big. It wasn't difficult to understand how it came to be seen as special, like a solitary island in a sea of wilderness. And once people found out about it, it was only natural that some of them would attempt to visit.

The area around the village was under perpetual surveillance by the state, but that surveillance wasn't perfect. The perimeter had to be structured in a way that nearby residents wouldn't notice, so it was set up over an exceptionally wide area. As a result, those who were serious about infiltrating the settlement didn't find it especially difficult to do. But of those who succeeded, not a single one returned home. So no one knew what went on inside the village, and its contents and purpose remained a mystery.

This was true even for the very government that kept it hidden and under surveillance in the first place. All they knew was that they had been told to monitor the place. And while that was strange, it wasn't an entirely unique situation. There were plenty of things in the world that were off limits, and the number of countries that had been destroyed for not respecting those boundaries were too great to count.

Although Japan's head of state changed, the system of government didn't. As such, the details of the taboo were handed down rather effectively. Even if they didn't understand why, keeping that area under observation was something that came to be taken for granted.

That is why they only came to know the reason for that taboo when the surveillance network around it was breached from the inside.

◇◇◇

Having finished her meal consisting entirely of instant food, Asaka Takatou made her way to the porch. It was pitch black outside.

"I wonder how they are doing this. Is it like a planetarium?"

It was a totally impossible sight. The village was deep underground, so there was no way they should be getting weather down there. Although Asaka had yet to get a handle on the exact details of the area, she could guess that it was a rather small, hemispherical shape. The day and night cycle was likely done through some sort of projection mapping. The movement of the sun in their underground world seemed to match that of the sun outside.

"Wait, am I going to have to stay here forever? Things are looking pretty grim."

While she'd been well aware that she would be living at her workplace, she had never imagined ending up stuck somewhere like this.

"Hey, what did the last person do at night?" she asked the young boy as she walked back into the living room.

"She went home before it got dark," the boy answered politely.

Asaka's job was to take care of this cute little kid, who was still overflowing with innocence. His name was Yogiri Takatou. He hadn't had a name of his own originally, so Asaka had given him one. She hadn't intended to give him her last name as well, but the boy had understood enough to feel that he needed one, so she'd let him take whatever name he wanted.

"Home, huh?" she murmured, looking through the instruction packet that she'd been given. Apparently, there were some lodgings for staff a little ways away from the mansion. "I guess I should probably go too, then."

"It's dangerous to go out at night."

"Of course these rural country roads are dark, but I'm an adult. If I had a flashlight or something..." she muttered, peering out at the night.

Relying only on the moonlight would make her uneasy, but if she had a light source of her own, she figured she could find her way. Or at least that's what she thought for a moment, but immediately changed her mind.

There was a dark figure beyond the window. The moment she saw it, she began to doubt her own eyes. The figure was an inky black, as if it were someone's shadow that had just stood up in three dimensions.

"Those things come out at night," the boy explained. "If you leave the windows open, they feel like they're welcome to come inside, so you have to close everything up tight before the sun goes down."

As Asaka watched, the shadows began to multiply. She hurriedly ran back to the porch and slammed the storm shutters closed.

"What are they?!"

They were only a hair's breadth in width. If they truly wanted to enter, the wooden shutters would likely prove no obstacle, but for some reason they simply stood outside and watched.

"I don't really know."

"Do they always come?"

"Yeah."

Judging from the way he had set about readying his futon for the night without the least bit of concern, it appeared this was an everyday occurrence for him. Most of his life seemed to take place in this living room.

"I guess you could call it being a shut-in..." Asaka murmured to herself.

Shortly after finishing dinner, they began preparations to sleep.

Maybe there was just nothing else for them to do, but it seemed like a rather dull lifestyle.

"Well, I suppose I can't go outside now…I guess I'll have to spend the night here…" Never mind going outside, she wanted to avoid even leaving this room if she could. With weird things like that lurking around, she wasn't going to let herself be caught alone. "Are there any other futons?"

"No, this is the only one."

"Well, I guess I'll have to deal with that, then." Yogiri was just a child, and the futon was fairly large. There was plenty of room for them to share. "Actually, I don't even have a change of clothes here, do I? I guess there's nothing I can do about it now."

In the end, her concern for the figures outside kept her from sleeping much at all.

◇◇◇

The next morning, Asaka was getting breakfast ready. It was the first time she had ever worn an apron, but it was handy to have on while doing housework. She wasn't all that excited about the Fifties-era housewife look it gave her, but since the only ones there were her and Yogiri, it wasn't that big of an issue.

"Hmm…does this actually qualify as miso soup?"

It was hard to say she was truly working when all she'd been doing was feeding him instant food. So Asaka had gone to the kitchen to attempt some actual cooking, but that turned out to be easier said than done.

"It's kind of hard to call it miso soup when it's just water with miso in it. There's stuff here to make soup stock too, isn't there?"

When she tested it, it had tasted like straight miso. She had tried to recreate the soup she was used to from her own home growing up, but she hadn't even come close. The ingredients on hand here were just too good. There were plenty of sardines and dried bonito, which looked ideal for making soup stock, but she had no idea how to actually make use of them.

"If we had the Internet here, I could look up some recipes, but…"

This place was completely cut off from the outside world, so it didn't even have normal phone lines. There was a rotary phone in the mansion, but it was only connected to the facility's own network.

"At least give me a rice cooker or something!"

Cooking rice with nothing but a pot and a stove was downright unreasonable. Piecing together her own limited knowledge of the subject, she tried using the portable gas burner instead. The results of her previous similar best-guesses were now sitting on the dining room table, although they were hard to look at. The fish was totally charred, and the eggs that were supposed to be sunny side up were completely unrecognizable.

"Yep, this is impossible."

Asaka's first attempts had been awful. The rice seemed ready, at least, so she brought that and the miso soup to the table. With that, a breakfast of a sort was good to go.

"It's bad," Yogiri remarked after a single bite, just as Asaka had expected. "The rice is sticky, but it's still hard."

"Is that really what you should say to someone who just made food for you?" Being honest with herself, she had thought the exact same thing, but being told that straight to her face was still upsetting.

"But it tastes awful —"

"Shaddup!"

"Uhh…what?" Hearing Asaka's distorted English, Yogiri grew puzzled.

"Listen, if a girl makes food for you, you should absolutely never say that it tastes bad! You won't be popular at all if you say such things!" she scolded him, putting aside the question of whether she could actually be considered "a girl" in this context.

"What do you mean 'popular'?"

"Unpopular means that no one will like you. You'll be treated like a hairy caterpillar. People will scream when they see you, they'll think you're gross, and no one will ever want to be your friend."

"Caterpillar…I know what that is."

"Good. I'm glad you at least know that much. In this case, it's clearly impossible to hide that the food is bad. So the person making it already knows they screwed up. But as a man, you should eat all of it and say that it was delicious anyway!"

"Okay…I'll do that. It's delicious…"

It seemed that she'd been able to convince him with a bit of forceful wording. Then again, acting all depressed about it would just make him feel guilty, which was unfair. And anyway, the food *was* so bad that even Asaka herself could barely stomach it. She could hardly blame the kid.

"Thanks for the meal," Yogiri said, polishing off all the food in front of him.

"Hey, are you serious?!"

The charred fish, the pathetic eggs, the miso-water and the crunchy rice were all gone. He had actually eaten everything. At this point, Asaka would have to eat everything as well or risk being a hypocrite. Swearing to herself that she would learn to cook as soon as possible, she powered her way through the awful meal on spirit alone.

"Okay, that's that. Please wait a minute; I'll clean up." Once she had finished, she collected the dishes and made her way to the kitchen. "This is quite the situation, isn't it? If they're going to force me to do on-the-job training, they could at least put someone here to teach me."

Quickly washing the dishes, Asaka retrieved the instruction manual from her pocket. Her job was to take care of $A\Omega$ and to give him a minimum level of education as a Japanese person. The packet provided nothing more specific than that. It seemed they were leaving it all up to her. In short, they had tossed her in without a second thought.

"What do you even want me to do?! This doesn't make any sense! Is this even legal? Is there any oversight here at all? Will I even get paid for this? Doesn't it seem like I've just gone missing to everyone else?!"

Of course, she had basically been kidnapped by an organization that operated above the law, so the law likely didn't care one way or the other about her. Getting caught up in all the small details wouldn't do her any good.

"Well, I guess for now, I can at least teach him at an elementary school level…"

He seemed to be about that age, so it was probably a good place to start.

◇◇◇

The morning would be spent studying. The afternoon would be reserved for playing outside. That's what Asaka decided for the time being. Now that breakfast was done, she wanted to get right to the studying, but first she needed to get a grasp of Yogiri's academic abilities.

"First, let's work on your writing."

In a way, it was a relief for Asaka. While she was indeed certified as a teacher, she was a total novice. She had no idea what to teach someone of Yogiri's age. So to start with, she wrote some examples for him to try to copy.

Just as they began, she heard the sound of the front door opening.

"Hey! Is someone here?"

"Probably one of the delivery people."

"Keep at it," she told Yogiri, standing up and heading to the entrance. A woman with a huge basket on her back was standing there. Without any sort of greeting, the woman took off her shoes and made her way into the house.

"Umm, can I ask who you are?"

As Asaka called out to her, the woman slowly raised her face to look up, earning a surprised exclamation. She was smiling, but there was no movement or life to it at all. It looked more like it was painted on.

"You are Asaka Takatou, correct? I am an Autonomous Humanoid Operational Mechanism. I have brought you food supplies."

Though her speech was fluent enough, it was completely lacking in emotion. Asaka had thought it strange that they had so many fresh ingredients on hand, but apparently this robot was bringing them in now and then. She remembered being told there was an autonomous robot working here earlier, but she didn't expect it to look so unnerving.

"If things like this are an everyday experience for him, I worry about his upbringing..."

While it seemed the company had made it humanoid out of

consideration for them, it felt like they were working hard in the wrong direction.

"Uh, excuse me, do you deliver anything other than food?"

"Yes, if anything else is needed."

"In that case, do you think you could get me an elementary school curriculum or some textbooks? Also an introductory book on cooking, a microwave, a rice cooker, and an electric kettle would be great. What else? We could use a television, a Blu-ray player, and some game consoles for our free time. Any games or movies are fine. Maybe some magazines, novels, and manga would be good too. And a change of clothes for me."

Asaka had rattled off a list of just about everything on her mind. There were likely plenty of things that she wouldn't be allowed to have, but there was no harm in asking.

"Very well. I will convey your requests."

Apparently having decided that their conversation was over, the woman stepped up into the house. It seemed this was a regular enough occurrence. Accepting it as such, Asaka returned to the living room.

"I finished," Yogiri said, proudly showing off his writing.

As she'd expected, if he put his mind to it, it wouldn't be that difficult for him to progress. At this rate, he would have no problem with elementary school material.

"All right, it's a bit early, but let's go outside. We don't have any textbooks yet anyway." She didn't really know what it meant to give him an "education in being a Japanese person." Kids these days likely didn't spend much time playing in rice fields, but for now, she figured they would try it and see how it went.

Obviously remembering what Asaka had told him before, Yogiri set about searching for creatures in the rice paddy.

"It's so strange. This all has such a nice rural feel, but we're still underground, aren't we?"

It was a standard countryside landscape, one that looked especially lonely, like it had been left behind by the flow of time. It was early autumn, so the rice fields were still full of water.

Yogiri crouched down at the edge of the field and stuck his hand into the water, trying to catch something. Given how deeply interested in the activity he seemed to be, it was like he had never done such a thing before.

"It's so light," he said, inspecting his catch. Most of what he had caught were green, transparent little creatures, which he scooped up and put into a bucket.

"What do you call these things? Are these the ones that are good luck for the harvest?" Asaka wondered to herself, adding an illustrated dictionary to the list of things that she wanted.

She looked out over the scenery around them. She definitely hadn't seen them yesterday but there were people working in the fields. She couldn't tell from this distance, but she assumed they were robots too. Despite their perfectly human-like movements, they all seemed to have the same pasted-on smiles as the automaton she had met earlier.

"This is what they call the uncanny valley, isn't it? Though if they can imitate humans that well, it's actually kind of impressive."

Japan was vigorously advancing the field of robotics, but there was no way they should have progressed to this point already. It wasn't her specialty so she didn't know the details, but they seemed to be at least several generations ahead of modern robots. They must have been developed in secret and put to work where no one would find them. As expected, maintaining this place must have been a tremendously expensive endeavor.

"It's not really feeling like I'll be able to leave here alive…"

Wouldn't she simply be erased in order to keep this place a secret once they had no more use for her? Asaka felt a vague sense of unease growing within her.

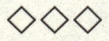

◇◇◇

Asaka was back in the room where she had first been interviewed. She had been called up to the surface to make the first of her monthly reports.

"Thank you for your hard work, truly. I never thought someone would make it a whole month. Your boldness is something that's hard to find in most people. What do you call it, your human ability? With that, I'm sure you could have found employment anywhere."

The man thanking her was the same white-coated young man who had interviewed her in the beginning. Asaka made a bitter face, the memories of her repeated failures to find a job resurfacing.

"Well, actually, corporations tend to prefer someone who has the ability to read the atmosphere and cooperate and communicate well with others, don't they?"

"Yes, it's become something of a modern problem. They've focused so much on finding people with good communication skills that they've ultimately developed a workforce that's only good at dodging responsibility despite their general lack of abilities. Companies these days are finding it tough to keep things going."

"You didn't call me here to talk about all of that, though, did you?"

"We don't have anything in particular to talk about at the moment, but we can't just leave you down there on your own forever, can we?"

"Wasn't this a very important assignment? Something about stopping the world from being destroyed?"

For such a heavy situation, it felt to Asaka that this guy was taking things rather lightly.

"AΩ is pretty quiet, isn't he? Even if we left him to his own devices, he would probably remain just as he is, or at least that was our conclusion. But that thing *will* keep growing, so there's no telling what might happen if we simply leave it alone. Our goal is to introduce a bias to the direction of that growth. I read your report. It appears he's reached the academic level of an elementary school student. That's quite impressive."

Yogiri's academic ability was genuinely incredible. Though he looked to be the age of a third grader, he was already working on sixth grade materials now.

Asaka nodded. "I think middle school material will be beyond my ability to teach, though."

"Well, I'm sure you'll find a way. We can also arrange a sort of correspondence school program if we need to."

"Wouldn't it be better to hire actual teachers? We could use some more people down there."

"If we could do things like that, life would certainly be a lot easier for us. Did I mention that you had a predecessor?"

"Masaki, right?"

"Yes, she lasted longer than others. Most people give up after the first night."

"I see. What are those things, by the way?"

At night, the shadows appeared. They didn't force their way inside if the doors and windows were closed, but they tended to moan as they circled around the building, which was unnerving enough.

"I have no idea. We don't know anything about them except what you and the others have written in your reports. We do know that there are beings out there trying to hurt $A\Omega$. I'm not too well-versed in the occult, but apparently there are a number of roadblocks set up to keep them away. For instance, there is something like a barrier preventing those who aren't invited from entering the house."

The whole concept was far beyond Asaka's understanding, but there was little she could do other than accept that it was real. She had eventually grown accustomed to the shadow creatures, so she had no issues sleeping at night now. If that's what this man considered "bold," she couldn't really disagree.

"How about the robots, then? Shouldn't you be able to do something with them?"

"Are you comfortable with robots stealing your job?" he smiled. "Well, in truth, those androids aren't at a level where they can teach people yet. They still lack that kind of adaptability. But, more importantly, how are *you* doing? Do you dislike your current workplace?"

"Of course I do. Why do we have to be stuck down there in such an isolated place?" she snapped. She felt bad for Yogiri, of course, but if she was going to be forced to live in some bizarre hidden village for the rest of her life, that was an even bigger concern.

"Yes, well. That is something we have to take into consideration. Right now, your results have far exceeded our expectations. Your evaluations have been quite satisfactory, so we'd like you to continue your work. We're currently thinking of the best way to set up a strong welfare support and care system."

As he spoke, he pulled a fat envelope out and put it on the desk. Realizing that it was being offered to her, Asaka took and opened it. It was filled to bursting with cash.

"Wait, this is —"

"Your salary for the month."

"Seriously? There are five stacks in here."

"Yes, it should be about five million yen after taxes. Of course, considering you're protecting the world, it doesn't really seem like all that much..."

"Well, uhh, no matter how much you pay me, if I'm stuck underground for the rest of my life, there's no real way for me to use it, is there?" Her initial reaction had been shock, but the reality of the situation grounded her rather quickly. No matter how enormous her salary was, it was entirely pointless.

"Oh, it seems like you've misunderstood. You're more than welcome to go outside if you want to."

"Wait, really?! Why wouldn't you tell me that from the start?!" she complained after a sudden spark of relief.

"Well, we can't just have you coming and going as you please, but if you let us know in advance, we can manage it. For instance, if you wanted to go somewhere right now, that would be fine. You've already come all the way up here, after all."

"Are you sure? But who would take care of him while I'm gone?"

"If it's just two or three days, it should be no problem. The robots can handle the cooking during that time."

"Wait, are you serious? Then what was the point of me learning how to cook?!"

After taking great care to follow the recipe book, Asaka's efforts had finally ended up producing something approximating food as of late.

"Don't you think that food cooked by a robot will taste strange? Cooking is all about the love put into it, isn't it?"

"It would be totally fine! Come on! Why didn't you tell me *that* from the start?!"

"Well, we figured you would either die or quit right away."

"Could you not say such disturbing things so lightly?! And wait, really?! I can just quit any time?!"

"It's rather delicate work, so having someone who hates the job would be problematic."

"But didn't you make me sign something like a slave contract?"

"That was just a waiver in case of your death. At this point, we've decided we can make good use of you, so we'd like you to stay for as long as possible. That's why I'm explaining all of this now. If there's anything you're unhappy with, please let us know right away. We'll do everything we can to provide what you need."

"Well, in that case…I need a break."

In the end, she decided to take a three-day vacation, and left the facility for the first time in a month.

◇◇◇

When Asaka opened her eyes, she was in an unfamiliar room. It wasn't the mansion underground, nor her own home, nor was it the hotel she had been staying in. She was in a stark white room, inside of which was nothing but a bed.

She tried to recall what had happened before she'd fallen asleep. In the morning, she had taken a car from the research facility to the station, where she boarded the bullet train to the city. On her way, she contacted a number of people. When she checked her mail, she found a huge amount of unread messages. She responded to most of them with an apology, saying her training at work was so intense that she just hadn't had time to contact anyone.

She'd also contacted her parents for the first time in a while. Asaka wasn't one to talk to them all that frequently, so they hadn't thought it strange when she'd failed to come home. She had told them that she'd found work but wasn't sure how long it would last.

After reaching the city, she immediately went in search of lunch. Since she had plenty of money, she decided to go for something luxurious, finding a *teppanyaki* restaurant to dine at. After eating her fill, she went shopping, determined to exhaust her supply of five million yen.

She didn't think she had worked hard to earn the money at all. Really, it seemed like easy money. As such, she felt no obligation to be stingy with it. So the first thing she went for was a handbag she had long admired but had never been able to afford. An item from a store so high-class, it had its own private security team to guard the entrance.

But she certainly couldn't go there in her interview outfit. So she first needed to get some clothes worthy of such a store. She spent most of the afternoon shopping for outfits, shoes, and watches, then bought the bag she had long been waiting for, and spent the remainder of her money on a suite in a city hotel.

The next thing she knew, she was here in this empty room.

"Nope, no idea how I got here!"

It appeared she had been brought there while sleeping, as she was still wearing the pajamas that she had put on before going to bed.

"Ah! What about my Birkin?!"

She had nothing on hand now but the clothes she was wearing. Everything she had bought earlier was missing.

"No, this isn't the time to be worrying about my bag!"

In a panic, she checked on her own physical condition. It didn't seem like she was injured, nor did it seem that anything had happened to her. But for a woman her age, this was a bad situation to be in.

"Was I abducted or something?"

If that was the case, it was likely the work of some organization. Kidnapping someone while they were sleeping in a fancy hotel was hardly something an ordinary person could pull off. And if she had been abducted, there was only one reason she could think of.

"It's something to do with that research facility. So, probably about *him*..."

"That is correct, Asaka Takatou," a woman's voice called out to her from somewhere beyond her line of sight. "*We have no intention of harming you, so please be at ease. We just wish to ask you some questions.*"

Side Story: The Agency

"That's a funny thing to say since you're holding me captive here, aren't you?"

"*That depends on your perspective. From our point of view, we've saved you. Though it may already be too late, in the end. If that's the case, we'd like to get some information from you before you die, to save this world.*"

"What? I have no idea what you're going on about. Are you sure you took the right person?" She figured it was pointless, but decided to try and play dumb anyway.

"*No, you have been confirmed as a Level C employee, so there is no mistake. We have a full list of the facility's employees. While their internal security is tight, it seems they have a weakness to hacking. All we had to do was wait for someone from the facility to leave.*"

"You're going on about a Level C employee, but I don't even know what that means." Did the workers at the research facility have levels like that? It would make sense, but she didn't know anything about it.

"*You don't know?*"

"That's what I'm saying! Why does everyone talk to me like I know everything that's happening?!"

"*Those who have met Lord Okakushi, or AΩ, as he is called within your facility, are designated as Level C.*"

"And?" While she obviously worked there, she had no idea what value it was to these people.

"*My, my, to have you work with that thing without even telling you that much. How cruel your employers are. Lord Okakushi can kill those he has seen at any time, you know.*"

While she found that hard to believe, it did make her think. The researchers at her workplace took every precaution to avoid meeting Yogiri themselves. In short, they didn't want him to see them.

"*It should be clear to you now who the true villains are. We are an organization working to prevent the destruction of the world, end this calamity, and seal it away forever.*"

She didn't fully understand what the woman was talking about, but Asaka knew instinctively that she had been caught up in a very bad situation.

◇◇◇

"Hey, where did Asaka go?" Yogiri asked the Autonomous Humanoid Operational Mechanism.

"Asaka Takatou is currently on holiday."

"I see."

How many times had he asked now? The robots always gave him the same exact answer.

Yogiri returned to the living room. He was bored, which was a new feeling for him. Not knowing who or what he really was, he had just spent his time mindlessly sitting around doing nothing before he met her, but he had already forgotten what that old life was like.

The living room was now full of things that Asaka had brought in. A TV, a Blu-ray player, game consoles, bookshelves, manga, textbooks, an exercise bike, dumbbells, board games, puzzle rings, a transformation belt, a magic stick, dolls, plastic models, writing tools, a bug catching net, a fish tank, a dog, a hamster, and a decorative plant. Most of her requests had been approved, and Yogiri remembered her getting excited every time something she asked for had arrived.

Sitting in front of the dining table, Yogiri flipped through a textbook. They had already finished going through all the elementary school materials, so there wasn't anything that he hadn't already read. Asaka had told him he wasn't allowed to play video games without permission, so that was off the table for now, and he had already read all of the manga they had on hand.

Nikori, their Shetland Sheepdog, came up to his side. Petting the dog made him feel better, but it didn't make him any less bored.

"I wonder when Asaka will come back. You miss her too, don't you?"

The dog replied with a bark. Yogiri decided that must have meant she was lonely too.

As Yogiri was playing with Nikori, the robot brought him lunch. Though it was made perfectly well, he couldn't help but feel it wasn't all that good. The feeling brought him back to before Asaka had come, when he was always eating alone. Her predecessors had made food for him, but after they brought it in, they would leave immediately.

He was so bored. With that thought in mind, he spoke to Nikori. "Wait here for a bit. I'm going to go look for Asaka."

As Nikori saw him off with another bark, Yogiri set about searching for his caretaker. Stepping outside, he looked around for some of the working machines.

There was a robot nearby in a field, so he called out to it, "Hey, where did Asaka go?"

"Asaka Takatou is currently on holiday." The same answer as always, but this time he wanted more information.

"I'm asking where she is now."

"I am unaware."

"Then tell me someone who does know."

As he said that, the machine went stiff. He didn't know what thoughts had gone through its head, but eventually it answered.

"I believe the researchers would know."

"Okay, please take me to them."

"Understood." Stopping its work, the robot began guiding Yogiri across the landscape.

Following the machine, the boy was led outside of the village, to the end of his tiny world. Though the road appeared to continue far into the distance, it was only an illusion. In truth, they had reached a wall with a door set into it.

"How do you open it?"

"It cannot be opened from this side. It must be operated from the control room."

Yogiri wondered what he should do, then immediately came to a conclusion. When he looked around, he saw that someone was watching him through a camera. Now that he had noticed that, the rest was easy. He could tell that whoever was watching was surprised when he suddenly turned to look back at them.

"I want to leave. Open the door."

If someone else had to open the door, then he would just ask them instead.

After a brief moment, the door opened. It really was quite easy.

◇◇◇

When Head Researcher Yukio Shiraishi arrived at the control room with security in tow, he found a scene of total chaos. One of the employees had opened the door that sealed off the underground village. Not stopping there, she had continued to open all the doors blocking AΩ's progress along the way. It was unexplainable. A scenario where the staff went mad and simply let AΩ out into the world was beyond anyone's imagining. They had no procedures for dealing with such a complication, so all they could do was address the developments as they came.

A young woman was operating the console intently. Occasionally, they would hear AΩ's voice, and she would do as he said, like an idiot. The other staff members who had tried to stop her were lying on the ground around her.

"Can't we lock her out of the console somehow?" Yukio asked the other employees standing nearby.

"We could, but…we can't. Anyone who tries to get in his way ends up like that! Would you take that risk?!"

"This was AΩ's work?"

There were no external injuries on the collapsed employees, and the woman operating the console wasn't particularly athletic-looking, yet everyone around her was lying motionless on the floor. They were likely all dead.

"Yes. Anyone who even tried to stop her died the moment she looked at them!"

"That's impossible…" Yukio muttered in shock. If AΩ was capable of that, there was no point in sealing it underground in the first place. Any time it wanted to leave, it could. He turned to one of the guards. "Do you have your gun?"

"Yes, but…"

"This is an emergency. I'll take responsibility. Please shoot her."

The guard was clearly nervous, but this wasn't a normal research facility. The fact that a situation like this might occur was the reason they had guns in the first place, and they were trained well in the use of them.

The guard pointed his gun at the woman handling the console. But before he could even put his finger on the trigger, he fell to the ground.

Yukio immediately threw in the towel. "Well, we're out of options, then, aren't we? I never imagined he would be capable of doing something like this."

There was nothing they could do. They could try to destroy the facility, but they would probably be killed the instant they made the decision. They didn't know the boy's objective, but he had clearly decided to leave, and no one could get in his way.

After a while, $A\Omega$ reached the surface. He had now seen everyone in the control room, making them all Level C employees. Yukio immediately became aware that it was a far more dangerous, far wider classification than they had previously thought. Judging from what had just happened, $A\Omega$ might be able to go through those he had met before to use his power. If that was the case, the danger he posed to the world was far greater than they had ever anticipated — and now that danger was standing right in front of them.

"Hey, where is Asaka?"

"She's on holiday, so she left the facility," Yukio answered him.

"When will she come back?"

This was also beyond their expectations. They had never thought he would grow so attached to his caretaker. While that meant she was even better at her job than they had imagined, there was no room for celebration right now.

"She won't be coming back," Yukio answered honestly.

They were aware that Asaka had been captured by the Agency. Yukio also knew that the higher-ups had decided to abandon her to her fate. They had felt she wasn't valuable enough to go through the trouble of trying to rescue her.

"Why?"

"She was kidnapped. She is probably still alive, though."

Surprise rose to AΩ's face. He looked like nothing more than an innocent child. "Aren't you going to save her?"

"Well..."

The facility itself didn't really have the manpower to undertake those kinds of operations. And even if they asked other departments for help, their opponent was a difficult one. The Agency that had kidnapped Asaka was a global organization, so it wasn't hard for them to find a place to hold her where the Japanese government couldn't reach them.

"Then I'll go save her. Do you know where she is?"

"Shouldn't you know already?"

AΩ could track the location of anyone he had previously met. That's what they had thought, at least, but from his expression, it seemed that wasn't always the case.

"Masaki got super scared when I did that, so I didn't do it to Asaka. She would probably get really mad at me. So please don't tell her about all the stuff I did here either, okay?" he said with a bright smile.

No one dared to disobey.

◇◇◇

It came straight at them. There was no plan or strategy, it just looked like it was moving directly towards its target. It was a young boy, dressed in old-fashioned Japanese clothes, entirely in white. The boy headed straight into the base, walking from the gate to the interior buildings like he was strolling through an empty field.

Of course, the soldiers guarding the area attempted to stop him, but they were all killed to a man.

"Hey, where is Asaka?" he asked each of them one by one.

If they didn't answer, he killed them. And anyone who tried to attack him died as well. The fact that the Agency had a facility within this base was a closely guarded secret, but keeping that secret seemed meaningless before the opponent now facing them. It was only a matter of time before they broke and gave him what he wanted.

Naturally, the entrance to the building was restricted to related personnel. The interior was also divided into sections, each of which had strict security measures in place. But before the strange boy, none of them even served to slow him down. The latest in cutting-edge electronic security folded just as easily as the heaviest physical doors that blocked his path.

"Well, even if they're Class 3, normal soldiers would be helpless against him," a woman dressed as a shrine priestess muttered, watching his progress from the control room.

"Anyone he sees dies? Calling something like that rare doesn't quite do it justice in this world," a man in a cassock noted.

"Maybe it's a kind of magic eyes deal. Simply put, you just have to kill him before he sees you, right?" a soldier with a sniper rifle interjected, focused intently on inspecting his own equipment.

But they never had a chance to put their thoughts into motion. As far as the boy was concerned, they were pebbles on the roadside. As he walked, they'd be kicked out of the way. They were nothing more than that.

◇◇◇

Asaka lay on the bed, staring blankly at the ceiling. There was nothing there in the room, so there was nothing for her to do. They had interrogated her, and she had answered everything they'd asked. It was a problem as far as her nondisclosure agreement with the research facility went, but in this situation, the contract didn't exactly mean much. Her survival was her number one priority.

In the end, her kidnappers had already known almost everything she had told them, so they'd ended up disappointed. They initially said they would release her if she told them everything, but now they were telling her to "wait a little longer." Though they claimed they were the heroes, they had no inhibitions about behaving in a way that was incredibly illegal, so she doubted she could trust them. Now that she knew about this place, they couldn't let her live. She wouldn't be surprised if they told her to die for justice's sake.

"I really should have found a more reasonable job..."

She had never thought that picking the wrong place of employment would have landed her in a situation like this.

"I wonder what Yogiri is up to…"

Though he was technically the source of her current misfortune, she could hardly blame him for it. Yogiri was himself little more than a victim of that place. Not only did he have no idea what was going on around him, the researchers there treated him like a monster to be locked away. For her part, Asaka could see him only as a somewhat naive child.

Getting up from the bed, Asaka stretched and looked around, feeling that she couldn't quietly await her fate in this room. The first thing that stood out to her was the bed. There were also two doors. One led to a bathroom, but it had no windows, so she couldn't escape from there. The other led to a hallway, but it was locked from the outside. She couldn't break the door down, and even if she could, she was under constant surveillance, so she'd be discovered immediately if she tried anything.

Her motivation left as quickly as it had come. "Looks like there's nothing I can do right now…" This wasn't a situation she could solve with hard work or clever thinking alone.

As she sat back down on the bed, she heard a noise. Pressing her ear to the door, she tried to figure out what was happening outside. It seemed there was some sort of panic in the corridor. She could hear the sounds of people running, something crashing, screams, gunfire, and explosions, distant at first, then louder and close enough that it became impossible to ignore. Something serious was going on out there.

"Maybe I can use this as a chance to escape?"

Though she still had her doubts, she began to feel a faint hope as the door to her room burst open. A woman entered, pointing a gun at her as she stepped inside. It was the woman who had been interrogating her.

Asaka stood there, confused, as the woman circled behind her, pressing the gun to her head.

"Hey! What's going on?! I thought you said you weren't planning on hurting me!"

"Quiet!" The woman used her free hand to squeeze Asaka's neck, cutting off her voice. "Follow me."

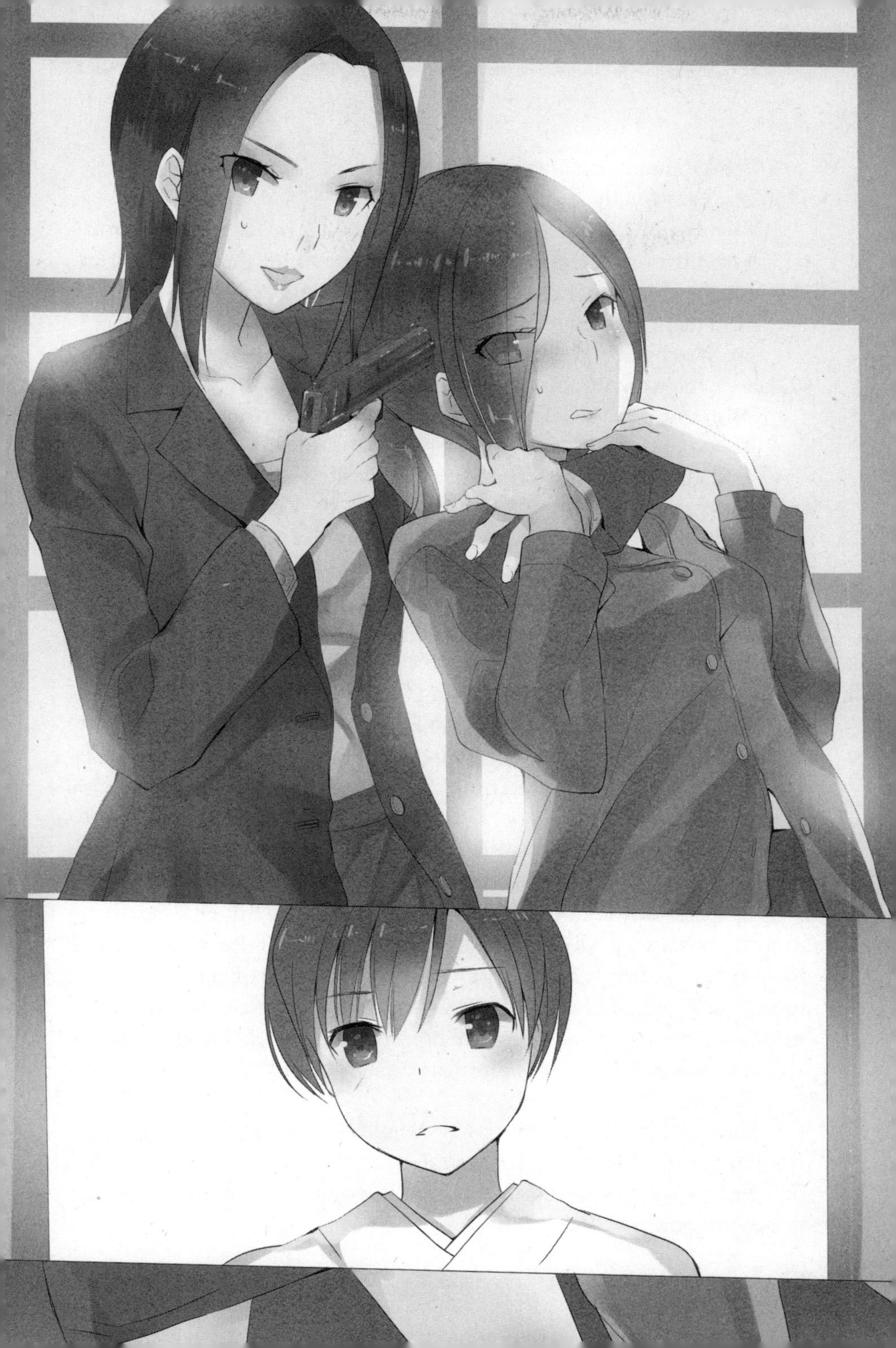

"It's kind of hard to walk like this..."

"Asaka! I finally found you!"

A young boy in white clothes came into view. There was no mistaking his little form. It was Yogiri Takatou, the child who was supposed to be awaiting her return in the underground facility.

Ecstatic to see her, his face lit up with a bright smile.

"Wait, why are you here, Yo—" Asaka was once again choked into silence by the woman tightening her grip on her throat.

"Don't do anything! Understand?! If you so much as move, this woman dies!" the woman yelled, pressing her gun to the side of Asaka's head.

Asaka finally realized that she was a hostage. "Ow! Hold on, what are you doing?!"

"You tell him too! Tell him not to do anything! If he does, you'll die —" The woman's voice suddenly cut off as she slumped to the floor.

Stepping up to Asaka, Yogiri gave her a big hug. Asaka herself had no idea what to make of the situation.

"What is going on here?"

"Let's go home. Nikori is waiting for us."

"Uh, we can just walk out of here?"

"Yeah, I came to get you," Yogiri said, grabbing her hand and pulling her along. As she followed him, she saw heavily armed soldiers lying all over the place.

"Don't tell me..."

They were all dead. It was obvious that Yogiri had done all of this. Even now, people were dying. Bodies continued to fall from hiding places around the hallway. As they entered the stairwell, more corpses tumbled down the stairs from above them. When they stepped outside, there was an explosion ahead of them. Even with their chain of command in tatters, the soldiers still had a sense of honor in their work, but they clearly had no idea what they were fighting.

"Yogiri..."

She paused. Telling him to stop would be easy, and he might even listen to her if she did. But that would mean the two of them would die. They had long since passed the point of being able to talk their way out of the situation.

The two of them headed straight for the exit. They hadn't done anything wrong. *They* were the victims here. She had been kidnapped and he was only rescuing her. But seeing the base collapsing into ruin all around her, Asaka couldn't help but wonder if it was really necessary for him to go this far for someone like her.

For the first time, it crossed her mind that Yogiri was terrifying.

◇◇◇

Once they'd left the base, everything had gone smoothly. A car from the main facility had been there waiting for them, so they'd gotten inside and were quickly whisked away to a government base. From there, they'd boarded a helicopter that brought them back to the research center in no time at all.

"We're home!" Yogiri shouted as he walked inside, where he was immediately greeted by Nikori jumping on him.

"Yogiri, go play with Nikori in the living room."

"Okay!" Taking Nikori with him, the boy went on ahead.

Asaka remained outside, a short distance away from the house, accompanied by Yukio Shiraishi. Figuring there was no point in hiding from Yogiri now, the head researcher had accompanied them down to the underground village.

"So, what now?"

"In all likelihood, nothing at all. We were unexpectedly shown $A\Omega$'s true power. The higher-ups won't be able to do anything until they come up with a plan for dealing with that."

"What, they're just going to let it all slide?"

"Well, there isn't much anyone can do about it."

"And me?"

"Ah, sorry, but I'm afraid we can't let you quit anymore," he chuckled nervously.

"This isn't a joke!"

"Truthfully, we've learned there's really nothing anyone can do to stop $A\Omega$ at this point. Actually, we knew from the start that hiding him underground was merely to provide a false sense of security. Once the details of this event get out, I doubt many people will target you anymore."

"Yeah, about that. Didn't you know I might be taken in the first place?" She couldn't help but think it was possible that all of this had been part of someone's plan to draw out the Agency, using her as bait.

"No, we never thought a low-ranking employee like you would be targeted. From now on, we'll be sending a security detail along with you on any excursions. We're working hard to make this a better place for you. So, how about it? Do you think you can continue?"

"Wait, are you saying it's okay for me to quit after all?"

"We don't want you to, really. But if we tried to force you to stay, there are concerns about how AΩ would react. Basically, we have to be very careful about how we deal with you going forward."

"Well, I can't say I'll stay here forever, but I have no intention of quitting just yet."

Asaka glanced at the mansion. Yogiri was playing with Nikori in the living room. He was dangerous. If he was left as he was right now, she could imagine something even worse happening in the future. In order for him to become a good person, there were many more things that he would need to be taught.

Asaka was afraid of him on some level, but more than that, she felt bad for him. She didn't know how much she could do, but she wanted to help him in any way that she could.

"Asaka! Can I play some video games?" Yogiri called out, having looked out and found her in the front yard.

"I'll be right there!" she answered, then turned back to Yukio. "I'll talk to you later, then."

Having said her goodbyes, she made her way to the porch. The situation had been resolved for now, so she couldn't help but feel a little relieved.

"Wait, aren't I forgetting something...? Oh! My Birkin!"

Asaka had lost every single thing she had bought with her first paycheck.

Afterword

Thank you very much for buying this book.

If you bought volume 2, that means you probably bought volume 1 as well, and that led to this volume being possible. Really, thank you so much!

With the way things are going, continuing this series should be no problem, so a great "thank you" to everyone who found this series interesting. It's said often enough, and it doesn't really have anything to do with you readers, but for a series to continue it needs to sell at least a certain amount. So thank you in advance.

So, this is the afterword. I normally run out of things to say by the time I get to writing these, but this time I have something to talk about, so I'll start from there.

When volume 1 went on sale, I started a Twitter campaign to pick names for some of the small-fry enemies. It was a really messy affair from start to finish, but in the end, the following two names won: Fehu Kazuno and Shiro. Congratulations!

They appeared and died in this volume already, so please look for them inside. Come to think of it, Fehu Kazuno is the writer of the series "My Sister is a Monster."

"So, wait, you ended up picking one of your friends?!"

You may think that, but with only four entries, I couldn't help it! This was the result decided on by the ultimate unbiased random number generator.

"Anyway, since they play around like this, I'd like to send in a submission, but I don't use Twitter."

I figured there might be some people like that out there, so I thought I'd try taking letters as well. We're recruiting small-fry enemies for volume 3 onwards. That is my secret plan this time.

If I share my lottery plan for picking enemy names in the afterword, that should inflate the word count quite a bit! And after this volume,

I can laugh about how few submissions I got, so I should be set for my afterwords for a while!

Here are the important points of the application. Please include the following:

The name of the character you want included.
Up to 140 characters about the character's background.

Don't feel like you have to write too much. There is no particular deadline, but I will select winners around the time I write the next volume. I plan on picking two or three names, but it may change based on the story, so I appreciate your understanding.

Please send your entries to the following address:

〒107-0052
Tokyo-To Minato-ku Akasaka 2 - 14 - 5 Daiwa Akasaka Building 5th Floor
Earth Star Novels Editorial Department Tsuyoshi Fujitaka

Some important things to consider:
Inappropriate names and those of characters from other works will not qualify.
Names that depart from the naming sense of the story's world too strongly will not qualify. So please read the book and think about it carefully.
If you tell me the character can shoot a laser that will destroy the entire world, that will be difficult to write into the story, so it won't qualify. Please try and make it something that sounds like it could show up in the story.
If you've read the book, you will probably already know how it works, but the characters will inevitably die before they've barely done anything, so please be understanding. "They died without saying a word," "They died the moment they appeared," "They died without even meeting the protagonist" are all possible situations.
If you want to include any setting information or pictures, please feel free.

Afterword

That should be about it. From volume 3 onwards, their classmates and other monsters will start appearing, so that might come in handy when you are trying to think of your submissions. You can also send fan letters of any kind to that address, so I look forward to all of your submissions. I heard that if you ask for fan letters in your afterword then you'll get a lot, so I figured I'd try it out. I've already published ten books, but I've never received a single one.

Next, I will talk about what was added compared to the web novel version of the book:
Added an interlude, discussing Lain's clone and Euphemia, one of Yuuki's bodyguards.
A bonus side story, continuing the side story from volume 1.
Added explanations and details about parts of the setting that were unclear.
Numerous corrections from proofreading.
And other such things. The main plot of the story has remained unchanged.

Hopefully that should fill up enough space. So my thanks.
To my director, my apologies for leaving things so close to the deadline.
To Chisato Naruse, who did the illustrations, thank you once again for your beautiful artwork. I'm especially thankful for the ten pieces of art you gave me for the Twitter countdown leading up to the release of volume 1. This must be what it feels like to respect someone so much that it hurts. The illustrations are on Miss Naruse's Pixiv, so if you haven't seen them, please go take a look. Every single one of them is great.
So, about volume 3. According to the sales figures of volume 1, as long as things don't go horribly for volume 2, it should be safe to say the series will continue. But don't worry, I won't be taking it easy yet.
I very much look forward to your submissions. If possible, let's meet again in volume 3!

Tsuyoshi Fujitaka
藤孝 剛志

Hello, this is the Illustrator for this series, Chisato Naruse. I very much enjoyed drawing for this volume as well.

Despite both being deeply connected to Yogiri's story, these two don't meet in this volume. I feel they would get along well, even if it might be a bit dangerous to have them together, but I wonder if they will actually get to meet in the future...